D1273275

Spring Harvest

Spring Harvest

By GLADYS TABER

G. P. Putnam's Sons   New York

© 1959 BY GLADYS TABER

MANUFACTURED IN THE UNITED STATES OF AMERICA

For
My Mother

1.

"IN years to come," said Michael, "we'll remember today."

Julie nodded, although the truth was she was not considering years to come at all. Time was now, while they walked the old Indian trail downriver. The white clover blossomed early that spring of 1914 and was breast-high along the banks. May sun shone on the wide river, and the Wisconsin hills broke green against the sky. Across the water, a herd of black and white Holsteins drifted toward home and milking time. There was no sound except the thunder of the dam three miles upstream.

Their current quarrel was finished, so they were now in the blissful state of reconciliation. Mike broke a branch of May apple to clear the path and Julie waited, loving him more than she could bear. ("I can't see why she wants to hang around that football player," said her father.) But to Julie, Mike was —well, just everything. True, in the picture taken for *The Clarion* he resembled a monster with his padded football uniform, headguard, cleated shoes. Crouched to spring, and with the fighting grin, he looked terrible. Now he wore sneakers, faded pants and sweat shirt and was not formidable. He was a tall, easy boy with sun-bleached hair, gray eyes, firm mouth and stubborn chin. ("He's pigheaded," said her father.) For a big man, he had an oddly light voice.

In short, there was nothing more distinctive about him than about many other college sophomores. But to Julie, he resembled a sun god. That was all there was to it.

Nevertheless, her pride made her go back once more to the quarrel. She wasn't going to be pushed around.

"If you'd rather take Marcy Lindstrom to the dance, it is perfectly all right with me. Perfectly."

He laughed. "You're jealous," he said, "but I love you anyway. You know very well I only took her last Saturday because you wouldn't speak to me. I was mad. Let's sit down and forget it."

There was a clearing at the edge of the water where picnic fires had left an open space. Julie sat down, feeling the stubble under her pleated skirt. The light slanted now, and she knew she should be going home in order to reach there before her father, but she could not go. When Mike kissed her, she could only move closer to him. Her heart seemed to stop beating, but she felt the strong beat of his. He smelled of sun.

"You're my girl," he said, "and don't ever forget it." His hands were gentle as he pushed back her hair. "You're such a little thing," he murmured, "no bigger than a bird."

Julie held his hand to her mouth and kissed the rough palm. "Don't ever leave me," she whispered, "don't ever."

He spoke soberly. "Well, the way things are with your family," he reminded her, "it's kind of hard to plan much. But I want to tell you right now that I mean to marry you, just as soon as I can take care of you. I promise. I'd take a chance on our getting married right now, if I had any money or a decent family to help out. But I'm a poor bet, the way your father looks at it, and you can't blame him. You've got pretty much of everything. And your family—"

"It would kill Papa."

"I know." He held her tighter. "And right now I better get you home or he'll have my hide."

"I want to stay with you."

"Someday," he said.

But as he followed her up the path, he didn't feel as confident as he sounded. His heart slowed, and the enchantment diminished. He was, he felt, so much older than Julie, much more than the actual seven months. After all, she was an only child, cherished, with a professor for a father who was known to be one of the tops at Westerly, even if he was hell to get on with. Her mother was simply wonderful. While Mike was an orphan, living precariously on the bounty of his aunt and uncle.

It didn't add up very well, he thought, his eyes loving her as she ran to the top of the slope. She reminded him of a wild pony he had broken to halter the summer he worked on Schotta's farm. She was all grace and speed, and her dark hair flung back like a mane. She stopped and waited for him. He always let her get there first, because it pleased her. She stood breathless, smiling, her dark blue eyes shining. Maybe there were more beautiful girls at Westerly but not to him. Her nose was wide, and he knew she pinched it with clothespins sometimes to narrow it, but he liked it the way it was. Her fair skin burned easily, and was often peeling. Her mouth could tighten with anger, but it was a kissing mouth, warm and passionate. She wasn't easy, he thought, with that hot temper, and she was spoiled in many ways. She could, often did, drive him into seething fury.

But she was his heart, and he didn't even want her faults any different.

He just wanted her for the rest of his life, and for after, if there were an after. That was the way he felt.

She held her face up, damp with perspiration. "Kiss me."

"No." It was up to him to do the managing. "You run home. I'll take the back streets. And fix your hair before you see your father."

"But Mike—it's so long until tomorrow," she begged.

"Get going," he ordered.

He stood watching her as she ran, dipped in sunset. When she rounded the corner, it was twilight. Mike went on, taking the back streets, avoiding the campus. He didn't want to meet Professor Prescott.

But Professor Prescott had been held up with a student who was about to fail Paleontology. The big lamps on Science Hall portico were already lighted as he put his papers away. The lab was dusky. He felt tired, and he did not believe in being tired. He didn't believe in being sick either, and if he felt he was "coming down with something" he fortified himself with aconite, quinine, seltzer, topped off with a raw onion sandwich and coffee.

In former days when he was a mining engineer, he carried a black medicine chest with him, with twenty-five bottles on each side. He dosed everyone he met who was ill, and there were still people in remote mountain districts in Colorado and Mexico who spoke of his miraculous cures. His method was simple, he just shook out a few pills and passed them around. And even now, when he was settled down as head of the Geology Department at Westerly, he dosed himself from the medicine case rather than consult a doctor.

He had given up his roving life when Julie was old enough to go to school. Sybil pointed out that a child raised in shacks at the edge of mines or traveling around on trains half the time would just grow up to be a heathen. They must, she said, stop living out of packing cases and have a home, somewhere in a small town with a regular school. And so here he was, trying to knock some knowledge into the heads of Westerly students. Actually he loved teaching, but seldom admitted it.

Now he had a moment of wishing himself back on some mountain trail, his pack horse easy behind him. The lab was stuffy and smelled of chalk. He lowered the shades, glad the day was over. He'd been up since five (he had gone out to shoot rabbits in the vegetable patch). Then he'd had finals and conferences all day and term papers to grade. And material to get together for the next catalogue.

As he went outdoors, he put the day's work out of his mind and began to worry about Julie. He had managed to get rid of the whippersnappers that dogged her all through high school, one after the other. She never seemed to mind very much. But since she had taken up with this Michael, she was different. He didn't like it at all. She skipped out after meals, she talked over the phone incessantly. Came in late from parties. Was always too busy to play accompaniments when he felt like singing. In church, you could see she wasn't listening to the sermon. He never listened either, but that was different. When he spoke to Sybil, she said Mike was a nice boy. A nice boy!

Well, Sybil couldn't understand his dreams for Julie, who was destined for great things. Sybil herself had never been to college, and was, of course, limited.

He had expected to marry a scholarly woman, preferably gifted in science. He had quite a list of qualifications before he met Sybil that night at a skating party. The river ice was black, the wind bitter. She flew over the ice so fast she nearly outdistanced him and when he finally caught up with her, she spun on her skates laughing. Flyaway black hair blew out under her bonnet, her face was rosy, her brown eyes bright. In the snowy landscape her jacket and full skirt were the color of a cardinal. And immediately he began his frantic courtship, overlooking her lack of a proper degree (she could not spell very well either). She was gay, sweet and wise, and he persuaded her to marry him.

He took her gifts for granted, her cooking, which was inspired, her skill as a needlewoman, which saved money during the lean years, her china-painting, which was charming. And her gift for friendship, which kept the house overflowing. To him, she was simply there, familiar as sunshine or rain or wild ducks flying.

When Julie was born, a frail colicky baby, something changed in his heart. He walked the floor patiently with her, singing. He guided her first staggering steps. He taught her, later, to use crayons and paints, and still later, he hunted Indian arrowheads with her, read *Evangeline* aloud, explained the Milky Way, showed her glacial scratches on granite boulders. She followed him close as his own shadow. When she went to school he checked her homework. He laid out her high school courses and she faithfully got A's in them. She was obedient from Sunday morning church to Saturday's dusting of his minerals and specimens.

But now, when he had said candidly that he didn't want that football player wasting her time, she gave him a look he had never seen before, cold, defensive, strange. It worried him.

As if he didn't know what was best for her, he thought as he left the campus. He only wanted her happiness, and college affairs could be dangerous. Only last week he caught his best Geology major kissing a girl in the Science lab. He must protect Julie. Put his foot down. He walked faster. He would tend to this business tomorrow, he decided, for tonight he had to go to faculty meeting at eight.

This was another worry, for some of the young members advocated a change in the curriculum requirements. They wanted more elective courses, more credit for stuff like Art and Music. This was ridiculous, anybody could see Greek, Latin, Physics, Mathematics, and Geology were the basic subjects. But there would be a battle. As he crossed Lawe Street, he met Michael idling along in the waning light as if he, at least, had nothing better to do.

"Hi." Michael waved a paw at him.

Alden humphed. Upstart, he thought, and hurried past. Actually he never really walked, he loped. In winter his overcoat belled out behind him, in summer his jacket flew open. He was a door slammer, and as he flew up the front steps of the house, the door banged harder than usual. He was ready for action and changed his mind about putting off the talk with Julie. Why not tend to it tonight?

He dropped his books and briefcase on the Chippendale chair in the hall. "Sybil, I'm home," he shouted.

She answered calmly from the kitchen. She could tell by his voice he was in a stir over something, and she sighed. But she kept on basting the roast beef, the heat of the gas oven bringing a flush to her face.

"Hello, dear," she said, closing the oven door.

"Where's Julie?" This was always his first question.

"Upstairs. She'll be down to set the table." She did not add that Julie had dashed in just five minutes before, for she was expert at holding her tongue.

"I want to talk to her," he announced firmly.

She glanced at him and yes, his color was high, hair tousled, ice-blue eyes stern. Oh dear, he must have had a run-in with someone, and he'll take it out on Julie. She began to mash the potatoes with hot cream and butter.

"Why not read the paper first?" she suggested. "I hear there's something about raising taxes in it."

Instantly he was deflected. "Confounded Democrats," he said, "they'll ruin the country." He vanished, banging the dining-room door.

Sybil took the roast out, and made pan gravy. No matter what a state he was in, Alden was always hungry. I wish he could grow up, she thought. I wish he could come to terms with life. Everyone says he is a genius—are they all children always? But at least he will have to realize sometime that Julie is growing up. I wasn't much older when we were married. And Julie must stop meeting him head on, compromise a bit. She's too fiery about everything.

She took off her apron and slipped into the downstairs lavatory (which was a luxury in Winnebago), washed her face, dabbed rice powder on, tucked the bone hairpins back in her hair firmly, adjusted her hair net. She was not a vain woman, but she noticed fine lines beginning around her eyes. She was

13

getting plump, too, and her corset pinched. But she was too busy to worry about herself.

She went back to the kitchen to make the salad, hoping Julie would come downstairs. But Julie had lost count of time, and sat at her window staring at the sky. One star was out. She wanted to write a poem for Mike, but after love and above she couldn't fit dove in. Rhyme was difficult.

"Julie, your mother is setting the table," called Alden.

She tore the paper up, smoothed her hair and hurried down. She knew she was flushed and her eyes too shining, and she tried to think of something dull and ordinary. Father was hawk-eyed. She stopped a moment on the landing, breathing hard. She had a feeling her own father was a stranger, an enemy. Of course she loved him, but lately she was afraid of him. Whatever would she do if he forbade her to see Mike? She would never give him up, never. But fear was there, sliding into her bones. If only her mother could help her—but wouldn't her mother be loyal to Father? Well, she must be careful.

She ran on downstairs and flung herself in Alden's arms.

"Oh Papa, I didn't hear you come in," she said. "I was doing math." It was the first direct lie, and it wasn't easy.

"What's the matter with your math?" He lowered the paper.

"Oh, nothing. I just knew you wanted me to get an A and finals are tomorrow." She lowered her lashes (a great protection).

"Supper's ready," called Sybil.

"What do we have candles for?" Alden asked. "I like to be able to see what I'm eating."

Sybil snuffed the candles and lit the ceiling light.

The Prescott family sat at the round mahogany table. It was a typical Winnebago dining room, with a big buffet displaying the silver service, a Brussels carpet, starched curtains. The furniture had come down from the Prescott family and Sybil found it heavy and ornate. The light was too bright, glaring down on

14

the linen tablecloth, the platter of roast beef, the bowl of mashed potatoes cradling melted butter, and the side dishes of asparagus, leaf-lettuce salad. The gravy kept warm in a silver gravy boat.

Alden sliced the roast, giving Julie the outside slice and ladling gravy with a lavish hand. He liked a simple supper such as this, and hoped there would be a simple green apple pie with whipped cream for dessert. He felt easier in his mind as he began to eat. He could put the young faculty in its place, he was sure, and as for Julie, she would be a good girl. Tempest in a teapot, he thought.

Julie felt easy in her mind too. He hadn't, for a wonder, asked her what she had done after her last class, where she went, and with whom. Everything was all right.

Sybil knew better; she sensed a storm in the air, and wished she herself could be out of it, in a quiet place. But of course she had no refuge from her own family. She brought in the pie and served the coffee.

"It's good pie," Alden remarked. "Why can't other women make a decent crust? It's perfectly simple, I could do it myself. We used to have gooseberry pie at my grandmother's. *There* was a pie."

"We had a nice meeting of the Literary Society today," Sybil said cheerfully. "We are halfway through *Pickwick Papers*. We're reading all of Dickens aloud."

"Dickens is greatly overrated," remarked Alden.

"But he is interesting to read aloud." Sybil's voice was mild.

"Women," he sniffed. "Why don't you take up something worth while like the *Iliad?*"

Julie nibbled at her pie. She wasn't interested in Dickens either. She was, at the moment, standing in the door of a rose-embowered cottage waiting for Mike to come home to supper. She had whipped up something special (she could only do

15

wieners and fudge) and the Victrola in the chintz living room played softly. "I'll be loving you—always—"

"Now then, Julie," said Alden, "I want to talk to you as soon as you have the dishes done."

"Yes, Papa."

No use putting it off, thought Sybil, better get it over with before time for faculty meeting. "I'll do the dishes," she said, "and just take my time."

Julie followed her father to his study and perched in the Morris chair while he sat firmly behind the desk, in command of the room. He cleared his throat, an ominous sign. Julie got that stiff feeling in her neck.

"I want to speak to you about this boy," said Alden.

"What boy?" Her eyes were innocent.

"Don't dodge. You know very well what boy. This Michael you keep sneaking around with."

"Oh that one." She shrugged. "I don't sneak around with anybody, Papa."

This was a mistake, right away. Contradicting him was fatal. "Now you listen to me." He spoke sharply. "You are too young to form—to form any attachment whatsoever. Is that clear?"

"Yes, Daddy." She was trembling. "Attachment?"

"Don't repeat everything I say," he snorted. "I want to explain to you, calmly and sensibly, why you must not chase after this football player."

"I don't chase anybody." Her voice rose. "I suppose you think nobody would date me on their own account. If that's what you think—"

"Don't get excited!" He whacked the desk with his fist. "And don't argue with me." He leaned forward. "I know what's best for you."

"Why?" Her smaller fist banged the arm of the chair. "How do you know what's best for me?"

16

"Because I'm your father!" He was shouting now.

They glared at each other, both with tight lips, fiery cheeks, steely eyes. They looked exactly alike, and they were feeling alike. Secretly they both wished the words unsaid, but it was too late. Rage and fear swept them equally, for Alden could not help being afraid of this child of his. As if he had to defend his position!

"I do not intend to argue." He spoke heavily. "I am just telling you to stop seeing this boy. That is all I have to say."

Julie got up and left the study without a word. Alden, prepared for the submission, the reconciliation scene, the mutual tears, was astounded. Well, he had laid down the law. She'd get over it.

In the kitchen, Sybil wrung the dishcloth out of ammonia water, heated the coffee, and carried a cup to the study. Naturally she had heard every word that they said, and she hoped the neighbors hadn't. Why did they have to shout so? This battle ended without a truce, she thought apprehensively.

"I settled things," Alden told her, breathing heavily. "There won't be any more trouble. Don't worry about it." He took the coffee.

"I wasn't worried until you got her so upset," said Sybil. "I wouldn't push Julie too far. She's your daughter."

"I simply told her what to do." He gulped his coffee. "You always take her side, but someday you'll be glad I made the right decisions for her."

"I wonder." Sybil spoke dryly.

She went to the living room because there was nothing to say now. She lit the lamp by the Martha Washington sewing table and began to darn Julie's black gym stockings. You could stitch up holes in fabric and it was almost as good as new. Holes in life were not so easy, she thought. She slid the china darning egg in. Sewing was an anodyne. But this was not like keeping Julie home from the Carnival or not letting her go to a party on Sunday. Or like taking away her teddy bear when she had marked the walls with crayon. For these weren't vital, but now Julie had a desire not all childish, and a will to battle for it. Alden was meeting a new antagonist.

She pushed back her familiar yearning for quietude, which of late ached in her bones. What could she do, practically? Well, she thought briskly, I can set the clock back Saturday night during the Prom. And suggest to Julie she get Marcy's beau to call for her, they can switch at the gym. For there is absolutely no need, thought Sybil wisely, in asking for trouble.

2.

The Conservatory of Music stood across the street from the Methodist church. Both badly needed renovating. The Conservatory was shabby outside and inside lacked enough practice rooms. The auditorium was inadequate, and the acoustics were nonexistent. Sometimes during concerts the echo was louder than the music. The organ often emitted shrill whistles of its own accord. The truth was, the Conservatory was a stepchild, and came off badly when appropriations were divided.

The best studio, in the front on the second floor, belonged to Professor Mark Allingham, since he had headed the Conservatory for fourteen years. He sat there at his desk on this Tuesday night in May, working on a concert program for Marjorie Knight, his top soprano. Marjorie was scheduled to sing for the Conservatory graduation. She hadn't been in top form for several months, had even missed some lessons, but she said Dr. Jim was giving her a tonic, so he wasn't really concerned.

Music was Mark Allingham's life. A bachelor, he had time

to work on it day and night. He never had to walk colicky babies or rush to the hospital while children parted with their tonsils, or baby-sit when Mama went to Ladies' Aid. He had no distractions, no responsibility except for his students. Phrasing, breath control, diction, tone production, interpretation, repertoire, occupied him. He was hard-driving, tactless, but gifted as a teacher. Even the girls who left his studio in tears seldom dropped their lessons.

His studio wasn't much. The carpet was down to the nap under the piano pedals. Shaky music shelves sagged with scores. Beethoven's bust was cracked, and the young Mozart in the picture had a dingy nightgown. An anemic rubber plant (gift of a student) was liverish. The walls were peeling, but then this was true all over Westerly. Money didn't exactly flow in.

Mark was too busy to mind. He had his regular students who were majoring in voice, and worked with them endlessly. The would-be sopranos (who were really contraltos), the tenors (with baritone range) and those who had no range at all but wanted to be singers, they filled his days. But the Conservatory was also open to non-college students (without credit) so there were many town people (chiefly matrons) who took lessons. Mark taught them too, accompanying them himself unless he cadged a student pianist. He staged the student recitals, planned the faculty ones, if necessary gave a piano recital himself to fill in. He also played the chapel organ and directed the Glee Club. It was no wonder he seldom attended faculty social gatherings.

He was thin, stooped from sitting so much on piano benches. He brushed his hair forward over the bald spot beginning to show. His face was pale, since he never sunned, and his eyes looked startling, for they were sea-blue and seemed almost to give out light against the pallor of his skin. His mouth did not fit the ascetic face; it was full and humorous.

Mark had one vanity, unusual for a professor. He kept his trousers well-pressed, his shirts starched, and he chose his ties with care. He never slopped around, and this led various women teachers from time to time to "set their cap" at him. Such a quiet well-groomed man obviously should be married. But the gentle trap never closed on him. He went his own way with his music and his students. It was true, a few people noticed, that he was very possessive with his students. Those rash enough to go against his wishes paid for it.

On this particular night, he decided to transpose the aria for Marjorie Knight. Lately her top notes didn't float out so easily. He wanted her to give a flawless performance. For years he had dreamed of a voice like hers which he could develop, shape, bring to full bloom. In Marjorie, he had it. It was a voice with incredible range, immense power, and purity. It seemed effortless and, thank God, she had perfect pitch. Moreover, she was intelligent, skimmed through technical difficulties, and she was beautiful in a dark, intense way.

She was not a regular Westerly student, but had, with Mark's pushing, taken most of the courses. She was, unfortunately, married to a clerk in the First National Bank of Winnebago, and Mark couldn't do anything about that. But Ralph was no real problem.

Now as he put away the aria, Mark decided that he would stay in Winnebago all summer and work with Marjorie every day. Her French was shaky and her repertoire still too limited. During the long vacation, the Conservatory was almost empty and they could use the auditorium any time. And he really didn't have any particular place to go. He was tired of going to Europe and coaching with famous teachers who didn't know half he did. New York was steaming in summer, noisy and dirty. He could accomplish something by staying in Winnebago and working on Marjorie's voice.

He locked the studio and went out, wondering whether he

was too late for the dormitory dinner (boiled beef, limp potatoes, bullet peas). He nearly fell over Julie and Mike who sat on the Conservatory steps (why were they there?).

"Nice evening," he said.

"Yes, isn't it?" answered Julie. Her voice sounded as if she had been crying.

He got to the dining hall as dessert was served (rice pudding). But the student waiter brought him a plate and he ate absently, hardly caring that everything was cold. He was planning Marjorie Knight's first big concert tour (a year more of concentrated work might do it). He'd better start on the program this summer so they could polish and polish. He'd write to Colter when she was ready (he knew him in Vienna long ago). Or was Pritchard a better manager? For that matter, he could manage her himself, except during the actual college term.

He wanted an accompanist who would never fail to support the one thin tone in her range, but who would never try to be a soloist. Well, he would try the prospects out. And then, finally, she must have exactly the right costume. Something velvety and sweeping, showing off her figure. Few singers had good figures, they either looked like poles or silos. The local dressmaker, he thought, could not create the right gown, and of course Ralph couldn't afford anything. If necessary he himself would borrow on his insurance to meet the cost. Still figuring, he left the pudding and went out of the dormitory. As he crossed campus, he met Julie and Mike again, this time sitting on the stone bench. He wondered uneasily if her father knew where she was. Even in the Conservatory, rumors flew. Mark had been told that Professor Prescott was breaking up the affair and, knowing Alden, felt it likely. Julie was a voice student of his, but she had cut a great deal lately. He hadn't reported her so far, for if she was in trouble with Alden, that was enough. He waved and walked quickly past them.

His flat was not really much. It was the upstairs of an old house and smelled of leaking gas. He flung up the window and brewed a cup of tea on the spirit lamp. The dormitory coffee was undrinkable.

He was just steeping the tea in his earthenware pot when the doorbell rang. It wasn't the downstairs bell either, but his own. He jumped, for nobody ever came to his sanctum, as he called it.

When he opened the door he couldn't believe it. It was Marjorie. As if she had stepped out of his thoughts, almost.

"Come in." He opened the door wider. He was confused. She must be worrying about the program, but it was peculiar for her to come here. Married women, or single students either for that matter, did *not* drop in on professors at night. This could start gossip, make trouble. He shut the door quickly.

Marjorie came in and sat down on the sofa. "I had to come," she said. "I've got to tell you now. I thought I could get through it, but I can't." Her voice was desperate.

"What's the matter?"

"I can't do the program," she whispered, "I simply can't do it."

"But you have to." He jumped up. "It is your—it is my—"

"I know." She twisted her hands together. "It is—it is hard for me to explain. And I was sure I could wait until college was over—but—lately I haven't felt well—not at all. The doctor told me I would after about the fourth month—but I only feel worse." Tears began to fall silently down her face.

"But what's the matter? What is this about?" His voice broke.

"I—we—I'm going to have a baby." She bent her head. "I didn't want to upset you!"

Upset! When he was small, he had crashed from an apple tree and broken three ribs. That was nothing to this blackness swallowing him. Upset! As he turned toward her, she looked frightened.

"I guess things like this do happen," she said timidly. "I guess they just do. I—there are things that just happen."

He mumbled something. Then he sat down and put his face in his hands.

Marjorie stood up, dropping her hands hopelessly. "It doesn't mean I can't sing later on," she assured him quickly. "It's just now, at this time. By fall, I'll be just fine. It will be just the same as always. I'll work harder to—make up to you."

He looked up, and she tried to smile but it was only pitiful. She moved over and touched his hand. "Please," she begged. "It will be all right, except for now." She went to the door, came back and said softly, "Ralph and I—well, we were wondering—we hoped—I mean you are—you have always been—we wondered if you'd be the baby's godfather?" The question hung limp in the air. She turned and went out, closing the door gently.

Mark cried. He cried for the lost years, the overwork, underpay, the frustration. He cried because he had fallen out of the apple tree. Then anger dried his tears. Marjorie, he thought furiously—washing bottles, ironing baby clothes. There would be croup, colic. Then no doubt another baby. Women got the habit so easily. Her career would consist of singing in the Methodist church at times when Ralph would mind the baby. He felt like a mountain climber plunging down a crevasse with the peak in view.

He threw the program announcements in the wastebasket, got his jacket and flung down the stairs. He had nowhere to go except the Conservatory where he turned in automatically. Two lights burned in Miss Nelson's studio and Mr. Parker's. Miss Nelson was practicing the piano and Parker was tuning his violin. He sneaked past, in no mood to speak to either of them. But he thought bitterly about them as he went to his own studio and sat at the desk.

Miss Nelson was the second voice teacher, inherited from past years. She was a spare woman (she reminded Mark of a heron) and she had no idea at all of how to teach anything. Year in, year out her students sang "The Fairy Pipers" and "*Ouvre tes yeux bleu*" and "My Mother Bids Me Bind My Hair" while she accompanied them, whacking the piano keys, nodding her head violently. She sang with them inaudibly, and when they missed a note her head bobbed wildly as she bore down on the fatal key with a fierce finger. Mark thought her sole qualification was that she could play Mendelssohn's Spring Song.

Parker was a different problem. He was an expert violinist, but indolent. When he was in the mood he could give a brilliant recital, and as he tossed his long hair and half-closed his eyes he made a fine impression, especially on the female part of the audience. But he was an indifferent teacher, letting his pupils saw away without comment. They bored him. Unlike Mark, he never dreamed of nourishing a great gift; he was a realist.

Nevertheless he was popular and a favorite with the faculty. He was a handy teacake passer, good with small talk, attentive to faculty wives, who later told their husbands how gifted he was. He was always ready to play a solo at any function (he played what he already knew). He was not yet married, but no constitutional bachelor like Mark. Currently he was edging up on a rich widow, and playing the field with a young instructor still dewy from an eastern college.

All these years, thought Mark, and I'll come no better off than Nelson and Parker. Just another small-town college teacher. He stared despondently at the transposed aria. May as well toss that out too. He was a saving man, saving everything from paper clips and string to old news clippings. Now, curiously, he prowled his studio throwing things away. He flung piles of old programs, reviews, copies of *The Etude*, boxes of pencil stubs, receipted bills from ten years ago, odd envelopes, yellowing pictures of former pupils. When he finished, dust blew like a mistral through the room, and he put the wastebasket and two cartons of the discard in the corridor for the janitor.

Outside again, he wandered aimlessly, now chiefly feeling tired. He wasn't used to large emotions. The campus was quiet except for the sound of the band coming from the gym. They were practicing the "Alma Mater" (why couldn't those horns stay on key?).

> Westerly—
> We love thee!
> Though far away we go,
> Westerly will ever know
> We are her sons and daughters
> As long as flow the waters
> From Winnebago to the sea.

Asinine, thought Mark—and how badly they play. "But let them flat every note," he muttered, and turned toward his flat. "Godfather," he snorted. "Godfather!"

3.

The wind rose, carrying a strong smell of sulphur from the paper mills across the river. This forecast rain, though the sky was clear as yet, the moon bright. The town was deep in night, few houses had porch lamps on. But in the darkened Conservatory Miss Nelson's piano light glowed. She sat rubbing a chamois over the piano keys, for she felt it kept them whiter.

She was now alone in the building except for the night watchman, and she should go home; she had nothing more to do. But she sat rubbing away, as if that might rub the worry from her mind too. The truth was, she was frightened to death as the end of the year loomed over her, and the annual Board Meeting. Every year she trembled until that meeting was over, but this time it was worse, for this marked her twenty-fifth teaching year. The number of pupils she had, diminished as time went on. Professor Allingham attracted them with new-fangled methods. He always got the best voices, and his students sang so many new numbers. She herself hadn't had a good voice in some years, and this year she had only leftovers that he could not fit in his packed schedule.

Moreover, he had Marjorie Knight who was a sensation not only at Westerly but beginning to be known all over the state. Marjorie was a true artist, and naturally every new student expected to sing like Marjorie if they studied under Allingham. In another year, when she gave her major recital, who would be willing to study with Miss Nelson at all?

I must be sensible, she thought desperately. I have given the better part of my life to Westerly, and surely the Board would not consider retiring me and engaging some young graduate. My years of experience must count. But the fear was there, heavy in her breast. She had skipped dinner at Kennicott because the gabble of young voices made her dizzy. Now she needed a cup of hot tea. She opened the cupboard and took out her dead straw hat and perched it on her gray hair. Her coat was frayed, she must turn cuffs and collar again, mend the buttonholes. These summer coats never lasted; this was only nine years old and she was careful with it.

She scurried across campus, her resoled slippers tapping on the gravel path. Here and there, a few students coming late from the library drifted in the shadows of the lilacs. During exams they had night permission until eleven. She noticed they went in couples and walked close together, talking softly. It gave her a queer pang. How would it be to have someone to talk to?

Her room was on the third floor at Kennicott, in the rear. In winter it was draughty, in summer steaming. But it was nice and cheap to live in the dormitory. She turned on the light and picked up the mail from the marble-topped table by the door, feeling the familiar panic. There just could not be an extra bill from the sanitarium right now! But it was, it was for new spectacles because her sister had broken the old ones. There were many extras, although they had not mentioned them when they took her poor sister Marylin.

But she could not bring herself to put her sister away in a state institution, no matter what scrimping it meant. As she put the kettle on the gas plate and rinsed her cup in the bath-room bowl, she put away the thought of a fresh dress for Com-mencement. Marylin couldn't very well go without glasses.

Miss Nelson's life had been a financial battle for a long time. Her father was not a good businessman, and after he and her mother died, all his debts came home to roost. She paid the funeral expenses from the life insurance and took on the bur-den. For this she gave up the summer of study in Paris, and the summer session in Chicago. And then Marylin began to hear voices and lost her job in the department store because she made the customers nervous by carrying on conversations with nobody. Miss Nelson accepted the extra burden, gave up her flat and moved to Kennicott which was noisy, uncomforta-ble, but cheap. The windows gave on the laundry so the room smelled always of starch and bleach. The furniture was left-overs from departing students. Her bathroom was big enough to turn around in but by the time she took her bath, the hot water was usually gone. The food was poor, but she couldn't afford hot dinners at the restaurant. As long as she had her salary, she managed. But suppose—well, supposing was no good.

Everyone is keyed up at Commencement, she told herself. So much confusion and parents and alumni pouring in, and then after it is over, things settle down. She took out a box of biscuits, poured her tea. This will be nice and cozy, she thought. But she was still hungry as she swept up the crumbs.

She undressed, put her hair up in leather curlers. In the mirror her long thin face stared back at her, new wrinkles in it and folds under her chin. Her skin looked gray no matter how much she patted glycerin and rose water on. Nobody could stay young forever, she told herself firmly. She felt like having a good cry, but it always made her head ache. And she remembered the time Father beat her with a buggy whip saying, "I'll give you something to cry for." Father had taught her a good deal.

Surely I'll have a few good students next term, she thought. I'll put on a fine recital, learn some new numbers, everyone will say Miss Nelson is a gifted teacher, couldn't very well spare *her*.

Blinking, she got out the dress for Commencement and started to let out the hem. When dresses were short she took it up, when they were long she let it out. This was a let-out year. Her kid pumps were still good, she decided, French chalk would freshen them. She hoped it wouldn't be as hot as it usually was, for her feet would swell and the pumps were tight at best. She'd had them a long time.

This year she had planned to buy a new print, have a wide-brimmed straw and new slippers; now she couldn't. But she would look respectable and dignified. And tomorrow she would go down to breakfast and drink a glass of milk and eat a bowl of oatmeal so she would feel fresh as a daisy. She was really getting too thin, and that was why she had those wrinkles.

The springs creaked when she finally got to bed. She said

her prayers lying down because she was tired. As she dozed off, she had a comforting thought. President Wallace is an upright man, she told herself, and he knows how hard I have worked all these years. I have never taken a single day off.

At the same hour, across campus, President Wallace was indeed remembering how faithful Miss Nelson was. He had come to a part of his job he hated, for Miss Nelson must retire. For the good of the Conservatory, go she must. Miss Nelson was like an old horse (and looked like one) who must be put out to pasture, and it was too bad there wasn't a pasture provided by Westerly. But her antiquated teaching, her complete lack of extra study during vacations, even the way she slopped around in the same clothes year after year, were all bad for the college. She was a liability, although not by any means the only one.

Why hadn't she kept up? She was not lazy. Could he have spoken to her a few years ago? It was too late now. He felt the burden of his office as he went across campus and walked slowly up the steps of the Victorian mansion supposed to be his home.

Dick Wallace, at forty-two, was normally full of vitality, an ambitious, driving man, expert administrator, a success. Since coming to Westerly, he had revamped the investments, raised money for the new Student Building (he had been going over the blueprints this night). He battled the Board for salary raises and the faculty for a more liberal elective curriculum. He had managed to ease the social regulations—not enough, but it was a step. He even kept the turbulent faculty more or less in hand. The next step in his career would be a big university. He was on his way.

But Westerly, the testing ground, had moved into his heart. He loved the shabby buildings, the elms shading the campus, the lilacs, and the river flowing below the hill. He didn't mind

29

the factions, bickerings, jealousies of the faculty; those were part of any academic scene.

He grinned as he thought of the battle of the Blue Books. The younger teachers wanted them changed, big enough so one Blue Book would take a whole exam. Alden headed the committee, so the books were not to be changed. No use spending money, said Alden. Mark Allingham, suave and reasonable, had not swayed him, nor had Dean Richardson, the third member of the committee. She was a wise and gentle woman.

He rested a moment against the gingerbread porch railing. He was a big craggy man and the railing sagged. The college, he thought dryly, he could manage, but his own life was a shambles. His personal problem stooped him, kept his mouth grim. He pulled in a breath of air, let himself in the house, braced for the usual welcome.

It came as his wife stepped across the drawing room, elegant in a lilac chemise frock.

"It's about time you came home," she said icily. "I waited dinner an hour. Of course you couldn't get in on time."

"I was in the middle of a special meeting," he explained wearily. "I'll rustle up a sandwich. Where are the twins?"

He moved toward her to give her a kiss but she backed away.

"I sent them to bed." She picked up her novel. "They can't stay up all hours waiting for you."

He sighed. Carol was punishing him by sending the twins to their room. She found so many ways to punish him, put him in the wrong. But as he looked at her it was difficult to believe how hard she was, for she was so lovely.

Perhaps her external beauty left no room for an inner warmth. She was as young as when he first saw her; living had not touched her. She wore her hair smooth and tight, pulled back like satin (never marcelled, never curled) to emphasize the porcelain oval of face and the luster of her dark eyes. Her mouth was thin, but who noticed that?

"I suppose you've settled the problems of the world," she commented.

"Hardly that." He tried to smile. "Just tying up odds and ends."

He went to the kitchen, found some cold lamb and made a sandwich, heated the coffee and sat at the kitchen table. He knew better than to expect her to fix him a tray, sit with him, and ask about his day. If he missed dinner it was not her business. She was not, as she often pointed out, a servant.

He munched the sandwich, wishing he had someone to talk to. Like Miss Nelson, he felt a need to communicate personally with someone. He was so lonely. The big things in his job he handled without worry, but the lesser things he would like to discuss. Such as Alden wanting the whole top floor of Science Hall for his museum, the rocks, shells, Indian arrows, the stuffed bear (which was currently being aired on the front lawn of Science). The bear must go inside before Commencement. Then there was the new wallpaper for Kennicott. The housemother chose a paper with flamingos. The Dean preferred a cherry red with ivory medallions and the Art professor (second floor front) wanted green because the vibrations were soothing.

Miss Phipps, the librarian, wanted new chairs for the Browsing Room and Mark insisted on three new pianos for the Conservatory. Bertie, the football coach, nagged for a new field house. There wasn't money enough for everything everybody needed, and how to manage was a problem. He washed his dishes and went in to say good night to Carol, knowing he couldn't tell her anything at all. But she told him.

She was sick to death of Westerly and everything in it. The laundress didn't iron the sheets properly, the butcher was late with the meat. Gas was leaking from the stove again and Minnie had broken a Spode plate on purpose. The twins were impossible. Carol had brought in a half-dead kitten. Dick tried

31

to paint his bicycle and spilled paint all over everything. Neither of them would do their homework.

"And, Richard, I cannot manage without another servant," she finished.

Most women in Winnebago had no servant at all, except the weekly cleaning woman. What did Carol do to keep so busy? She took no part in college activities, or in town either. She went grudgingly to church, but never helped with church suppers. She paid almost no attention to the twins beyond scolding them.

"We can't afford two servants," he said.

"Then why not get out of this hole and take a decent business job?" she cried. "I didn't marry you to get stuck in the backwoods all my life!"

Dick had learned to listen with the top of his mind, so he could nod at intervals or shake his head. On the bottom level, he considered how to answer the wire from Mayhew Gilbert, the richest trustee. Gilbert did not want Dr. Burghley to deliver the Commencement address, as planned. Dr. Burghley was a radical, a pacifist, and if such a man were featured at Westerly, he Mayhew Gilbert would think again about the donation for the new gymnasium.

Dr. Burghley had already accepted. Should he be withdrawn? What would his friends say? And the Alumni Association had asked for him. Was it better to accept Gilbert's bribe —money was needed—or stick to a principle?

"Of course you don't care what I think." Carol was in a rage. "You just sit there like a log. I won't put up with it, I tell you."

Without answering he got up and left the room. There wasn't anything he could say. It was true she didn't fit in here. And as far as his career was concerned, she had nearly ruined it when they first came. She snubbed the faculty wives, refused invitations, and when he insisted she go with him to a faculty dinner, she made it clear she was bored to death. She had an unfortunate way of talking about her glamorous life in New York before they were married, lacing her conversation with famous names (all men). Then she had a cruel way of flicking her eyes at the women, emphasizing their dowdy clothes and old-fashioned hairdos. Consequently, she was not invited to join the Literary Society. The phone stopped ringing, except for Dick. The faculty women ignored her.

She had trouble getting good service, too. In Winnebago, everybody was as good as everybody. You couldn't talk down to tradespeople or servants. Most of the country-club set was a step away from lumbermen and farmers, immigrants who made their own way. The richest woman in town was the daughter of a millworker who invented a new process for treating the pulpwood. Her brother was a mail carrier married to a Swedish girl who had "worked out." Family dinners alternated between the mansion on College Avenue and the frame house on Locust Street.

Carol couldn't understand this society, and as Dick went to his study he wondered again why she had lowered herself to marry him, since she was a snob, and he was a poor graduate student. He was finishing his Ph.D. that year, on the money left him from the sale of a piece of farmland inherited from an uncle. He met Carol by merest chance, at a benefit luncheon for crippled children. A classmate told him the food was good and the society girls who staged the luncheon were pretty.

Carol, passing the rolls, was casually introduced to him. She wore a sea-colored dress. Perhaps she was tired of the sleek men and wanted a change. He took her to a concert, but she didn't care for music. Presently his funds ebbed away on theatre tickets and indigestible food at fancy places. Orchids were her favorite flower; her preferences in perfume were expensive. But he was in a dream, squiring this beautiful, exciting girl. Surprisingly, her parents were pleased. He never knew until the twins were born that they preferred any man to the European drifter, four-times divorced. Dick was single, honest, respectable.

Carol hated Marbury, where he had his first position as History professor. She hated Elliot, where he was head of the department. (But would he have climbed so fast without her nagging? That was a point.) She had hysterics when she found she was to have a baby and when it turned out to be twins, she threatened to throw herself out of the hospital window.

Since then, Carol had had her own bedroom. The closeness, release, gathering of strength, that came from love were not his. He was expected to knock on her door if he wanted to see her, and he entered as a stranger. It might have been easier if she had offered mental companionship, but there was nothing. Not even ordinary kindness.

He didn't often indulge in regrets, but spring was hard to bear. On a sudden impulse, he went downstairs and outdoors. Carol was already in her room, doing her exercises and creaming her face. He swung across campus to Kennicott, and knocked at the Dean's door.

"How nice to see you," she said without surprise. "Will you join me in a cup of coffee?"

He sank wearily on the sofa. "I was just walking," he said.

"I just made it." She handed him a cup. "I finished my grades a few minutes ago. I think you take two lumps?"

Fancy her noticing! As she passed the sugar, he saw how slender her hands were. He looked up, really seeing her for the first time as a woman. In her dove-gray dress (which matched her eyes), and with her hair combed softly into a loose knot, she looked lovely as Parma violets. It surprised him to make the comparison, for he hadn't observed any woman in so long. The contour of her face suggested a Renaissance portrait, but one he had never seen. Conscious of staring at her, he glanced around the room. The Dean's apartment was on the first floor,

34

at the left of the entrance hall, and the windows overlooked the garden, now sweet with spring flowers and budding roses. There was a bedroom and a bath and a small kitchenette at the rear. The living room was comfortable with polished eighteenth-century pieces, a plain gray carpet, filled bookshelves, and a fine collection of porcelain in the breakfront. The portrait of the Dean's grandmother presided over the mantel. The face was gentle, the eyes remarkably like the Dean's. A fire was laid in the fireplace, in case of a cool night.

The whole room was designed to make a homelike atmosphere for students who came to confide their troubles, for anxious parents whose daughters were in the various jams common to the young. Here, too, tea was served to visiting ministers or lecturers, and committees met and conferences were held with the housemothers. President Wallace decided it was the most satisfying place in Westerly.

"You are right about the wallpaper," he said suddenly.

"It was only a suggestion. Wallpaper isn't so important." She smiled.

Then he was telling her about Dr. Burghley, and Miss Nelson, and the Browsing Room, and many other things, even about the problem of Johnny Green, the quarterback, who handed in a Chamber of Commerce leaflet for his last theme.

"We can't have plagiarizing," she said, "even by sons of trustees. But he has a good mind. Couldn't you suspend him for the rest of the week? I could tutor him this summer, and he can do odd chores in return. I've heard one trouble is that his father doesn't give him an extra nickel and there is considerable family difficulty."

He gave her a grateful look. She made it sound easy.

"As for Dr. Burghley," she commented, "I think you might have to take a stand on this. You don't want to be a figurehead. But you could write a sympathetic letter, and put it to Mr. Gilbert that it would be bad publicity at this late date and so on. And add that nobody ever listens to the Commencement sermon anyway, so it wouldn't do any harm."

He laughed. "I think you should be running Westerly," he said. "Thank you."

"I'm always here," she smiled, "and I love Westerly too." She added, "I'm sure there are some discarded armchairs in the Kennicott attic that could be redone for the Browsing Room temporarily."

"Thank you," he said again, and went out into the troubling sweetness.

Dean Richardson, he thought, was what Westerly needed. She managed to run the Greek Department better than it ever had been, and at the same time handle endless problems with students, faculty, parents. She was a gifted administrator, and it was a mystery why she stayed on at a low salary. Somehow he must get that raise through; he could never get along without the Dean.

"I could have stayed forever," he said to himself.

4.

"I don't know what to do," wailed Julie, "but Papa can't make me give you up. I'd die."

Mike was troubled. "You are pretty young. And I'm a nobody."

"What do you mean nobody? You're on the Dean's list. You're on the team. You're on the *Clarion* staff. What more could you want?"

"A Prescott background." He grinned.

They walked slowly along the back street. They were both tired of walking and sitting and walking and sitting and dodging around. It wasn't much fun never to go to a nice house and play records and have sandwiches and cocoa. It kept them jumpy, too, watching for Alden or someone who would tell him. Julie was miserable, and transferred some of her resentment to Mike who seemed to always defend her father. Maybe he would get tired of her.

"I'm due at Gamma meeting," she told him. "We're voting on last-minute pledging. Lizbeth Fowler's coming up. You know we rushed her off and on."

"I know. And she wears thick glasses and old middy suits, but the Gammas sure could use a boot in their scholarship rating. Bottom of the list, aren't you? She's a nice girl. Sits next to me in Philosophy and helps me a lot."

"I'm glad you find her so interesting."

"Well, you sorority girls can be awful snobs," he commented.

"Thanks." Her temper flared. "Don't bother to come any farther."

"What's wrong now?"

"Nothing at all. Nothing. Gamma's a bunch of snobs, and dumb."

"I simply make a remark about a nice girl. I simply said—"

"I heard you. Now I'll run along and join the rest of the no-account ones."

"Oh hell," he exploded, really angry too.

"Why don't you pick up the wonder girl and buy her a banana split?"

"I think I'll do just that." He turned and walked away.

Julie couldn't believe it. She stared after him as he swung away with no backward glance. Was he really going off with that grind who'd been helping him with Philosophy (one of Julie's hardest subjects)? She remembered with a sick feeling that it was Mike who had first told her Lizbeth was a good egg and ought to be pledged by somebody.

She went back to campus and sat down on the stone bench.

Almost anything seemed to set them off lately. She was so nervous over her father, she snapped at everything. And Mike showed the strain by just talking back to her. Well, she had to get to meeting or get a demerit, so she dragged herself miserably to the third floor of the old Lawrence house, where Gamma had three rooms. She was late and the room was crowded. Girls sat on the overstuffed sofa, understuffed chairs (courtesy of a departing grad) and on the floor. Julie slipped into a corner as Marcy Lindstrom finished a report on Pan-Hellenic.

Marcy was the prettiest girl at Westerly, having the clean loveliness of her Swedish heritage. She was also a top student, the only Gamma except Julie to make the Dean's list. She was a practical girl too, hardheaded, and Julie's best friend.

"I'm posting the marks on the mantel," Marcy was saying, "where the scholarship ought to be. Next fall, we'll have a study committee to work with anyone below a B. Any discussion? Then we'll proceed to the matter of pledging Lizbeth Fowler. Any discussion?"

There was discussion on that, all right. Everyone took the floor at once until Marcy banged the gavel madly.

"It's not that I personally have anything against her, but is she the Gamma type?" asked Hazel.

"She looks like an old bird nest," said Bess.

"Why not fix her up?" Ginny was the hopeful one. "With a good hairdo and we could lend her some clothes—"

"She gives me the creeps," complained Lucy, "lumbering around with her head down."

"But we need a Phi Bete," said Laura, the practical one, "and it won't be me." Laura barely passed.

"I think you're all stuffy." Amalie was firm. "We can't all be May Queens like Marcy. I'm for giving her a chance. All she needs is a man, and we can put the bite on one if we work on our own men. It doesn't matter who he is."

The argument swung back and forth and wasn't, actually, any sillier than many of the faculty ones. Only Julie said nothing, but nobody noticed in the babble of voices.

At last Marcy ended the discussion and the voting box was brought. Marcy put the smooth balls in a basket on the table, the box to the right. The balls were white, made of ivory—or bone. But one was black. The Gammas filed by, reaching secretly for the ball they chose. They were quiet now, only the balls clicked into the box.

When it was her turn Julie walked slowly, closed her eyes and reached blindly for a ball, and dropped it. The tellers took the box and went to the kitchenette to open it. When they came back, one of them held up the black ball. Lizbeth Fowler would not be bid.

Marcy dismissed the girls and Julie walked to the dorm with her. Julie was staying for supper because this was one of the better nights with spring lamb and mint sauce. While they washed up Julie confided her troubles again, but Marcy knew them by heart.

"I think you better step soft with Mike," she said, brushing her hair. "He just might walk out on you one day. It isn't going to wreck the world if he buys one banana split for that poor Fowler girl. I wonder who blackballed her? It's a shame."

"I didn't watch anybody," said Julie truthfully, "and I hardly looked at the basket."

"Can't be helped now," said Marcy practically. "There's the bell. Come on, I'm starving. Hope they have seconds."

After supper, they went back to Marcy's room and ate chocolates (Marcy's steady was well-heeled). They discussed Gamma's deplorable rating and the low state of her finances, and what Marcy had heard from somebody who heard that Marjorie Knight was going to have a baby. And whether Liz knew she was voted on and blackballed. And what Julie better do about Mike.

When Julie got home, it was after nine-thirty. Her father called sharply from the study. "Julie, is that you? Where have you been?"

"I had Gamma meeting and stayed for supper with Marcy," she said shortly.

"Why didn't you telephone and ask me?"

The emotions of the day boiled over. "Why—why—why— why can't I live in the dormitory?" she cried.

He dropped his pen and stood up. "And what is wrong with your own home?"

She flung out her hands. "In a dorm," she cried, "you live like a human being at least! You aren't treated like a baby! In a dorm"—she winked back the tears—"you can be more a person!"

Sybil heard them, and flew down from the sewing room where she was running up petticoats for the missionary barrel.

"Julie, you'd better get up and do your homework," she said.

Julie turned on her. "Homework. Bed. Get up. Go to classes. Set the table. Wash the dishes. Do your homework and get to bed. A fine life that is! What fun do you ever want me to have? I'm the only girl at Westerly who can't stay to the end of a dance. I'm the one who can't go to Madison for the game. I'm the one who is supposed to sit at home. I might as well be dead!"

Sybil braced herself. "I don't think you have such an unbearable life." She spoke quietly.

But Alden was wheezing again. Sybil had to remind herself that he had broken his nose in a hockey game at Johns Hopkins and he needed a lot of air when he got angry. It wasn't really a dramatic device, although it sounded like it.

"Leave me!" Alden banged the desk. His snowflake paperweight bounced. "Leave me. I work day and night for you and your mother, and this is the gratitude I get!"

"Now, Alden," Sybil spoke calmly, "I don't know what this

is all about. But do try not to get so worked up. It isn't good
for you."

She knew better, but she was tired out. She had run two
club meetings, worked on the church missionary drive, visited
the hospital, entertained six faculty wives at tea, and had a
bad session with a Geology student about to flunk Geology 25.
She had to finish those petticoats tonight, although she wondered whether the heathen liked to wear them. And here was
Alden exploding again, and Julie looking like a Valkyrie. It was
too much. But to accuse Alden of being worked up was a bad
error.

"Worked up—" He labored for air.

"I'll leave." Julie was sobbing. "Nothing would please me
more! I never want to see Westerly again."

She didn't, Sybil noted, say she never wanted to see them
again, and that was a good sign.

"How sharper than a serpent's tooth." Alden sank into his
chair and put his head in his hands.

Sybil went out quietly and turned on the kitchen light. She
might as well get ready to restore them with food. She toasted
bread and sliced onions thin, made fresh coffee. Their voices
were muffled now, so she couldn't hear what they said. She
didn't care, at the moment. She also had a sudden yearning to
leave. To walk out and never come back.

Julie went up to bathe her eyes, and Alden came in sniffing.
He sat down and began his sandwich with gusto. Spooned sugar
in his coffee.

"What was it about?" asked Sybil.

He gave her a sheepish grin. "I don't know. But Julie has a
pesky temper. Comes from your side of the family, I expect.
Your aunt Grace was flighty."

His face was rosy, innocent, his eyes bluer than ever. His
collar was damp with tears—his and Julie's, and his tie

screwed around. Sybil found it impossible to be angry with him long, any more than she would with a child.

"Good sandwich," he commented. "Why don't we have the Peters for supper tomorrow night? I haven't seen Dr. Jim all week. I want him to run up to Fremont with me before Commencement. Some fellow up there claims he struck oil. Can't be, but I said I'd look around."

"Tomorrow is Clio Club day."

"Well, you needn't fuss for Ella and Jim. Just something easy like fried chicken and biscuits and creamed asparagus and a pie or something."

"All right," said Sybil.

They turned out the downstairs lights and went to bed. Sybil brushed her fine long hair while Alden retired to the sleeping porch to undress, for he was a modest man. Sybil pinned up her hair, tied the silk net on, got into her nightgown, and knelt to say her prayers. Her head ached again, but maybe that was because she hadn't worn her spectacles while basting the petticoats. The glasses kept falling from her small nose and she found them a nuisance.

Alden came out, his nightshirt billowing about his legs. He padded to the bathroom to throw the towels around and make a mess of the tooth powder. Sybil laid out his clothes for morning, wishing he would give up his long underwear now it was so warm. He said it protected him from germs, and germs were the only thing he feared, either on earth or in heaven. Inconsistently, he ran about when it was thirty below with his fur-lined coat open, scooping up snow and sleet as he ran.

Sybil got into the great walnut bed that she, as well as Julie, had been born in. Her mother had died in this bed too, a gentle, flowerlike woman chiefly concerned with not bothering anybody while she was dying. It was the bed Sybil and Alden first slept in, after they came back from the horse-and-buggy honeymoon. It had been stored during the wandering years, and now it was settled for the rest of their lives.

Alden banged his toe against the rosewood slipper chair.

"Confound it," he muttered. He climbed in bed beside Sybil "Better get some sleep," he sighed, "or we'll never get started in the morning. Hard day coming up. I have a lot to do."

Sybil did too, but she didn't mention it. The life of a faculty wife was not exactly a bed of roses around Commencement time.

"Remind me I have to do something about my bear," Alden said, beating the pillow into obedience. "He's all aired out. When I get that top floor I'll be able to fumigate now and then."

Then in one of his unexpected changes of mood, he leaned over and squeezed her so hard she almost cried out.

"That was a pretty dress you wore today," he said. "Your hair looked nice too. You're the prettiest woman in Winnebago. You haven't changed at all."

Suddenly he let his arms fall, turned over, and slept, as a child does, instantly and wholly.

Sybil, awake, watched the moonlight invading the room.

5.

Dr. Jim Peters drove back from Black Creek just as the sky grayed toward dawn. He had been called at midnight because the Novak baby was having convulsions. During the twenty-five-mile drive out, he almost dozed at the wheel, for it had been a busy day since six the morning before. But then, it was no different than most days.

After he treated the Novak baby and urged Mrs. Novak not

43

to give her pig's knuckles to suck, he started back, now fully awake. He was glad he had the fine Cartercar instead of old Daisy when it came to speed. The Cartercar didn't have to be saddled but only cranked a few minutes. Still he missed Daisy's companionship, for she was a good horse and nice to talk to as they clopped along.

He had seen many changes, he thought, in his fifty-one years. In town, street lights and pavements, for instance, a new front to the hotel (the food was no better), new buildings on campus. Some barns and carriage houses in the residential section had become garages. Daisy's harness and blanket still hung in his own and the smell of leather and ammonia still lingered. He had taken out the box stall to make room for the car.

Sleeping porches were now popular, and Ella nagged him to turn the upstairs porch into one. But he liked the big front bedroom although the new street light glared in the windows. Let Ella get new furniture downstairs to replace the sound Mission if she wanted, but keep the bedroom as it was.

Winnebago was quiet, except for twinkling lights from houses where men were on the early shift. The town had two focal points, the paper mills and Westerly, but it was the mills that were its lifeblood.

Dr. Jim drove down Main Street, past the watering trough where Daisy had always stopped to lip the water. He reached home, drove the car into the barn, cut off the engine, and lumbered in to bed as fast as possible. He got tired easily nowadays, but he fell asleep instantly, forgetting his aches. His last waking thought was it would be a wonder if the Novak baby lived to grow up. What could you expect with ten children in eleven years?

Around six the phone yammered again and he cleared sleep from his throat with a cough. "Be right there," he said. He washed, pulled on his worn suit, grabbed his bag and hurried out to the car. She started easy, still warm from the long night drive.

At St. Mary's he pounded down the corridors, nodding at the Sisters who glided by. How he'd like to get them out of those robes and into uniforms! The smell of incense drifted out from the chapel and he thought maybe the prayers did more than the pills, at that.

"We thought we might wait until morning," said Sister Mary Concepcion, "but then it seemed—"

"Right," he said crossly, smiling at her.

She understood this shaggy, brusque man very well. She had stood beside many beds while he cursed and sweated and snapped at the staff. He was a soldier for Christ, she said, God rest his soul.

In the room, there was nothing left to do. The Cheyne-Stokes breathing racked the air. Dr. Jim felt for the pulse while Sister Mary Concepcion laid a cool cloth on the forehead of the dying woman. The interne stood miserably at the foot of the bed. Dr. Jim flung up the window and the breeze diminished the sweetish odor of cancer.

"You could cut cancer out," Dr. Jim said aloud, "but how do you find out in time? There's got to be a way. Maybe I'll live to see it."

Time. Everything was time. Maybe death was simply an end to battling time. Now he was hoping for enough to get home, have a bath, put on clean clothes and maybe get some breakfast before beginning his rounds.

At home Ella was, as usual, waspish. She looked fresh and well-starched but had no greeting except the sausage was cold, the pancakes not fit to eat.

"No sense running around night and day," she commented.

He did not answer. Ella was a capable housekeeper and undeniably a good woman, but she had never understood what

45

being a doctor meant, and she had not a grain of sympathy for his patients.

"That suit is a disgrace," she said in an acid tone, "and you need a haircut."

"I'll get to it in time," he placated her. "We'll take the evening off and I'll dress up for the Prescotts'. Sybil puts on a whopping good dinner."

"I suppose I don't."

"I didn't mean that."

"If I didn't have to keep things warmed up for hours, maybe my meals would taste better."

"Your cooking is fine."

"I hear Julie's running around with that Hewitt boy"—she slid the sausage on his plate—"making talk."

"Pish and tush," he said amiably, "Julie is just honey, and the bees all go for honey."

"Jim, what a way to talk!" Ella was strictly raised, and Jim was too outspoken for her. "She ought to behave herself."

He was glad to get out of the house again and go on his rounds. He roared at patients who gave up easily, encouraged the desperately ill. "Sure, you'll be playing golf any day," to a hopeless case. "I don't give a hoot in hell if you're comfortable, I want to get you well"—this to a borderline case. And "If I catch you moving a peg, I'll spank you," to a farmer's wife gored by a bull.

Somehow he always made them feel better as he bullied them. Even the terminal cases managed a smile when Dr. Jim stamped in. The load was heavy this time of year, although nobody knew why. He was late again getting home to shuck his tired suit and clean up. Ella was already in her rose print (which made her spare figure look like a clothes tree) and was winding her hair around what she called a "rat." Her cameo brooch rode high on her bosom.

"Have a good day?" he asked, struggling into a stiff shirt.

46

"I'm all worn out," she said. "All the housework and the washing and the weeds in the garden."

"We could afford a woman one day a week."

"They're all shiftless," she snapped, "can't turn your back on them."

He whacked his red hair back (it did need cutting). They could have help, he reflected, if Ella could get along with them. He made enough, even with half his practice for free.

Besides he was Westerly's doctor and that paid regularly.

"Well, let's go, Mama," he said cheerfully.

Supper lights were on as they chugged down Lawe Street. The day had been warm and the lilacs were fully out. Their fragrance overpowered the fumes from the car. Ella clutched the door handle, for his driving, she said, made her nervous. They weren't much alike, he thought, rounding the corner. He smelled lilacs and she smelled fumes.

He looked forward, however, to a good evening. He liked Alden, who was a high-strung man but interesting, and so healthy. It was refreshing to spend some time with him, he was tough as a boiled owl. And Sybil—ah, there was a woman. She made a man feel important. She listened. Few women ever did. And she seemed to follow what was in a man's mind, and understand it. Her cooking was the best in town, but that wasn't it. She was, he thought, a woman to both rest and stimulate a man. And Julie was the kind of daughter he wished God had given him. She was volatile and difficult like Alden, but also sweet and warm like her mother, and probably would be as sensible when she grew up. Maybe if he and Ella had been able to have a child—

He parked the car and Ella tiptoed out, arranged her chiffon scarf elegantly, and preceded him to the house. The truth was, she felt uncomfortable with the Prescotts and this made her what Jim called uppity. She did not see why Sybil had a healthy and beautiful daughter, though wild, while she herself

47

had worked so hard on those baby bootees and bonnets only to lose her baby. Of course that was all Jim's fault. If he hadn't been on a night call delivering an eighth baby to that farm woman, he might have saved their own.

"But it was so early," he had explained. "No reason to expect—how could I know?"

Nevertheless her secret resentment grew like wild mustard, and as soon as she was up and about she moved to the guest room. She developed her headaches at that time, backaches, pains in her heart. She did her duty washing, baking, cleaning, answering the phone, going to church, but that was the end of it.

Now as she walked stiffly up the steps, she felt the bitterness sweep over her. Sybil had everything, no wonder she was so calm and easy. She had no problems. She could even have meals on time, for her husband lived on a regular schedule, not dashing around the country at all hours. As Julie opened the door envy knifed through Ella, and she hardly managed to say good evening.

"You look peaked," Jim said to Julie. "Eat oatmeal for breakfast."

"Well, I am busy—exams—" Julie said.

Alden and Sybil appeared and the usual greetings began, plus comments on the weather, inquiries as to Ella's headaches. The house had a delicious smell of frying chicken, creamy gravy and cinnamon and apples from the pie just out of the oven. Dr. Jim sniffed. He was hungry. He grinned at Alden, smiled at Sybil. Alden wore his usual baggy trousers, jacket with rubbed elbows, bright blue tie and high-laced shoes. Sybil wore a leaf-brown dress and with her fine skin, soft hair and deep eyes was not easy to look away from. Julie looked pale, and needed a tonic, that was plain.

The table was spread with the lace tablecloth and the candles were lit. Alden wouldn't object to them when Dr. Jim was there to discuss the Fremont trip and talk about what the Democrats were up to. While he served, Ella and Sybil talked about the next church supper. Ella didn't think they should have ham and potato salad but meat loaf and mashed potatoes. She also thought twenty-five cents an hour was outrageous for the woman who helped clean up. Julie said nothing. She's got the wind up, thought Dr. Jim, helping himself to gravy.

Sybil was bringing the pie when the phone rang. Julie flew to answer it and came back saying it was for Dr. Jim. Giving a reluctant look at the pie, he went to answer it. He loved Sybil's pie.

"I'm sorry, I'm called to the college," he said.

"What's wrong?" Alden asked. After all it was his college.

"An accident," Jim said evasively. "I'll give you a ring if I can't get back to take Ella home."

Ella frowned. How stupid of him to rush off in the middle of dinner.

"I hope it isn't anything catching, this near Commencement," said Sybil.

"Who knows what is catching?" He gave her a wry smile as he went out.

He pushed the car this time, taking the damp river wind full in his face. It was clouding up and the sulphur smell came strongly.

He ran into Kennicott and saw with relief that the Dean was standing by the door.

"Nobody knows when it happened," she said in a low voice, "but sometime today Lizbeth Fowler killed herself."

He was used to anything, but this was a special jolt, it made no sense at all. All he could say was, "What the hell."

Without further words, she led him upstairs to Lizbeth's room. It didn't take long to figure what happened although the why was a mystery. She had been dead, he figured, some time. She must have taken the pills the night before—at dinnertime.

49

He lifted the empty bottle with a piece of gauze and stowed it in his bag. It wasn't, he noted, a Winnebago prescription. Then he asked questions while waiting for the ambulance.

Nobody had seen her all day, the Dean told him, but that wasn't unusual, for she was a solitary girl. She missed breakfast, but often did. The corridor monitor discovered her when she made the after-dinner check on the rooms. The monitor was now recovering from hysterics.

"I'll see her in a minute," said Dr. Jim. "Go on."

Lizbeth was a top student, the Dean continued, but not popular. Her parents never came to see her, she spent Christmas at Westerly. She had, said the Dean, unpacked the laundry that came in the afternoon before, and listed the laundry to go out today. Why would a girl about to commit suicide list her laundry? The Dean stopped, choking.

"There has to be a reason," Dr. Jim told her, "back of it."

"Nobody knows. All I can think of is that she was not pledged to Gamma yesterday—she must have waited for the summons and it never came."

"Doesn't seem enough, but one never knows," he commented.

When the small burden was borne away, he finished his report in the Dean's living room while the Dean phoned the President and tried to reach Lizbeth's parents. As he dated his report he rested his head in his hands. What a waste, he thought. What had gone wrong? Why hadn't somebody prevented it? Then suddenly he fell asleep, and the Dean caught him before he slid to the floor.

Her eyes ached with tears, but they could wait. She pressed her hands against her temples, forcing herself to think, plan. It was her job to take care of this tragedy with a minimum of damage to Westerly. Keep the dormitory quiet, tend to the parents, manage the paper, pack Lizbeth's belongings.

Jim woke, stumbled to his feet, apologized. "I'll talk to the

parents when they come," he said. "Not much to say, is there?
She didn't suffer. Take this pill"—he held it out—"and get to
bed. No more to do now."

"Yes, thank you, Dr. Jim."

He picked up his bag. "I've seen eighty-year-old patients
fight for life," he commented, "then a healthy girl throws it
away. What do you make of that?"

After he left, Miss Richardson undressed, took the pill,
turned out her light. How could she have helped Lizbeth? Why
hadn't she noticed something wrong? She had failed—busy
with Commencement, the end of the year, reunion prepara-
tions. Why hadn't her parents felt their daughter was so unhappy? Or her classmates commented?

Somehow we are all to blame, thought the Dean, all of us.

6.

Julie woke up when the phone rang the next morning, and
yawned her way downstairs, just in case it was Mike. Her
mother was at the phone, saying in a shocked voice, "It doesn't
seem possible. Oh, I can't believe it! Let me know if I can do
anything."

"Who's sick now?" Julie pushed her hair back.

Sybil was white. "It's the Fowler girl," she said. "It's—it's
not possible. She's dead."

"Nonsense," said Julie loudly. "I saw her day before yesterday and Mike—" She stopped short.

"It's true. She killed herself." Sybil was beginning to cry.
"Oh the poor, poor thing. She was gone when Dr. Jim got
there."

It had to be a mistake. People didn't die until they were old.

It was monstrous, thought Julie. Why they had voted only yesterday—then she fell back, her hand over her mouth. They had blackballed her. Could that be—no, it couldn't. But suppose it could?

"Oh Mama," she whispered, and fled back upstairs. Horror went with her right into the pink bedroom. For if being blackballed was the reason Liz wanted to die—then who was responsible? Whoever dropped in the black ball? She tried, now, to remember walking to the table, choosing the ball. But did she look? And did she mean to choose the black ball or didn't she? Surely she meant to reach for a white ball.

But she had been so miserable about Mike. She could have been the one. If so, she was as good as a murderer.

This was Julie's first experience with remorse, for even if she were not guilty of blackballing, she could now wish she had taken Liz for a coke once in a while, chatted with her on the libe steps. She had never, she realized, gone out of her way to be nice to anyone outside of her immediate world. She'd never even been kind. And now she wept partly because of finding such a lack in herself. She could never make up for the past, but she determined to stop being selfish.

Finally she sopped cold water on her face, got dressed, and went downstairs. Sybil was calling the Riverside greenhouse for flowers to be sent to Marston's Funeral Home.

"Just anything springlike," she said, "not a wreath, please."

Julie refused breakfast, except coffee, and went off. Sybil sat in the living room to marshal her thoughts. This wasn't the first suicide at Westerly, but the most unreasonable. Poor Liz had no outward troubles, she was just inconspicuous, one of those shy ones who went through college without making an impression one way or the other.

The wild ones, the troublemakers, got all the attention. There should be one person, thought Sybil, assigned to be a kind of campus mother to those like Lizbeth, to reach out and draw them into the group. Being young was a hard job at best. Life is a hard job, she amended.

She hoped the confusion of Commencement would minimize the talk about the tragedy. It probably would for, once the shock was over, Lizbeth would hardly be missed, when she wasn't noticed while she was alive.

The May world was green and she went out a minute to breathe the sweetness. She had a tiring day ahead, and suddenly she longed to be walking again by the sea, where she had grown up. The river did not rest the spirit as the ocean did, it lacked the wideness of distance and the eternal tides. Someday perhaps she might go back—but it wasn't likely.

She went back in to do the housework and make a casserole of the leftover beef ready to heat up for supper. There was pie enough for Alden. Pie, pie, pie, she thought, I am so sick of pie. Why can't he be satisfied with Spanish cream or a dish of fresh strawberries?

Meanwhile Alden was in a bad mood as he loped along to Science Hall. Everything had gone wrong. Dr. Jim had gone before they settled on the Fremont trip. He had to take Ella home, and she was a tiresome old fuss-budget. Julie was acting like a sick dog. And here that Fowler girl had killed herself. One of his best students and he never saw a healthier girl. As he arranged the fossils for the day he argued violently with events. Couldn't tell what was going on these days. No sense to that girl dying, she should have known better.

Westerly needed discipline, that was the trouble. A firm hand. Shouldn't allow students to go around killing themselves.

When class began, the empty seat made him nervous and he almost forgot his lecture. The students were unmanageable, whispering every time he turned his back, the girls sniffling now and then. He announced an oral for the last class (which was unheard of). There, that would give them something to think about!

On a lower floor, in Botany lab, Julie was trying to draw the pear bud again. Everybody else had drawn theirs and passed, but her drawing was returned with TRY AGAIN on it. She knew hers looked like a potato with mumps but she couldn't help it. And as she eyed her particular pear bud, she knew it wouldn't hold out another day. It just would not be a pear bud tomorrow.

When Mike opened the door she thought it was the professor, and covered her miserable paper with her hand. But it was Mike, the first time she'd seen him since the quarrel. It seemed years ago. Mike looked calm and pleasant, and she knew she looked dreadful, red-eyed, pale.

"Thought I'd find you here," he said, leaning over her. "Busy?"

Now if she could fall in his arms, pour out her fear about Liz, be comforted, safe. But then suppose he drew away in horror?

"Yes, I'm busy," she said.

"Guess that settles that." His eyes rested on the smudged pear bud. "I just thought I'd look in. See you some other time."

He closed the door quietly. Julie laid her head on the drawing board and finished the destruction of the pear bud. Why hadn't she begged him to forgive her?

She pulled herself up and took a new sheet of drawing paper and sketched in the outline carelessly. She didn't care whether she got A or not, Father might as well be mad at that as anything.

She knew she must go to her music lesson or lose credit for the whole semester. Nobody but Professor Allingham would put up with so many absences. She was half an hour late at that, and said so when she came in the studio.

Mark was ready to put his foot down, for he too was not in a benign mood, but when he looked at her wretched face he changed his mind. She looked ill, he thought, and near the breaking point. What's the matter with Alden, can't he see it? I suppose he's doing it, pushing her. Normally Julie had a glow but she was an unlighted candle as she got out her score.

"Julie," he said cheerfully, "you can't afford a cut, but I'm rather involved just now. Suppose we just run through a couple of scales so I can mark you present."

"Thank you," she murmured.

Her vocalizing could barely be called vocalizing but he only said, "That's fine. I need a cup of tea. Will you join me?"

She sat down with a sigh until tea was ready.

"I expect we all have troubles," observed Mark. "For instance I've had a hard blow this week. Hope you don't mind crackers—I haven't anything else at the moment."

The tea was hot and comforting and she ate seven crackers. A little color came in her cheeks.

"You have a good voice," said Mark casually. "Too bad your schedule is so full, but that's the way it goes." He poured more tea. "But the best voices I get," he added, "add up to one thing. Marriage, babies, no more practice."

"I never thought of that." Julie was surprised. "I guess that must be hard for a teacher. I guess everybody thinks they have the worst problems—" she put down her cup—"I mean people like me."

"Problems are universal," he commented, "it's facing them that is individual."

She thought about this as she hurried home. Maybe I don't face things, she thought, I just get in a panic. If I were brave, I'd ask every single Gamma and find out about that blackball. I'm just scared to.

Sybil came home just in time to put the casserole in and found Julie moping in the living room. She didn't dare ask what was wrong, for Julie would look at her coldly and say, "Why, Mama, what could be wrong?" It was Mike, of course, and Liz Fowler's death, but somehow she sensed something else, for there was a hunted look in Julie's eyes. She couldn't be that much afraid of her father.

Supper was, for once, peaceful. Alden was absorbed, Julie silent, and even the phone did not ring. Afterward Alden went to the study to work on his farewell lecture of the year and Julie went to her room as soon as the dishes were done.

Sybil sat by the window in the living room, sewing fresh lace on the neck of her brown dress.

The sky was pale with afterglow and it reminded her of the delicate water colors she used to paint. She had burned them when they began to move around, and with them the sheaf of unrhymed poems she had written. Looking out at the light, she wondered where her dreams had gone? Was it enough to keep house, be a good faculty wife, fill missionary barrels, preside at teas? Was it enough to be a buffer between Julie and Alden?

Who am I, really? she asked herself.

Was she a person to anybody? Not to Alden; he never had realized her as a person. No longer to Julie, for the wall around Julie was harder than any stone. To her friends she was a help in time of trouble.

I am the loneliest woman in the world, she thought suddenly. I am absolutely and unbearably alone. All of the time.

And every woman, she reflected, needs to be a person once in a while. To have someone look at her directly and listen to her as if she were quite separate from everything else. But I, she thought, have never been really cherished.

Alden had been romantic when he was courting her, but looking back down the years, she knew there had been nothing selfless about it even then. And during the hard years he had ducked every crisis, always away hunting or on a field trip or climbing into some mine. Expecting a good hot meal when he came back, bubbling with excitement over his adventures. She tried not to think of the son, born in an adobe house with no doctor (Alden was away) or the second baby who died (Alden was on a field trip).

When Julie was born she fared better, for a neighbor happened in and rode for the doctor. And as Julie progressed through colic, measles, mumps, scarlet fever, Alden had seemed to change. For this last-born one, he would give up his own plans temporarily. For the first time he seemed to reach outside of himself. He was possessive, but indulgent. Julie was his darling, his little dove as he called her.

She must make an effort to be patient with him now that the dove wanted to try her wings. It was hard on Alden not to be the center of Julie's life. But it was time for Julie, nevertheless, to be more than her father's plaything. And it left Sybil an outsider in the conflict yet always in the middle of the battlefield, using her wisdom to avoid scenes, bind up wounds, soothe, placate, protect them both.

"Where are you?" Alden called.

"I'm coming." She laid down her sewing.

"I want to read this lecture to you."

"I'd like to hear it," she said untruthfully. Often she could make a comment or two that pointed up what he was saying, but now she didn't feel up to it. She tried to listen but her mind wandered.

"It's fine," she commented.

He walked around his desk, strutting and looking proud. He looked, she thought, not over twenty-five.

"It is good," he agreed happily. "Is there anything to eat?"

She resisted an impulse to tell him she spent over half her time being sure there was something to eat. If he asked for pie, she thought she would scream. But he was satisfied with a light snack of scrambled eggs and bacon in a toasted sandwich. And the inevitable coffee.

"I did not like this suicide at all," he said suddenly, as he

57

bit into his sandwich. "It ought to be looked into. I am going to tell President Wallace."

"It could hardly be considered his fault."

"Somebody ought to have prevented it. It isn't good for Westerly."

"It wasn't very good for her either," Sybil said mildly, "and not very good for her father and mother."

"It's all their fault," he said perversely. "They should have given her a good talking-to, the way I do to Julie when she gets notional."

Sybil wanted to laugh. But she said soberly, "I am sorry for all of them."

"Well"—he finished his sandwich and had more coffee—"I don't like it. I don't like it at all."

The truth was, she reflected, Alden never admitted death into his mind, and this death was even more difficult than death due to illness. He resented it and therefore had to blame someone, everyone. It had to be someone's fault. As soon as he settled down on whose fault it really was, he would feel better.

"We can't do much about it now," she said.

"Well, somebody is to blame," he echoed her interpretation of his thinking. "Got to get to bed. Have a hard day tomorrow."

He had a wonderful faculty for shutting one area off and plunging into another. He had already forgotten about the Fowler girl as he thought of tomorrow.

Sybil had one of her sleepless nights and dozed off toward dawn. And waked at five-thirty in the morning as Alden rummaged for a shirt (which was laid out on the chair). "Can't find anything," he muttered, banging a drawer shut. She kept her eyes shut for once and let him undergo the trial of dressing without help. Finally he bounced down the stairs making all the noise he could. He hated to be up alone, he wanted everyone else up too.

By six, she was downstairs beating the pancake batter and

he was running the lawn mower under Julie's window. He came puffing in as the first cakes were done.

"Time you were up," said Alden. "No use wasting the best hours of the day. Where's Julie?"

"She'll be down soon."

"When I was her age, I got up at daybreak," he grumbled. "People are getting weak these days."

"I expect they are," she agreed, thinking life with Alden would weaken a Marathon runner.

"I'll settle this museum business today," Alden said, sloshing syrup on his pancakes. "I've an offer from Minnesota for a fine stuffed moose. Do you realize most of the mammals as we know them will be extinct before long? The bison, where is he? Westerly must preserve them." He finished a third helping, pecked her cheek, and bounded off. Julie came in then for coffee. After she left, Ella phoned.

"Well, I suppose Jim and Alden will go off to Fremont"— Ella sounded shrill—"but I haven't heard a word about the plans. Of course I don't matter."

"I don't know either. I think the suicide has upset things."

"I hear the wretched girl killed herself because she was blackballed by Julie's sorority. Did Julie tell you?"

"No." Sybil tried not to sound irritated. "I doubt whether anyone can know what the reason was. I wouldn't make it my business."

"I simply thought you might know something," Ella snapped.

When Ella hung up, Sybil went to the kitchen to set the light rolls for luncheon Thursday. They had risen once, drawing away from the edge of the bowl. She punched the dough down, kneaded it, put it back in the bowl covered with a clean towel. Yeast makes them light, she thought, and life has yeast in it too, but you need the right temperature to leaven the dough. Is the yeast hope?

59

7.

"Today we shall review the concluding events of the Reformation," began Professor Peake.

Julie wrote the heading in her notebook. But Martin Luther didn't seem very important, and by the time class was over, she had nothing in the book except Michael's name. She would borrow Marcy's notes. Just as the bell rang, she passed a note to Mike who sat in the front row. (Professor Peake assigned them alphabetically since his memory for names of the students was poor, although his memory for history was incredible.)

Please meet me in the usual place, Julie wrote. Then she ducked out before Marcy could catch up with her. Maybe he wouldn't come. Why should he bother? But she hurried around the service driveway behind Kennicott where a giant lilac hung full clusters of bloom. From the far side one could not be seen. She waited, her heart jumping.

"I got held up," he said, pushing the branches aside. He looked at her, waiting. She braced herself. She was telling him the truth, maybe losing him forever. But she couldn't stand it not to tell him.

"Mike"—her voice was shaky—"I thought you better know. I'm not sure, but I think maybe I'm to blame for Lizbeth's dying."

"Are you crazy?" he asked.

She told him then, not sparing herself. When she finished, he pulled her to him. "So that's what's been in your silly head," he commented. "I never heard such nonsense!"

"How do you know it's nonsense?"

"In the first place, you never blackballed Liz. You're a spitfire, but it's not in you to be mean."

"I can't remember."

"In the second place, I happen to know who did. I got private sources. So get that load off your mind."

"Are—you—sure?" She drew a long breath.

"Sure I'm sure. It's not on your head, any of it. I'm sorry as hell about the miserable business, it makes me sick-angry. But not at you. Forget it."

Then Julie cried and he mopped her face.

"Gosh, you cry a lot lately," he observed, and kissed her. "Quit building walls between us. Doesn't work."

"Oh Mike, keep me." She leaned against him, weak with relief.

"That is my idea." He grinned. "Let's cut the rest of the classes and take the day off. Who's going to notice so near the end? I got paid for putting the Wallace screens on, let's spend it."

At the moment, Julie forgot her father. They wandered down Main Street and stopped for hamburgers and French fries and coffee and pie at Joe's. They sat in a booth, screened by a row of paper tulips. The Victrola played their own song, "I'll be loving you—always—" and they held hands, and laughed at silly jokes and then discussed seriously how much money they needed to live on after they got married.

"We could get a flat," Julie suggested. "I'd save on everything."

Mike grinned. He'd spent already most of his pay for the job on the seventy-two screens at Wallace's. But actually he didn't want Julie to be practical, that was his job.

They walked all the May afternoon, ending downriver where he could kiss her almost enough, but never enough. They had never been as happy. Afterward they went back to the Sweet Shoppe and had hot fudge sundaes (with nuts) and danced to "My Little Dream Girl." By the time they idled back toward campus, supper lights winked out in the dormitories, and Julie remembered her father with terrible suddenness.

"Sometimes I hate him," she said flatly.

"But you love him too"—Michael held her hands—"so fly home now and don't get into trouble. Meet you after Latin tomorrow."

"Oh—Michael—"

"I know. This is another day to remember. We're pretty lucky."

Julie ran through the violet dusk. After a full day practically on her feet, she could still run like a deer. Now, coming out of the enchantment, fear ran with her. What could she tell her father? She thought of a number of things, none of them plausible. Julie was still not adept at deceit. She stood a moment on the porch, smoothing her hair, catching her breath, and hoping nobody would notice her soaked slippers. Running cross-lots was a mistake, she thought.

"That you, Julie?" called her mother.

"Yes, Mama." She slipped in.

"Well, thank goodness you're home." Sybil came to the hall. "You'd better clean up fast and we'll eat. Your father is still at a meeting, something about a moose."

Reprieve was a tidal wave.

Sybil did not ask where she had been; she never pried. She saw Julie's flushed face, dilated pupils, flyaway hair, damp slippers. Julie looked like a sparkler just set off, she thought, so she and Mike had made up again. They'd been downriver, for leaf mold clung to Julie's skirt. It would surprise Julie to know how much Sybil could tell, even with no confidences.

It would be easier, however, if Julie wouldn't shut her out, she thought, dishing supper. They ate in the kitchen, since Alden wasn't there.

"The committee decided on a new aisle carpet for the

62

church," she said casually. "It's high time before someone breaks a neck on the holes."

"Could get sued." Julie passed her plate.

Thank goodness, her appetite was back. And a blessing Alden was held up at college. Another crisis avoided. She drew a breath of relief.

"Your father wants to start on the camping trip right after Commencement is over," she said, passing the quince preserve.

"Why do we always have to do just what Papa wants?" Julie looked up. "I hate camping. You hate camping. Why can't we take a cottage at the lake the way decent people do?"

So Michael must be staying in town for the summer. Sybil drank her coffee thoughtfully. This wouldn't be easy, for Julie would find it hard to slip away.

"He likes to go," she said mildly, "and you know how hard he works all year."

"Stuff," said Julie. "Not half as hard as you do or a lot of other people. Why should he run everything? Why should you put up with it?"

"Maybe someday you'll understand." Sybil dished the pudding. "Getting what you want isn't always the most important thing in a woman's life."

Camping was hard, she knew that. Camping with Alden was exhausting. He wanted to tear off to inaccessible places to hunt fossils, so they jounced over dreadful roads, often stopping while he chopped a way through. They were always hot in the car, bitten by mosquitoes at night, and they never got any rest, for Alden routed them out at six every morning to get started. They carried the tent, a running-board box of cooking utensils, canned goods and the gasoline stove (she was deathly afraid of it). The bedding jammed the back of the car, and Alden's gun, fishing tackle, and duffel bag as well as their suitcases piled the back seat to the roof.

"We'll see a lot of the country," she comforted Julie. "He

63

wants to go up to the Calumet region this time, and it's cooler there."

"Scenery!" Julie was scornful. "We never get a chance to look at it. We just go past." They also always went past all the post offices in the towns they bounced through. Communicating with Mike was almost impossible. She was just trapped in the car or in a leaky tent.

"Oh Mama," she wailed, "can't we once—"

They looked at each other, a moment of real communion trembling between them. Both were dreading the early starts, the taking down of the tent, getting on the road, driving all day, unpacking, pitching the tent, cooking supper by smoky lantern light, tossing on the hard cots and rising to do it all over again the next morning while Alden jumped about hurrying them. Sybil longed to tell Julie she knew how it was about Mike, and Julie wanted to comfort her mother, but they couldn't.

Julie washed the dishes and went up to her room, ostensibly to study for a final but really to sit and dream of Mike. Sybil wondered if she had time to do one gold border on a dinner plate before Alden came home. She wanted to finish the set with wild roses on an ivory background and bordered in gold. But she had just picked up the gold leaf when she heard Alden bounce in, so she went down to feed him. He had a hard day, he said, but he won out over the museum. Westerly would have the best museum outside of Milwaukee. The trouble was the trustees never wanted to spend a penny, but he'd get what he wanted.

"Now I need a mastodon," he said. "Where's Julie?"

"Studying," said Sybil.

"Glad to hear it. Have to keep her from running around like a gadfly, flighty like your side of the family."

"Flighty?" Sybil raised a dark eyebrow.

"Like your aunt Grace," he said, "going to Paris and all that."

He went to his study and Sybil washed the dishes. She wished she had someone to tell about the kind of day she had had. Well, it was natural that Alden and Julie were so absorbed in their own lives. After all, they were both Prescotts.

As she turned out the kitchen light she saw the moontrack on the river below, the edge like gold lace. She went out and sat on the steps. I wish I had something special—something more than china painting, she thought wistfully. It was a beautiful night, a nice night to walk under the stars with someone, maybe not talking, just feeling companionable. The dew was heavy and the grass sparkled in the street light. The mills were running full-time and she could hear the sound faint from across the river. The thunder of the dam came to her also, the two sounds weaving a pattern. Downriver a hound bayed.

"What in the world are you doing out here?" Alden stood in the doorway. "It's time for bed. I finished my report, putting in for the mastodon."

Sybil laughed. In the night, her laughter was clear and silvery.

"What's funny?" Alden sounded impatient.

"Oh, nothing," she answered, coming in, "I just needed to laugh, that's all."

As she followed him upstairs she could see no light under the crack of Julie's door, but she could feel Julie was awake, watchful.

In their house, they got up with Alden and went to bed when he was ready for bed. Now he dropped his wrinkled suit on the floor, went to the sleeping porch and got into his nightshirt. Sybil took her bath, knowing Julie and Alden would bicker over the bathroom in the morning. By the time she eased herself into bed, Alden was snoring. She moved gingerly, for she was scared of the Colt revolver he kept under his pillow. He

65

insisted on it, in case of burglars. So far as she knew, theirs was the only house in Westerly so armed. Alden, she thought wearily, was far from being a typical academic man, but perhaps nobody was really typical if you knew him well. She said her prayers and tried to ignore the snoring.

Julie was awake, as her mother had guessed. She was too happy to sleep. She sat at the window, looking at the night. The world had a silver glaze. Yesterday she wanted to die, tonight she felt she would live forever. She wouldn't have to go into a convent (if they would take a Methodist) or wither away because Mike married some other girl. In the glow of the moment she felt she didn't even need to bother about her father. He would have to give in. True he never had, but this time he must. Mike was so wonderful that even her father would have to recognize it.

They would have a simple wedding, just a few friends, not more than sixty, with chicken salad and rolls for the luncheon. It wouldn't cost much.

As she took a last look from the window a star fell, sparking the sky with light. An ill-luck omen, but not this time, not after today. She went to sleep holding a snapshot of Mike in one hand.

8.

As Dick Wallace left the house the college band was playing "Shine On Harvest Moon," which wasn't very fitting. Once more, he had to get away from Carol's temper. In fact, it seemed to him he didn't spend much time at home day or night any more. Except to sleep. This was bad for the twins. They were defensive, surly, out of hand, but Carol seemed able to prevent him from being with them, even if he tried. Well, he thought, you marry a face, a figure, but you have to live with the inner woman.

Somehow, this Commencement, he felt the burden of his marriage more than ever. Would it have been any different if he had given up his career and accepted a made job from her father? He doubted it, but he would never know. In any case, you couldn't go back and live time over.

The campus was beautiful, he thought, with lights on and the ivy-covered buildings green with young leaves. The sound of laughter came from the dormitories and it rested him. He had little laughter in his own life. But he walked briskly, hearing young voices. This was his place, this was his job. He found the town pleasant, too, with the wide shady streets and comfortable, ugly houses set back in smooth lawns. He enjoyed the people, farmers, millworkers, businessmen, and the unpretentious women. It was a place to put roots deep. He never yearned for the city as Carol did. He enjoyed the college plays and an occasional stock company's visit better than city theatre, and he never had liked dining places even when he courted Carol.

Passing Kennicott, he found his steps turning in, and he knocked tentatively at the Dean's door. She did not seem surprised, and closed the door, shutting out the sounds of the dormitory.

"I have a little forbidden sherry," she said. "You're in time to join me."

"I won't report it." He smiled. "As a matter of fact, I think some of the young faculty members do a good business in secret wines. After all, I don't pry."

They sat sipping the sherry, not talking. He felt the tensions ease and his pulse quieting. It was like dipping in a calm sea and being upheld by the depth of the water. When he got up to go, he thanked her. "How many find you a harbor?" he asked.

"What a nice thing to say." She was pleased.

His problems seemed easy to solve as he walked home. Possibly he could think of something for poor Miss Nelson to do. Maybe in a year or so he could get the pension approved. The French teacher, frizzed and bangled and with an abominable accent, could then be retired, and the Latin professor who forgot what the students were translating. And others. The modernizing of the plant itself would take time, but wasn't impossible. The Administration Building was the worst, boiling in summer, icy in winter. The old floors were gummy with the oil of years, peeled walls, light fixtures that were antiquated. But he would put on a new drive, and he was good at raising money.

The curriculum must be changed, and this meant every department up in arms. But patience and persistence would make even Alden admit you couldn't base four years on Geology. He would begin next autumn with a committee to study the curriculum, with the Dean heading it. He'd put Alden on, so he could let off some steam before the report went to a faculty meeting. Then Professor Peake, a mild man living in the Reformation.

The town was settling down for the night. A few people still sat on the verandas; a few students idled on the library steps. A hunting cat slid by with a mouse. Dick took an extra turn around Drew Street, chiefly to postpone getting home. Then he let himself in quietly and went to his room. Carol did not look up from *Lavender and Old Lace* or speak to him. He preferred the silent treatment, he thought wryly. Besides she had said everything once tonight. The sword outwears the sheath, he thought.

His desk was frosted with papers but he was in no mood to work. He didn't want to bother with his Commencement speech either, time enough for that.

What he wanted was to be back in Dean Richardson's apartment, feeling the peace which her presence gave. It was more

68

than peace, but he couldn't analyze it. He only knew he wanted
it too much.

9.

The habit of dropping in at the Dean's was easy to form. It
was perfectly logical to discuss Commencement problems with
the Dean, and if part of the time they talked of other things,
nobody would know. It was so satisfying to Dick to talk about
himself, his dreams, his college days, his childhood. He did not
realize how much else he told her. He knew he looked forward
all day to seeing her.

But one evening as he looked at her, cool and lovely in a
blue dress with a froth of white at the neck, he suddenly felt his
heart beating loudly. She was listening to him, smiling. He put
down his cup and stood up.

"I didn't realize how long I've stayed," he apologized, finding
it hard to speak. "I—mustn't overstay my welcome."

"You couldn't," she said.

"Well, I'll go along and give you a little peace." He spoke
stiffly. "I can't tell what—good night, Louise."

From the door he turned and looked at her, and her eyes fell.
The moment of recognition was no more than that. He was
gone. But she sat with her hands clasped in her lap, listening
to his rapid footsteps. Did he mean to call her Louise? Or was
it an accident? She got up and opened the window, feeling suddenly hot. Commencement, she thought sensibly, makes everybody jumpy, keyed-up, and this one especially so, because of
Lizbeth Fowler.

On the surface, this death could change nothing, but ripples from a cast stone did not subside at once. Was it because of Liz she had been tense, had a hard time sleeping?

"I must go away," she said aloud, "instead of staying here this summer. Someone else can take care of Johnny Green. I must take my savings account and go abroad. Why should I hoard it, just in case of a long illness? I must get away."

Dick—President Wallace—wouldn't drop in daily during vacation. She couldn't expect him. She pushed the thought away, reassuring herself that she was only tired. Dr. Jim could give her a tonic. He would bark at her, fish around in his cabinet, hand out a brown bottle. But his best tonic was himself.

She would take a walk. She had been correcting papers most of the day and going over last details with the housemothers the rest of the time. The dormitory buzzed, but nobody bothered about study hours now, and she wasn't going to. She pulled a lilac scarf around her and went out. The night was like music and the breeze cooled her cheeks. There were almost too many stars. She walked a long time, moving lightly. Finally she made her way to the top of the path to the river and sat down on a fallen log. A good many young lovers sat there, and discouraged students came there to cry. It was called the Sitting Log, and when the superintendent of grounds proposed to lug it away, there was a petition about it.

As she sat quietly she thought, for the first time in many months, about Alex. If she had married Alex would she be, now, in a shabby studio, or would he have been a successful painter?

She remembered his bright, restless face and the lock of dark blond hair that fell over his forehead, his reckless laughter and violent passion. He was a wanderer by nature and probably wouldn't have settled down to teaching art, raising a family. He dreamed great dreams, but there never was any drive toward realizing them. He was a most impractical choice, but he loved her.

So now she mothered the students; not her own children. They came and went and tomorrow swallowed them up. She and the rest of the faculty grew older but their world was always the same age.

She began to think of the day Alex died. It was brittle with cold, deep with snow from a blizzard, but Alex wanted to go sleighing. She knew better than to cross him, so she stood shivering in her gray cloth coat while Mr. Jones backed the horse into the shafts. The horse was jumpy, having had no exercise for three days. Horses frightened her; they rolled their eyes and blew noisily and kicked. But she climbed bravely into the sleigh and Alex tucked the mangy robe around her. She would have tried to climb mountains this day, for she knew he was going to propose.

Mr. Jones stood with folded arms, eying them doubtfully. "Take her easy and slow," he advised. "She's on the gay side."

Alex laughed and swung the whip like a banner. She put her velvet boots on the hot brick and held her muff to her face as they flew over the glazed street.

"Fun," shouted Alex.

The wind stung her eyes and two tears froze on her lashes, but never mind. This was the day. She did long to ask him to go slower as they left town, for barns and silos and farmhouses slid by at a terrifying speed, and the sleigh rocked.

"I have a surprise for you," called Alex, "when we get to the lake."

Then he made a sharp turn onto the hill road. The horse stumbled, the sleigh rose on one runner, turned over, and she was flung clear with the laprobe and brick following her. She landed in a bank of snow, and after a few moments fought her way out.

"Alex!" she screamed.

But Alex was under the sleigh, one runner pinning his neck down.

It was all a long time ago, she thought, shivering in the warm night. Perhaps things happen in a certain way because they are destined to. No one knows. Perhaps Alex had to die, in some curious way demanding it. But why was she now going back to that time, taking a long and futile journey? She was living now, with every day as full as it could be. And if not as full as she wished, that was part of the pattern.

Poor Alex. She would never know whether he loved her or whether she loved him. It was like lightning, summer lightning, that left no trace.

At last she felt the chill of dew on her feet and went back to the campus. It looked like a fleet of ships sailing, lighted, on the sea of night. She often had this feeling, and often wondered what destination this fleet had. She broke a branch of lilac as she walked toward Kennicott. Already the fragrance was musty, the lilacs were going by. And in a few days, she thought, the year would go by. No more cold towels would be wrapped around aching heads as students tried vainly to learn in one night what they had a semester to absorb. The squealing, the banging of doors, the sobbing farewells, would be over. And the alumni would move in, yesterday's boys and girls, now plump, middle-aged, graying. They always brought their children too. The one thing the faculty had in common, she thought dryly, was a hatred of class reunions. Just when college was over, they had Alumni Weekend.

The dormitory staffs grumbled at cleaning, making beds, polishing the plated silver, doing extra laundry. The cooks were furious at getting up luncheons and dinners just when they wanted to pack up and go home. Assigning rooms was a headache when four or five graduates wanted the same room.

In the men's dormitories, there was extra packing away to do. Back-slapping led to pillow fights, cigar ashes drifted over everything. Barbershop quartettes usually ended in a free-for-all. Of late years the "boys" who lived in Chicago or Milwaukee smuggled whisky in to prove their emancipation from rules. This resulted in broken busts of Lincoln, shattered windows, and last year a broken leg as an ex-football star demonstrated the mousetrap play at the head of the stairs.

Tomorrow, the Dean decided, she would call an extra meeting of all heads of houses and tactfully suggest "packing away breakables for the summer." She would arrange for as much outdoor eating as possible, so the men could work off their high spirits throwing wieners at each other and no damage would be done to carpets. If they wanted to draw plans on the paper tablecloths it wouldn't matter. She only hoped fervently that it wouldn't rain.

She was back in her regular way of planning, managing. A moth blundered against her skirt and she bent to brush it off. Then she saw President Wallace, walking as if he were beating against a storm. He drew up abruptly.

"What are you doing out this time of night?" he said, as if she were a student who had not signed out.

"I wanted a breath of fresh air," she said. "Such a nice evening. It seemed a shame to be inside."

"Yes, it is a shame," he agreed. "So many things are."

They stood in a terrible silence, looking at each other. There was enough light for her to see the look on his face.

"You must go home, Dick," she said, putting her hand on his arm. "You have to get some rest."

"I could, if I were with you," he said huskily.

Then he plunged away, bending his head against the invisible wind.

She moved slowly to Kennicott, and crept into her apartment. It looked unreal. She had a sense of not belonging there. "I must not think," she said aloud, "just make lists and plan for tomorrow—" She undressed and went to the bathroom and found the water tepid, the hot having been used up. She liked very hot water or very cold, she didn't like lukewarm anything, she thought. In the mirror, her face was pale and strange.

"Lightning cannot strike twice," she told herself. But it was not easy to pretend any more. From the beginning there had been a communion between them, and a recognition. "I have been here before, but when or how I cannot tell," she said.

She drew the shade to cut out the insidious moonlight. Instead of her regular prayers, she bowed her head and murmured, "God help me."

She could not sleep and was, on the whole, thankful when a knock came at her door. A frightened monitor managed to say between gulps that somebody had upset a candle, and the fire just would not go out, even with glasses of water thrown on it and everything.

The Dean grabbed her robe and slid into her slippers. She was used to night calls—homesick freshmen, girls with indigestion caused from too much cake and candy when boxes came from home, girls who got locked in the showers. But fire in the old frame building—that was different.

"Get a mop pail from the kitchen," she directed quickly, "and a broom. Hurry up."

The monitor scurried down the hall and the Dean flew up three flights of stairs. She was tight with purpose. She was not going to call the fire department if she could help it. On top of the Fowler death, a fire would practically ruin the college. As she reached the third floor (there was always one floor on which everything happened, and this was it) she seized a throw rug. Smoke drifted from Room 124, and a bevy of girls crowded the hall, helpless as mice.

She sent the monitor to collect blankets, organized a relay of mop pails and water pitchers, ordered two girls to stand on two of the trunks in the hall holding a soaked sheet over the door. Then she went in the room, got the window shut, and choking and half-blinded dragged one cot mattress and heaved it in the middle of the fire. The stench was dreadful. But she opened the door wide enough for a pail of water and began to soak the mattress. Fortunately the fire centered on the desk and hadn't reached the lace curtains. At last the flames were smothered. She hoped the ceiling below would hold, but after all she had mainly soaked blankets and rugs and the mattress.

She gathered the girls together in the hall and spoke firmly. "We shall not mention this," she said. "It's going to be a secret between us, what with Commencement, Alumni Weekend and reunions coming up. Put the burned things in the hall closet. I'll tend to the rest in the morning. Get to bed. Just double up any way you like."

She scrubbed herself, put on a clean gown, and weariness washed over her. This fire, she thought, she could put out. The other would be more difficult!

10.

Michael walked down College Avenue on his way home that Friday night in May trying to figure out his problems. Money was the first one. No matter how hard he worked mowing lawns, taking off storm windows, beating carpets, he never had enough. There were always books to buy, lab fees, Student Government fees. He needed a new suit, and where would that come from?

On the rare times Julie and he sneaked away to the motion pictures to see Theda Bara or Warner Baxter, it cost twenty cents, plus the soda or sundae afterward. He had to have enough for the violet corsage for the big dance, and for the

75

ritual stopover for ham and eggs at Joe's. His girl had to have the best.

He could, he knew, get a job at the sulphide plant as a night sweeper, but if he went to college all day, and worked all night, he would never see Julie at all. This was unthinkable. If he could scrape up enough to get through Commencement, he thought wearily, he could work the clock around while she was on that camping trip, maybe save enough to take her to the lake, rent a canoe, and picnic. Buy a decent suit for fall.

There was no use asking his aunt and uncle for a loan. They had, they said, "already put him through high school," although he had worked every spare minute those four years too. They had expected him to go to work in the mill and "make his own way." Only he knew the cajoling, the groveling, for that was what it was, that had enabled him to enter college at all.

"What was good enough for me is good enough for you," said Uncle Ned. "My father never went any farther than the sixth grade. *I* got through eighth. That's plenty. Let me tell you this fancy schooling and playing football won't bring in the pay checks."

"And after all we've done for you," Aunt Nellie told him, "you ought to be grateful."

Michael did not know the origin of his stubborn strength. He had been an angry teen-ager, ready to hit anything and anybody. When his aunt and uncle were too much to endure, he walked out and did the town. Hanging around the pool halls, he picked fights and slugged anyone who was available. He was known as a mean fighter. Then after he had flattened a few, he would go back to the mean house on Union Street and sneak upstairs, supperless, and sit on his cot to shed great, heavy tears. Fighting didn't really help.

But he never lost his determination to get through Westerly. Was it the memory of his mother, who "went out" as a scrub-

woman when his father lost his job as a railroad engineer? Or
was it because his father had been so cheerful as he lay on the
sofa coughing dark blood? "I'll be better," he always said. "I'll
get back to work. Then you'll have a bicycle. Next Christmas
will be a real Christmas."

He was hungry as he crossed the railroad tracks that bisected
upper Main. He knew what the prospect was for supper, all
right. His aunt and uncle would be out, and he wondered sometimes where they went so often. There would be a dish of cold
beans and a heel of bread in the icebox. They wanted him out,
and they figured that if he were hungry enough he would get
to work.

As he turned into Mott Street he was in the Fifth Ward, a
world away from Elm Street and College Avenue. In this part
of town the houses were small, box-shaped. Instead of big
lawns with iron stags gracing their smooth green, there were
tiny yards, unpainted porches. The women worked barefoot in
the back gardens at dusk, raising vegetables, strawberries,
gooseberries, and currants to feed their families. Chickens
clucked in small pens. The men worked in the mills eleven
hours a day or night, and children peddled papers, or ventured
into the other part of town to sell eggs.

And in this part of town Michael was always Mike. Mike
was going to college, and the neighbors were both resentful
and proud of him. At eighteen he could have held a job in the
mill. Someday things will change, thought Mike, climbing the
worn steps, but first there are people like me who don't fit. He
dropped his books on the rickety hall table and went to the
kitchen. There was a note on the sink.

A man comes to see you, it said. *He comes again. He is
overnight at the hotel. I told him we don't know where you
are. Mow the lawn. Wax the kitchen floor.*

He put the coffeepot on the stove and opened the icebox
door. There was a dish of cold beans, a cold boiled potato, and

77

a piece of veal, stiff with grease. The hell with it, he thought, and hunted until he found the package hidden behind the head of cabbage. Two pork chops (not for him) were soon fried with onion, and he sliced the potato and browned it in the pan. As he ate, he decided supper was worth whatever he paid for it. His exams were finished, the year behind him, and he felt reckless.

He drank his coffee and worried about his second problem, not having solved the one about money. The second one involved Professor Prescott, and was no easier to manage. Could it be that if he had plenty of money Alden would accept him? Or was it because he was not good enough for Julie? Who would be?

"Why couldn't I fall for Hilda Anderson?" Mike asked himself. "She's pretty, and cheerful. Clever, too, with a good job already, typing. I'd be welcome there."

He had dated Hilda in high school, and eaten a good many suppers in the Anderson kitchen. Hilda was as good a cook as her mother, and the sauerbraten and stuffed cabbage and fricasseed chicken she fixed were a revelation to the lanky boy. Maybe he might have gone on with her.

But she was not Julie. So he sighed as he cleaned up the kitchen and waxed the floor. His aunt was a fanatic about cleanliness, and scrubbed the floor daily. The house smelled of yellow soap and ammonia. He mowed the lawn, what there was of it, and went up to his room. I've got too much to learn, and too far to go, he thought. But I'll get there somehow. I must. And when he finished college and got a job nobody, not even Dr. Prescott, could keep him from marrying Julie.

From the first time he saw her, this was his goal. He remembered that day when she sat by the window, her notebook open on the chair arm. She wore a navy middy suit, and a red ribbon in her hair. As he slid into the chair next to her he discovered she smelled of violets.

This is my girl, he thought. He did not hear a word of that lecture, but sat hunched in his chair watching her light fingers move across the page, and the way her hair made a silky shadow as she bent her head.

This, then, was why he had not become involved with Hilda, or with the girls who swayed against him at dances or bicycled past the house at dusk or knitted sweaters for him. He had not been interested in them because he was meant to find Julie. He'd been lucky. He had enough strikes against him without having some girl turn up to make trouble.

He hadn't been picked up by a cop, either. A few beers, a few fights, shooting craps and playing pool added up to a fair enough past. He was tough and wary, but when the gang broke into the drug store he took Hilda roller skating. He had no parents to bail him out, and he never forgot that.

He heard the front doorbell ring and ran downstairs. Somebody must be sick, and since this was one of the few houses with a telephone, he was often asked to get Dr. Jim.

But it was not a neighbor. This was a tall, well-dressed man, much too prosperous to be on this street except to foreclose a mortgage.

"Michael Hewitt?" His voice was prosperous too, genial and assured.

"Yes."

"Call me Rusty"—the man held out his hand—"and I'll call you Mike. I'm Russell Farley, District Manager for Kennesaw Pulp, but I'm Rusty to my friends."

"Come in." Mike stepped back.

"Thought I'd drop in and take a look, as one football player to another. Left you word." He sat down in the parlor, pulling his expensive trousers up to preserve the crease.

"Why did you want to see me?" Mike was confused and suspicious.

"I just happened to be in Winnebago on business. We've

79

been keeping an eye on your record down at State. That ninety-five-yard run in the Thanksgiving game was the kind of play we like. Now I'm known as the best broken-field runner State ever had. Swivel-hip they called me. But you gained more yardage than any man in the Conference this past season. And you can pass and punt."

"Well," muttered Mike. Lord how he wished Julie were here. She would know what to say.

Rusty leaned back on the sofa. His eyes flicked about the room, missing nothing from the cheap varnished furniture to the antimacassars dotting the top of the sofa. This was easy. He leaned forward and spoke confidentially. "What are your plans for next year?"

"I'm going to college. I want a college degree," Mike answered.

"Fine." Rusty lit his pipe and relaxed. "Have you ever thought of transferring to State?"

"No." Mike was getting the idea. "I like Westerly."

"There are advantages in a bigger school. You know—more opportunities."

"We have some wonderful professors here," said Mike, "and in a small college they have time to help you."

"Any trouble with your grades?"

"Not so far." He grinned. "Mostly A's, a couple of B's."

"Fine." Rusty tamped his pipe. "Now I don't want to overstay my welcome, as the saying goes, but some of us were talking about next year's team at State. We'd like to have you on it."

"You mean I should quit Westerly?"

"Let me put it this way," said Rusty, smiling. "Some of us in the Alumni Association know it isn't easy to manage expenses at State; so we have established a few, a very few, athletic scholarships for outstanding football players. You would be highly eligible for one of these."

"But why should I transfer?" Mike asked innocently. "I'm satisfied here." (Julie was here, wasn't she?)

Rusty stood up, flushing. "I don't know whether you are dumb, or smart as a fox," he said sharply. "I am offering you your whole expenses at State, plus living in a frat house, meals, and the rest of it. You can take whatever courses you want, nobody cares. All you do is play on the State team, and don't forget State is one of the Big Ten."

Mike's stomach was tight, the way it was when he had to make a touchdown. This was the big deal. This would end the money problem with a bang. Sure, he could take courses enough to graduate, but the adviser would pick the easy ones, so he would have plenty of time for practice. He'd have a decent room, good meals, expense money for books, lab fees, the works. It was laid out open and easy as a punt to the coffin corner when the wind was right, the interference good. Nothing to it.

"I sure do appreciate it. I sure do." He spoke huskily. "I never have played except for fun—I mean, I like football. But I guess—" He lifted his stubborn chin and looked directly at Rusty. "I guess I could play better on three squares a day, as far as that goes. And more free time to practice instead of pushing lawn mowers."

"Right," agreed Rusty, "you don't have a thing to worry about. We send you an application for a scholarship, and you sign it."

"I guess I have to think it over. But I appreciate—"

"You don't have to feel obligated to anybody. We got a trade-even deal. You'll earn your way. We need a new bowl, a new field house, a lot of stuff. But who kicks in fifty thousand on a losing team? We need to win. So you wear the blue and white, and run with the ball against Minnesota and Michigan. What have you got to lose?" His eyes swept around the parlor again.

Only Julie, thought Mike.

"I won't rush you." Rusty was hearty, touching Mike's shoulder. "Talk to your folks and send me a wire at the Blackstone in Chicago in a day or so. Send it collect."

Michael said good-by. He went out after the cab had gone, and started to walk again. Everything was solved. Nothing was solved. Well, there couldn't be anything wrong about taking this offer, could there? So he would barter his strength and skill for a diploma. Westerly didn't buy players. But everyone knew a lot of schools did.

The Westerly team played hard, but not for money. It was different. After winning a game, when Mike was lifted on the shoulders of the crowd and borne from the field in triumph, he could look over and see Julie, shining like a star at the edge of the crowd. After the snake dance the bonfire blazed, the band played the "Alma Mater." Then he walked Julie home, and kissed her, and her hair smelled smoky from the fire.

"Oh Michael, you were wonderful."

He felt like flying.

Playing for business would not be the same. Nor playing without Julie in the stands. Julie would watch someone else.

The practical thing would be to go to State and get his diploma. Any dope could see that. But any dope did not have Julie. He walked past the Prescott house, looking up hopelessly at Julie's window. She might have been in Mars for all he could reach her. So he moved on back to the campus, feeling a rage and confusion about his whole life. As he passed Kennicott he saw the lights on in Dean Richardson's apartment, and on a sudden crazy impulse he knocked at her door. She was his faculty adviser, wasn't she?

She opened the door quietly. "Why Michael, come in." She did not sound surprised or shocked.

"I saw your light," he said, as if that explained everything.

"I was just reading."

"I'm in trouble," he told her.

82

"I happen to have some hot coffee," she said. "I like a cup when I read. Sit down."

He handled the fragile cup carefully. The room was so beautiful it made him feel he should be dressed in his best.

"Now tell me about it," said the Dean gently.

He looked at her and saw the understanding eyes and told her everything. Just telling it was like unloading a cement bag from his chest. After he finished she said nothing. She leaned her head on her hand, fine lace falling away from the slender wrist.

"I think you have a hard choice to make," she said finally. "It would be easy if you had only to decide between your sense of honor and a practical living. But you have so many things to consider."

"I just can't figure what to do."

She refilled his cup. "I think you will know what to do, and make the right choice. It may be that life has a pattern laid out for us and we must follow it. I do not know. But we do have to be honest with ourselves." Then she said, surprisingly, "You miss having a mother. I miss having one, too. A mother is a kind of touchstone."

He put his cup down awkwardly and stood up. "Julie's the main thing"—he spoke firmly—"if I can only figure what is best for her."

"Yes, I know. Love is sometimes a dreadful responsibility."

"I didn't mean to bother you."

"Perhaps you helped me." She smiled. "Being needed is a good thing."

As he plunged along the dark streets (had he been walking forever?) a late freight crossed upper Main. He had a sudden impulse to swing onto that train, ride out and away. Yes, away from Julie too, he thought fiercely. But the freight rumbled on, the caboose light red in the night. And Michael went on. He could no more be free of Julie, leave her, than walk out of his own bones. Tonight he almost hated her for making his life so difficult, and it had never, in his memory, been easy.

But he felt better since talking to the Dean. True, she hadn't advised him, only listened without criticism, smiled, and looked at him with tenderness. He felt that she thought of him as a man, not as just a college boy.

Her room, smelling of lavender, filled with beautiful things, gave him a sense of wonder. Someday he would make such a room for Julie. A room that would fit her.

He must try to catch her after French in the morning and in the ten-minute break between classes, tell her about State. He couldn't hope to see her that night because she had to serve at the church supper. He would just have time enough to tell her about Rusty coming, and then the bell would ring and they would have to rush off in their separate directions.

The moon was high as he turned into the Fifth Ward. Clouds floated around it—could it rain on Commencement Day? Someone, up late, was playing "Always" on a tinny piano. Maybe it meant something special to hear their own song as he went up the steps of the house he hated. He was lucky, for his aunt and uncle had gone to bed. He had to strike a match to get to his room.

In the morning, he thought drearily, he would face the battle of the missing pork chops. But now he didn't care. He fell on his bed without undressing, and slept.

11.

The rehearsal for Commencement was terrible, Mark thought. He wanted to beat his head on the music stand. The best tenor flatted, and he had hay fever, so he kept spraying his throat and nose between numbers. The bass had been working on his father's farm planting pole beans and was dog-tired. He sang like a foghorn. The contralto had a case of poison ivy caught on a picnic at the lake, and he wondered if she had also eaten it, the way she croaked. The substitute for Marjorie cackled.

And the numbers Miss Nelson accompanied made his teeth ache. How could anybody hit so many wrong notes with such finality? Every time she swooped her bony hands in the air and brought them down, he shook. Marjorie could have saved the whole thing, for her rich voice pulled the others along. She might at least have been considerate enough to hold off on this baby business until after next week. But nobody ever thought of anything but themselves, he thought, thinking of himself.

Even the good part of the program was small comfort, for that was Jan Wolski's violin solo. Not even Mr. Parker's teaching had damaged Jan's clean vibrant tone. He played with a kind of madness, his angled face white, his eyes glittering. But Mark reflected sadly that Jan was graduating, and that was the end of him. He was going in with his father to raise Holsteins. A lot the cows would care about his violin playing.

The program itself was endless, as always, for you had to include everybody's students, good or bad (oh God, that harpist). The Glee Club had a number, to cap the climax. Was it for this I have spent half my life? Mark asked himself as the tenor stopped to spray again.

"That's all," he announced. "Remember we meet at seven-thirty sharp Thursday night. Be on time."

As they rattled away, he ducked downstairs into the men's room, avoiding Miss Nelson who fluttered toward him. He definitely had all he could bear of Miss Nelson. He was sorry for her because she was going to lose her job any minute, but for the good of the Conservatory she should have been retired years ago. You couldn't estimate how much talent she had ruined in the years of bad teaching.

When the auditorium quieted down, he came out, and walked downtown. It was no comfort to know the captive audience would applaud every number. They were fathers and mothers, aunts and uncles, and friends, and they would clap heartily for their own.

How did I get stuck here? he asked himself. I could have done better. Why didn't I gamble on myself and go to New York? I was afraid, he admitted, that's why. I settled for security. He turned into Joe's for a hamburger and coffee, hoping to shake off his depression. He was, after all, better off than most of the faculty, for he earned extra money in summer giving private lessons.

But at Commencement he invariably had this lost feeling. The misty-eyed seniors, the swarming parents, depressed him. It was the only time of year when he wondered whether he would be better off married, and with a family of his own. He had once courted a girl named Nina, who could not sing, was bored by music, but cooked chicken with wine exactly the way he liked it. It wasn't much of a courtship, and he was relieved when she went off with a paper salesman named Riley. Riley was now a district manager of sales, and he and Nina lived in Evanston in a neo-Spanish house, with four children, two dogs, a cat and a turtle. He had once stopped there when he went through Evanston, and he shivered as he remembered it.

The hamburger was overdone, the coffee brackish. But it was better than the tearoom where they served creamed things on waffles. He had grown accustomed to dropping in on Marjorie for a good meal, and then rehearsing with her while Ralph read the paper. But now Marjorie wasn't cooking those delicious meals. She was nibbling at soda crackers and warming up something for Ralph to eat at the kitchen table.

He went home, and the smell of cabbage climbed the stairs with him. Cabbage upset his stomach and he never ate it, but

86

he lived with the smell of it. Tonight it seemed to invade his
rooms, and he flung up the windows. Then he followed his
nightly routine, which never varied. He took his bath, washed
his socks and underwear (to save on laundry). He folded his
trousers neatly (to save on pressing). He put on a smoking
jacket (he didn't smoke) inherited from his father. It was bro-
caded and with satin lapels. Then he got the tea things ready
for his nightly cup of tea, and sat down with the Harmony
grade sheet before him.

But his eyes were too tired to focus. He needed glasses but
could not bring himself to the admission. Glasses were for the
really middle-aged. He pushed the grade sheets aside.

Tomorrow he would drop in and ask about Marjorie. It was
Marjorie's fault that this Commencement was particularly
dreadful. When she sang, his life was justified. And when she
sang, he felt young, untroubled.

He closed the windows (he believed night air was un-
healthy) and went to bed. Commencement would soon be
over, he thought. It would be better then.

12.

After rehearsal Miss Nelson fortified herself with the cold lamb
at Kennicott. Then she went upstairs to soak her hands in hot
water with Epsom salts added. She had, of late, much trouble
with swollen joints, so that often when she played, the second
and third fingers bumped together. Now she spread them wide
in the basin, and sighed. Her hands had always been her chief
pride. Even as a child she was not pretty, but her favorite uncle
once said, "Your hands fly around like butterflies." She never
forgot that. The last few years she rubbed them with cocoa

butter, patted them with glycerin and rose water, was careful to wear mittens in cold weather. She was never without pain in the joints, but she bore this better than the way they looked.

As she sat with her hands in the basin on a chair before her, she tried to push back the anxiety that nibbled at her. So far, she reminded herself, President Wallace had merely asked her to drop in one day at her convenience for a conference. It could mean almost anything, but she knew she shouldn't put it off. She ought to get it over with and then begin to make plans, if worst came to worst.

The trouble was, there were no plans to make. The thought stupefied her. She must work at something, somehow. The wrist watch they always gave retiring faculty wouldn't help her. Maybe she wouldn't even get a watch since times were tight, they said. But times were always tight with her.

She got up to add more hot water to the basin, and dipped her reddened hands again. Where shall I turn? she asked herself miserably. What will become of me, and of Marylin? Now I must be calm, think things over. Perhaps a furnished room off campus and private pupils? But where would she get a studio and a piano? She couldn't even rent the back room at B.P.O.E. hall. Also, she wouldn't have the minor benefits of being a faculty member, such as free manuscript paper, pencils, music books, free printing of recital programs. And quite a few free dinners.

She couldn't teach in the high school, for there was some new regulation about educational qualifications. And after a lifetime of piano teaching, she certainly could not take up typing, even if the swelling went down in her joints. Nowadays you were supposed to type without looking at the keys. She couldn't move fast enough to be a waitress, even if she could balance trays and keep the orders in mind. She was too old to be a housemother, even if managing a dormitory of noisy girls didn't frighten her. Westerly preferred young widows for this position, or mothers whose children were grown and on their own.

I ought to have saved something, she thought drearily, but how could I? I was so careful, except that one time. And that seemed so sensible. That nice Mr. Swift from the West gave me a fine certificate printed in gold for that mining stock. He said it was a nest egg, but the egg never hatched. Mr. Swift vanished, leaving no address, and all she had was the memory of a wonderful dinner at the hotel, with roast beef and baked potatoes and peas (a lovely night that was, to be sure).

Something dreadful must have happened to poor Mr. Swift. But he left no address. He tucked her money (cash) in his leather wallet and promised to send her a report from the mine. Where was it? She still had the certificate, in her glove box in the bureau, and suppose now she learned suddenly it was worth a lot of money? Maybe as much as two thousand dollars? The thought made her giddy. She would take just a bit of it and go to Chicago to hear Mary Garden, she decided.

She emptied the basin and dried her hands, which were puffy from soaking. She went to the window and looked out, smelling the lilacs. In books human troubles were simultaneous with floods, earthquakes, blizzards, but in real life you could reach the point of despair when the weather was cruelly indifferent. It was an exquisite night.

A good cup of cocoa would make her less shaky. As she fixed it she decided she could not send Marylin to the county farm, no matter what happened. The very thought gave her a shaking spell.

"I am just imagining things," she said firmly.

Surely some Board member would speak to President Wallace. "Great asset to Westerly, that Miss Nelson. Part of the good old tradition." This comforted her. She did not go so far as to have her salary raised, but she went to bed in a more tranquil frame of mind. She slept flat on her back. Years ago someone had told her this kept the lungs from congestion.

She woke at dawn, which was tiresome, for if she got up so early she was apt to nod during her lessons.

This time, she decided to get up and wash her white cotton gloves, mend the runs in her good stockings, sew the hook and eye on her dress. The sky was pale fire and birds were singing in the maples as she padded to the bathroom to wash up. After she finished her chores she had a daring thought. Why not go to the drug store for a poached egg and buttered toast and tea? This would give her a fine start for the day.

The drug store was just opened when she went in.

"A nice day," she ventured.

"You may call it nice." The counterman set the water on to boil. "Kids coming in all hours, and expect us to be open day *and* night so they can eat their heads off. Next thing old grads jamming in, wanting three-decker sandwiches. I hate Commencement." He swished a dirty towel over the counter.

"Oh dear me." She took a sip of water. "I thought—well, it does bring business, doesn't it?"

"Business," he snorted, slapping down her egg, "business. Who gets paid for extra business? Not me. I get paid same in December, same in May. Believe me, no justice."

"Perhaps there never is," she said suddenly.

She ate her egg slowly, saving the yolk to the last. As she finished her tea Mark Allingham came in, looking as cranky as the clerk.

"Oh, you here?" he asked wearily.

"Well, I thought—"

He sat limply on the stool next to her. "Scrambled eggs, bacon, not too done, toasted roll, coffee with milk," he said. "I had a bad night."

"So did I," confided Miss Nelson.

Mark slanted a look at her. A few more years and I'll be

where she is, he thought suddenly. Somebody will come along with newer methods, young. And it won't matter a jot that I'm the best.

"Let me buy you a refill on your tea," he heard himself say, with surprise, "and one of those Danish pastries."

Miss Nelson chirped happily. She was still hungry, but she could not afford to spend another penny. "Thank you," she said.

The pastry was big and squshy with frosting. She ate every crumb, surreptitiously licked her fingers.

"I hope the weather holds for Commencement." She pushed the bare plate away reluctantly. "Ten years ago it rained. Remember? All the gowns were soaked."

Mark felt uneasy, jolted from his customary selfishness because this poor old thing was still concerned about a Commencement ten years ago.

"Well, Miss Nelson," he said heartily, "we have weathered a lot of Commencements, weather or no," and laughed at his joke.

Why should she care about the weather this year? Even a hurricane wouldn't save her job. So why, for heaven's sake, did she care what happened?

"What are you planning to do during the long vacation?" he asked, and could have bitten his tongue.

"I—well, I haven't exactly—made up my mind." Her confusion was pitiful.

Perhaps it was his own sense of frustration, or possibly his loneliness, but he made a decision quite inconsistent with his orderly mind.

"I asked," he said thoughtfully, "because I wondered—you may have heard that Marjorie Knight is expecting a baby [who hasn't?] and so I thought—if you were going to be here during the summer, you might play accompaniments for her after the baby is born—to keep her in practice. It was just a thought."

"Oh yes, yes, indeed I could!" Miss Nelson cried.

The cool top of his mind said, Marjorie is done for, but she might at least practice a little, and Miss Nelson could play for her. It might take Marjorie's mind off baby tending.

"I would be honored." Miss Nelson was red as a radish.

He felt more cheerful. It was queer, he had gone along for years waiting for Miss Nelson to be dumped. And now he was throwing a plank out for her to cling to, and it made no sense, but he felt better for it.

"I'll speak to Marjorie," he promised as they went out. "I am sure she'll be delighted. I have to be away, myself, part of the summer, and she shouldn't let her voice go."

You see, thought Miss Nelson, he really does respect me or he wouldn't turn her over to me for the summer.

This would surprise President Wallace!

In her studio she sat down at the piano and ran a few scales, tossing her head in the air. But gradually, as she practiced, the assurance ebbed. Her hands were still knotted, in spite of all her care. And it occurred to her perhaps Professor Allingham was only being kind. She got out the chamois and polished the keys again. The truth is, she thought honestly, I have no gift. I cannot teach students to sing well. Something always happens. They flat or tighten up. That is the truth.

The clang of the bell roused her. She had her annual appointment at the beauty parlor. The rest of the year, she washed her hair in the bathroom bowl and set it, unsuccessfully, but today she would have a marcel. She scurried along with her head bent, for she was nearsighted and the old sidewalks were deep with cracks.

Julie and Mike almost knocked her flat, for they also had their heads bent. Mike retrieved her with the famous football arm and Julie picked up the shabby purse.

"Oh, I am so sorry," they all said at once.

Miss Nelson straightened her skirts.

"We're just on our way to a cup of coffee," said Julie. "Won't you have one with us while you catch your breath?"

Oh my, thought Miss Nelson, agitated. Breakfast with Professor Allingham and coffee at eleven in the morning! What a whirl!

Swinging her purse recklessly, she said, "I don't mind if I do!"

Julie gave Mike a look. Mike nodded. He had heard the news too. Everybody had except Miss Nelson, and she must suspect. He took her arm, feeling how thin it was.

"Cakes too," he said, "to celebrate Commencement." And there went his last dime.

Miss Nelson walked proudly, for here she went down Main Street with the most talked-of students at Westerly. They looked as if they had been dipped in sun, she thought. They went to Joe's and took a table, and Miss Nelson ate two cakes. She couldn't think of any suitable remarks but Julie and Mike chatted about grades and exams and the weather.

She was forty minutes late for her hair appointment, but Greta was nice enough to fit her in. As the marcel iron sizzled, Miss Nelson relaxed. Greta's husband made wigs in the back room and brought one in to be admired, and Miss Nelson said coyly, "You may make one for me someday." They all laughed.

Her hair was still fairly thick, and when waved looked very well, she felt. It was not hard to brush over the thin part, not really. "One does grow older eventually," she said.

"Nothing to worry about yet," said Greta, putting the iron on its stand. "We are only old as we think. Ja?"

Miss Nelson felt jaunty as she walked back. Certainly she was not old.

13.

On the morning after Mark's struggle with rehearsal, Winnebago housewives were cleaning up for Commencement, for it was a fine day. Ella Peters came out for a breath of air after sweeping the parlor carpet. The Peters' house was on the corner of Elm and Linden, a pleasant yellow house with green trim and elegant with a cupola. The veranda ran around two sides of it, and was a good vantage point from which to watch the length of the block in both directions. Ella sat down in the green wooden rocker and began to watch the streets.

Usually she had her washing on the line before the neighbors were out of bed, but today she was late. One of her headaches was coming on. She hated spring, and her headaches were more frequent then. This time she told Jim to get breakfast at St. Mary's so she could lie down and put cold cloths on her head. But after he had plowed off, she felt well enough to fix two boiled eggs and two slices of buttered toast and have her coffee. She washed up, did the house, and now rocked jerkily back and forth. How she disliked Commencement! Jim was never home, for the silly students were worse than ever. They got poison ivy, they bicycled into farm trucks, tried to swim in the lake, though any fool knew you could not swim until July when the water warmed up. They got upset eating midnight snacks. To top it off, there were the girls who decided they were getting plump, and lived on orange juice or bananas until they collapsed. The whole college "acted up" during these May days, and she blamed the faculty for being lax.

It was true that a heady excitement swept over campus as the lilacs bloomed. Couples went by Dr. Jim's all day on the way to the river. The girls giggled, sometimes the boys burst into whistling. Pins sparkled on blouses, pins which might come off in September when things calmed down. Some girls, Ella heard, wore one fraternity pin outside and one inside under their camisoles. The mooning around was disgraceful.

But Ella couldn't understand the magic of spring. The fact was, summer loomed ahead for most of the students as a time of hard work on the farms. It was a prosperous valley. Holstein herds fattened on rich pasturelands. The cheese, butter, cream, were famous. But everybody worked hard and outside help came only at threshing time, when neighbors traded their services. Many of the girls worked in the kitchens with their mothers, some helped with haying.

Summer meant work and meant parents. No vague explanations about homework could be offered. Even the sons and daughters of the mill executives were asked to account for their time, and most of them had jobs in offices, for idleness was not a part of the social system in Winnebago. Moreover, as if working were not enough of a trial, most of them were separated from their current sweetheart. Some of the students lived in Winnebago itself, many came from farther north or farther south, a few came from the next state, and occasionally even from the East or West. With the closing of Westerly they were cast back into a world they no longer liked. They found, also, that they had outgrown their friends who stayed at home, and had little in common with those attending one of the Catholic colleges.

The day students were no better off, for their best friends invariably went off to Waukesha or Waukegan, or their parents dragged them away on camping trips (like the Prescotts). Some of the wealthier town families had cottages on the peninsula between Green Bay and Lake Michigan, and some of the faculty went there too, living in modest cabins. For the

95

few students left in town, the empty campus was a bitter reminder that fall was years away.

But to Ella, they all acted plain crazy this time of year. She felt her forehead, and the skin was dry and cool. She had got up to go in the house when she saw a couple coming down Linden, from the direction of the river, not going toward it. At *nine* in the morning! Her lips pinched, she watched them come, holding hands. It was Julie Prescott with the Hewitt boy her father had forbidden her to go out with. As they drew near the house Julie stopped and pointed to her left foot. Ella could see very well, by craning her neck. The laces were untied. Michael knelt down to tie them and, right in broad daylight, kissed Julie's ankle, and Julie bent over him holding out her hands. It was enough to freeze the blood in a body. When he stood up, Julie pulled his hand to her cheek shamelessly, and then they moved on until Ella could not see them.

Hussy, she thought. Professor Prescott's daughter, carrying on in a public street like that. A hussy, that was what she was.

She went in the house quite dizzy with rage. Julie, with that innocent look and those soft eyes! What would Alden say? Wait until she told him! She sat down at the kitchen table, and pain jumped again in her temples. Could she call Alden now? No, he would be in class already. No use phoning Jim, and she knew better than to call Sybil. Sybil would suggest gently that this was not, after all, Ella's concern. No, she'd have to wait and catch Alden when he came home from college. Well, he would put a stop to this kind of business.

The day stretched ahead. Aside from answering the phone for Jim, there was nothing for her to do except wait for suppertime. Spring house cleaning was finished and not a thing remained to be cleaned, waxed, or aired. The washing and ironing were done and put away. The pork roast was ready for supper and even the peas were shelled. Finally she decided she could clean out the top cupboards in the kitchen again, although they had been done two weeks ago. The white elephant bazaar was coming in June and she could choose some odds and ends for that. The cracked soup tureen, those chipped bone dishes, and the unmatched cups and saucers would do nicely.

The phone rang as she lugged the stepladder up from the cellar. She let it ring. Probably some patient had a cold. The ladder was rickety; she must speak to Jim about it. As she reached the top of the ladder, the phone rang again. From the top rung she could just reach the shelves of the cupboard. She leaned forward to grasp the tureen, and reached too far. The tureen slipped and she tried to catch it and then the ladder swayed and she lost her balance and crashed to the floor, splintered bits of china cascading about her.

Nobody knew how long she had lain there before one of Jim's patients opened the back door to shout "Anybody home?" Ella was doubled up beside the ladder, her pinched face splashed with blood, her sharp lids shuttered. Forgetting his own symptoms in a hurry, the patient lifted her and carried her to the walnut sofa in the parlor (for which he was cursed later by Dr. Jim). He dragged the Paisley shawl from the piano and draped it over her, then ran to crank the phone frantically.

By the time Jim got home the house was full of patients, for news spread in Winnebago like a grass fire. Among them was a mother with a small boy coming down with measles, spotty under his freckles.

"What's this?" Jim boomed at them. "Get out, all of you!" They melted away, the small boy sniffling. (This was the beginning of the measle epidemic, for his mother was so shaken that she simply turned him out to play when they got home.)

Dr. Jim got the ambulance, after an infuriating delay. The driver said it had a flat tire. "I'll flat-tire you," roared Jim, and the driver flung on a new tire without stopping to vulcanize the old one. By the time they carried Ella in to St. Mary's, the staff surgeon was scrubbed, the Sisters swishing about, the

97

emergency X-ray ready. And in the chapel, three Sisters off duty said their rosaries and beseeched the Holy Virgin to protect Dr. Jim's wife.

Ella had moaned once. Dr. Jim charged down the corridor after the stretcher, sweating and swearing. He ran into a food cart, bumped into an interne and nearly knocked Sister Maria flat.

"Dr. Jim, we are praying." She put out her hand to steady him.

Somehow the words stilled him. He already felt, from his preliminary examination, that Ella's spine was broken, but he moved steadily ahead.

When Ella came from the curious fog she had been in, she opened her eyes and saw, facing her, the crucified Christ, framed in gilt. What in the world was he doing in her bedroom? But it wasn't her bedroom. The bed was not her four-poster but a narrow hard one. There was a varnished bureau across the room, a straight chair by the window. And a Sister stood by the window, shaking down a thermometer. Heavy robes almost hid her, but Ella could see dimly a young, pretty face framed in the rigid coif. Why, this must be the hospital, and however had she come here? Or was this another of her nightmares? She tried to sit up, and then realized she was encased in what seemed like a cement wrapping.

"Please don't try to move," said the Sister gently. "Just lie still. After all, everyone has to lie quietly once in a while."

Up to this moment, Ella had never trusted Catholics, as she was constantly saying to Jim. He said they were the best blankety-blank nurses he had known, and the Sisters weren't always giggling around handsome young internes the way most nurses did.

"I—fell," murmured Ella.

"So you did."

"The soup tureen—"

"Don't worry about it." The Sister held up a syringe and let a bubble rise. "You can serve right in the bowls. My mother has a fine recipe for a meat and vegetable soup. I'll give it to you one day to try." The needle slipped in while Ella thought about the recipe.

"I am Sister Teresa," the Sister said, "and whenever you want anything at all, I shall be right here. Now you must rest."

Ella slept, or rather went into a waking dream. She was waltzing—she loved to waltz—and Jim was saying, "Ella, how about marrying me?" Then it was another time and Jim was saying, "I guess we'd better adopt a baby, since you want one so much." And this dissolved into another scene. He was shouting, "My God, Ella, can't you understand? You always *knew* I was a doctor! No, I won't be home for lunch, I'm operating."

When she drifted into a drugged sleep, she slept heavily. Waking toward dawn, she saw Sister Teresa standing at the window clicking her rosary. Somehow it was a comfort. She tried now to remember about her fall but the whole day was a blank. The days that followed were hazy also. She sipped broth from a bent glass tube, looked at flowers sent by Dr. Jim's patients. When Sister Teresa suggested she share them with less fortunate patients, she was oddly pleased. She was proud of having so much. She began to enjoy the attention, being waited on, hovered over, a new and pleasant emotion. She bore the weight of the cast without complaining, although it felt like a coffin. But Sister Teresa praised her courage, and she smiled bravely. She had no idea she was on the critical list, but she was proud of all the attention she had from Jim, who kept dropping in to lean at the foot of the bed, scan the chart, and say hello.

She pleased him, too, with her cheerfulness and the first day she asked for an egg, he dropped a kiss on her cheek. "That's my good girl," he said.

Of course since he was at St. Mary's so much, he had time to drop in, and she saw more of him than she had when she was at home. And now she was a patient, he took her pulse, badgered Sister Teresa about her diet, checked the bedcovers. Lying flat in the cast, Ella for the first time in years drank the intoxicating wine of praise. And she flowered. One day when Sister Teresa brushed her hair, she asked for a mirror and looked at her face. There were no scars from the broken china. Her skin was clear and the days of lying quiet seemed to have smoothed the wrinkles from her face.

She was proud of the visitors. The only bad time was when Mrs. Wallace dropped in to pay a duty call. Mrs. Wallace looked cool in a leaf-green dress, and her inspection of Ella was not pitying.

"We do hope for a speedy recovery," she said in her distant voice. "So hard on everybody to have this happen right at Commencement. Especially for Dr. Jim, what with the measle epidemic too. Of course, if Dr. Jim had examined that boy, everybody needn't have been exposed, but of course Dr. Jim was too busy with your accident. Why did you get up on that ladder? I've wondered."

When she swept out, Ella cried. Sister Teresa hurried the supper tray in and sat down to feed her.

"We have a treat tonight," she said gaily, "a nice lamb chop. Dr. Jim says you love lamb chops." She wiped the tears from Ella's face.

"She—upset me," sniffed Ella.

"I wouldn't let her." Sister Teresa cut the chop. "We find visiting hours are difficult when that one comes. We say extra prayers. But this is a secret between you and me."

Ella opened her mouth for the first delicious morsel. Sharing a secret was a tonic.

"You have opinions about the visitors?" she asked curiously.

"Oh my, yes." Sister Teresa twinkled. "Opinions are the

natural part of everyone. Now try this mashed potato. God, however," she added thoughtfully, "God forgives us."

The friendship between Ella and Sister Teresa grew. Up to now, Ella had never liked another woman, she distrusted all women. She was always afraid Jim would find them more attractive than she was, and she felt inferior to most of them who had been able to bear children. Sybil, whom she might have liked, she was frankly jealous of.

But now she found no reason not to like, even be fond of, Sister Teresa, who was a nun after all, and no threat to any woman. And Sister Teresa had a bright spark of humor as well as great tenderness. She even managed to feed Ella without making it a chore, dispensing bits of gossip about the hospital and nurses and doctors. Under her influence Ella began to take an interest in the people around her. She could hear a lot that went on, too, for in the heat of the day her door was left open, with a screen in front. And since everyone knew she was a critical case, the internes poked their heads in, other doctors stopped to chat, and ambulatory patients came in to admire her flowers.

She had no responsibility, no compulsive housework to do. The one worry that remained was that Commencement was five days away and Jim's robes and hood were packed in a chest in the attic, layered with moth balls. They would smell, and be wrinkled. She spoke to Jim about it.

"Don't give it a thought," he said. "Sybil is doing mine when she does Alden's. Julie already took them over."

Instead of feeling angry at Sybil she was suddenly grateful to her. The mention of Julie brought a dim memory of something she was to say about her, but it flickered. Something about Commencement no doubt, she thought, dismissing it.

"You just be a good girl," said Jim. "Sybil is bringing her cleaning woman over once a week until you get home, so the house is all right too. You look very pretty today," he added.

Ella was practically floating, cast or no cast. The minute he left, she called Sister Teresa and said, "I want you to phone Mrs. Prescott. Ask her to buy me a new bed jacket. Blue. Blue is his favorite color. I want a blue satin ribbon to match, for my hair. And a bottle of violet perfume. She can charge it at Ingold's."

Isn't she wonderful, thought Sister Teresa, cranking the phone, wanting to fix herself up for him? And so brave about her suffering—and never walking again. May God bless her.

Sybil promised to get the bed jacket, ribbon and perfume, and Sister Teresa said an extra prayer in the chapel for Dr. Jim's wife.

Sybil thought it was amazing, but if Ella had a notion to fix herself up, that settled it. She herself had not a moment to go uptown and shop and take the long streetcar ride to St. Mary's. Why did people always build hospitals at the edge of town, she wondered, and up a steep hill? She commandeered Julie, who was extremely reluctant.

"Why should I drop everything and take that mean old trip for her?" demanded Julie, who remembered Ella's sharp tongue very well.

"Because I can't, that's why," Sybil snapped.

"Well, if she was silly enough to topple off that old ladder, I don't see why she has to get waited on all the time." Julie was fretful. "I already got those old robes out of that smelly attic." She switched her skirts impatiently. "You'd think she was a hero or something."

"Go." Sybil waved a hand at her. "Just go."

Julie went off sullenly. She got the jacket, ribbon, perfume, and waited for the streetcar. She hated to go to the hospital, a horrible place full of sick people and those Sisters gliding about. Besides, she was always carsick. As the familiar oily smell rose in the streetcar, she bit her lips and tried not to notice

SPRING HARVEST

it. But the churning began in her stomach and sweat trickled down her forehead.

She hadn't seen Mike all day, so she was miserable enough already. He was seeing about a summer job in the sulphide plant. She wished he didn't have to work. And she was frightened at this offer from State. Suppose he weakened, accepted it, and left Westerly? She might as well die. She worried about it until she went past her stop and had a block to walk back in the heat.

As she reached St. Mary's the ambulance slid past, and she saw an interne leaning over a sheeted form. It made her stomach feel worse, and she ran up the steps. Skidding along the waxed corridor, she had a vision of how it would be if Mike were ill. But no, Mike could never be. But if she and Mike were separated, it would be a kind of dying.

Sister Teresa opened the door, smiling.

Julie clutched the packages awkwardly and tiptoed in. Why, this couldn't be Dr. Jim's wife! Why, she can't move at all, thought Julie, in horror. Oh how hideous!

"Now this is nice of you, Julie," Ella said.

"Well, let's see what has come." Sister Teresa spoke cheerfully. "Oh my, how pretty!" She lifted the bed jacket. Blue was her favorite color too, and this was the shade of her first party dress, and she had worn a satin rosette in her coppery curls. But the only blue for her now, she reminded herself sternly, was the blue of the Virgin's robe. She would confess her unsuitable thoughts to Father Moran.

"It's what I wanted," Ella smiled, "not dark blue, but light. Like forget-me-nots. And the ribbon matches."

"How are you?" Julie asked.

"Much better, thank you," Ella answered. "They spoil me here. Thank your mother for the wine jelly. It tasted so good."

Julie said good-by and walked soberly down the corridor. She

103

couldn't understand it, but Dr. Jim's wife looked happy. How could she, stuck in that cast, maybe for always?

Somehow it made Julie humble. She didn't have anything like that to face. She could run, dance, play tennis, ride a bike, swim—do everything. She was ashamed of being so snappy lately, moody and perverse. Suppose she were sealed in a cast and might never walk again.

"Bringing spring in?" Dr. Jim spoke cheerfully as he met her. "We'd like that more often in here."

Julie smiled, and went on, as he hurried to Ella's room before checking on a terminal case. That Julie was a beauty, he thought, as he opened the door to Ella's room, a proud filly, but she'd turn out fine with Sybil for a mother.

"My, how dressed up we are!" He smiled at Ella. "Looks like a party going on!"

Ella flushed. The lacy bed jacket was draped over her thin front and the ribbon tied back her hair, now soft and loose.

"I had broiled chicken this noon," she said proudly, "and ate it all."

He kissed her, and smelled the violet perfume. It was odd how it affected him, for she usually smelled of yellow soap and ammonia. It was also odd that he had spent years insulating himself against a shrewish, nagging woman and now had an uncomplaining, friendly patient. His compassion almost revived the love he once had felt for her. She was trying, consciously, to please him, and it warmed his heart.

When he left, he stopped in the locker room to smoke his pipe, and summon his strength to bluster at the rest of his patients.

Now, for five minutes, he was himself. Marriage is a funny business, he thought, tamping the tobacco with a blunt thumb. You can hate anybody and you can long for peace as a child longs for home. But marriage is a third presence and you can't get away from it. Now he was beginning to see Ella as he once had, a woman who needed him as he once had needed her. He wondered whether she would ever walk again. Well, a day at a time, he thought, and dumped the ashes in the toilet bowl and went out to join battle again with his old enemy, death.

14.

Everybody said there had never been such a spring. But in this crop-conscious community, they added that more rain was needed. Even when it had rained hard for two days, the farmers would come to town on Saturday with their eggs, peas, butter, and cream, and would shake their heads at the clearing sky. "You'll notice when you cultivate, the ground's dry two inches down."

This spring the first hot weather was earlier than usual, so the trees were already in full leaf. The lilacs bloomed so fully that the branches bent from the weight of the clusters. They were beginning to go by now, but the bridal wreath was out in every yard. The old-fashioned single roses were in bloom, and ruby spears poked up, promising a wealth of red, white, and pink peonies. The air smelled all night long of new-cut grass.

Winnebago was beautiful to those who lived there, for the ugly Victorian houses had an air of graciousness. It was a green town with its arching elms, great maples, oaks, and birches; green also with spreading lawns, and shrubbery. The wealthier inhabitants imported Colorado blue spruce for the middle of the front lawn, while the Fifth and Sixth wards brought in native pines from the woods.

The soil was dark and friable. Gardens bore richly. Even Alden had a vegetable garden, although he impatiently dug things up occasionally to see why they were not growing faster. The women put up the garden produce against winter. Even the wealthy women with hired help filled their cellars with jars and glasses and bottles. Canned vegetables from the store hadn't much flavor, and shipments of fresh fruits and vegetables from warmer climates were rare.

But they had no complaints. Winnebago was the best town in the Middle West, they asserted. It was growing. The mills ran day and night, and there was work for everyone. They had culture, too, for Westerly brought musicians and literary men and women to town in winter, and in summer there was Chautauqua.

The men in the mills were content, having jobs the year round. Their work clothes were worn, but clean and neatly mended. They might walk with a slight stoop from long hours bent over the machines, but there were plenty of saloons where they could get good German beer. Their children went to school, and many framed diplomas hung in the parlors, often beside a portrait of the Kaiser. Their sons and grandsons would marry daughters of mill managers, and their grandchildren would alternately visit the big houses with the cupolas and the small ones with chickens in the yard.

A few from the old country thought the college was a playground. But most of them, as they passed the campus swinging their black lunch boxes, stopped to look with pride at the gilded chapel dome and the ivied walls. And at Commencement there would be many of them, in stiff black shoes, tight clothes, and choking collars, sitting in the chapel with their plump wives who sweated in unaccustomed flowered prints and whalebone, their eyes brimming as their sons and daughters graduated.

But all of this made no impression on Mike's aunt and uncle. Commencement was two days off, and at ten o'clock that night they were still at it with Mike. The argument had gone on ever since they heard from him about the offer from State. He thought wearily that they sounded like a cracked cylinder on a phonograph. We have made a home for you and taken care of you. School costs money and times are hard. (The mills ran twenty-four hours a day, he thought.) If you want to waste your time, and these people will pay for it, you can take it or get a job and make a decent living.

There were brief lulls while Mike scraped greasy dishes, washed them, waxed the hated floor. Then they were at him again. They could rent his room to a millworker. They needed the money. They had put up with him as long as they could.

As he stood facing them, shifting from foot to foot, he fought his temper. His thoughts ran like a millrace. They'd miss him, all right, when they began to pay out money for all he had done. The years of chores—scrubbing and waxing floors, doing dishes, hanging out the wash.

And firing the furnace, beating carpets, putting on screens, taking off screens, hanging wallpaper in the parlor—well, it added up to his keep, he figured. His uncle claimed to have a weak back, and his contribution to the household was to sit on the porch in a rocking chair and call to Mike to bring him a bottle of cold beer. His work wasn't too heavy; he sold tickets at the railroad station.

This time, Mike decided to attack.

"What happened to the insurance I signed over when you took me?"

The silence seemed loud. Then his aunt, her nostrils turning white, as they always did, spoke fiercely.

"It went supporting you."

"So how?" He rolled his fists up tight. "So all gone?"

"Every cent." She faced him.

"Seems I paid twice for my schooling. Once in work and once in the life insurance. You ought to be satisfied by this time."

"Now Mike"—his uncle was nervous—"we don't mean to turn you out or anything, we just feel you ought to quit fooling around."

"Any day I don't work twice as hard as you," Mike said, "I'll really quit."

He turned on his heel and went to his room. He'd had it. For this scene followed a bad time with Julie. She had stormed if he loved her he would stay with her. She had sobbed that she wanted him to be happy. She had sniffled that maybe he would remember her now and then after he had deserted her.

He tried to figure things out, be sensible. He had, he knew, lived cheaper in this hellhole than he could boarding. How could he support himself at Westerly without a roof for free, and grudging meals? He couldn't get the insurance back, in any case. Suddenly, as he sat with his head in his hands, he remembered that when he was cutting pines to sell for Christmas trees he had come on a trapped weasel. It was alive, and gnawing at its leg. The beady eyes were defiant. He was glad now that he snapped the jaws of the trap, although it was a silly thing to do. Weasels ate chickens, were predatory, and there was a bounty on the pelts. But the look in those eyes was too much for him. Now he was trapped, and would anybody open the trap and let him limp away?

I've got to go, he thought, right after Commencement, if not before. I've got to find a place to go. He could hear his aunt and uncle arguing downstairs, his aunt's voice shrill, his uncle rumbling. He guessed they were worried about the insurance money. Also it had occurred to them that if he left, they would have to hire someone to do the work around the place. He wouldn't even turn over his summer money. This made him grin. Then he laughed until he had to muffle the sound in his pillow. Finally he went to the bathroom and ducked his head under the faucet. Then he pulled his cardboard suitcase from the closet and began to pack. The suitcase was all he had left to remember his mother by, except a small gold locket with a round curl in it. It was his baby hair, dark gold.

The suitcase would hold all he had—socks, underwear, sneakers, sweatshirts, work pants, two notebooks. Also the notes from Julie, tied up with the ribbon from their first dance program. He carried the few snapshots he had of her in his pocket. Most of them were cloudy and you could hardly make out the subject, but he cherished them.

His football togs were in the gym locker along with his tennis racket. He could pick them up any time. His best shirt and a few handkerchiefs were downstairs in the laundry hamper and he decided grimly not to leave until they were ironed. And better leave his high school pennant on the wall until the last minute. He locked the suitcase and pushed it far under the bed, put the key away in his pocket.

By now, he was able to think with his natural good sense. Flinging from this house dramatically would be a relief, but would also leave him without a place to sleep. He could not afford the luxury of anger. In the morning he would settle on a job for the summer, take whatever paid the most, regardless of the hours. He would drop around to see the Dean about doing odd chores at Westerly in return for a bed at Kennicott. Kennicott stayed open, for the college help lived there during the summer. There was plenty to do, painting, cleaning, repairing, waxing floors, mending leaky faucets, gluing broken chairs.

If that didn't work out, he'd check for a fraternity house needing a summer caretaker. As a last resort, he would ask at the big houses or see if the hotel needed a bellhop. The main thing about the summer job, he reasoned, was it had to be housing in return for work with time enough left over for a paying job at the mills or on the road crew. He didn't care what it was particularly. That rose-covered cottage Julie dreamed of seemed a long time away at the moment, but he was not defeated, not by any means. Given part of a chance, he would make it.

Across town, Julie was no better off than Mike. Alden had found her last note to Michael. He was upstairs hunting for something, as usual, and since Julie's door was open, he just stepped in and glanced at her study table. His conscience was always clear as a bell, so he took up the note, carried it to the bedroom and read it. There were a good many blobs on it but he made it out, even to the lines crossed out with a stub pen.

My darling—he read and began to flush. With the next sentences he felt as he had the day he almost drowned in the river. She loved him, she said, she would always love him. Farther on, she said she hated him, but she hoped he would be happy after he ruined her life. All she wanted was his happiness (Alden didn't catch the echo of his own words). He was selfish, mean, had never truly loved her at all. But why expect him to sacrifice for her? She would be happy waiting on tables and living over a drug store. In case he had anything more to say, she would be at the usual place after class. She felt it was safer to return the locket personally so he could give it to some girl at State.

Never in his life had Alden read anything remotely like this. The fact was that the tenor of the missive remarkably resembled the type of reasoning of the Prescott who was reading it. He breathed so heavily, he opened the window and leaned out for more air. His emotions were terrible, for on the one hand Julie had defied him, on the other it appeared this upstart had dared to make her miserable. The reference to State was a mystery, and this enraged him further. Finally it was evident Julie had accepted a present from Michael.

As soon as he had pulled enough air into his lungs, he charged downstairs to the kitchen. He found a peaceful scene. Sybil was putting sugar violets and roses on cakes for tomorrow's tea. Julie was rolling dates in powdered sugar. The pleasant domestic scene exploded as he waved the paper in the air.

"What's the meaning of this?" His voice was choked.

Sybil dropped a paper funnel of frosting. He wasn't, she thought, taking time to work up to violence, he was already there. I'm sick to death of it, she thought. I cannot stand it another minute.

"What's the matter now?" asked Julie wearily.

"Matter! Matter!" he bellowed. "You write such letters to this nincompoop behind my back, and then ask me what's the matter?"

Julie dropped the bowl of sugar and jumped to her feet.

"You—you—you've been sneaking and prying like a—thief! How dare you? Do you call it an honorable thing?"

The attack shook him. He sneezed, blew his nose, sneezed again. It didn't add to his dignity. Also he had absent-mindedly wiped the blackboard with his handkerchief earlier in the day, and now a cloud of chalk came from it so that he nearly strangled. But he finally got his voice back. "My own daughter!" He waved the letter again. "Disgracing me. Deliberately disobeying me."

Julie gave him a fierce look. "I wouldn't have expected my own father to be a sneak thief," she said, "but now I know better."

Sybil walked out on them, still carrying the frosting spoon. She went to the back yard, scaring a fawn-colored rabbit away from the clover. She sat down in the slatted glider where she could see the river, basted with gold. She was out of earshot and glad of it. This was a larger conflict than ever before, she felt, and much blood would be drawn. She wondered whether any woman in the world had such an impossible job as hers. Hard enough being the mother of Julie; hard enough, God knew, being the wife of Alden. But to be both was more than any woman should have to endure. Inconsequentially, she felt it would be nice to be that rabbit. Rabbits bore their young, raised them, and they all went their way. Presumably the father rabbits didn't thump around the burrows.

The night itself was serene. The stars seemed low enough to be tangled in the river willows. The air was cool with dew, and the street was quiet. Such a night was meant, surely, for murmurs of love, or the quiet companionship of a man and woman long sharing their lives. It wasn't meant for turmoil.

She was sorry for Alden, for his pride had suffered a dreadful blow. Sorry for Julie—oh, she ached for Julie. She only hoped they could rock along until Julie finished college. Sometimes it seemed doubtful. Alden could push Julie too far.

It was a pity that Julie couldn't temporize, manage things. Sybil herself had learned early to ease around crises, keep a quiet tongue. She got her own way by devious means. If Alden wouldn't give her money for a new hat, she used the grocery money and served enough really cheap meals to make it up. She was a master hand at sauces and casseroles, and then one could always get calves' liver for a quarter, and often sweetbreads and brains for nothing, as well as kidneys. She paid her tithes for church from money she saved by doing Alden's shirts at home, and he never knew the difference. He also never noticed the new hat, but might say she looked nice that day.

Women could always manage this way, she thought, but somehow Julie's generation seemed different. They worked so hard at being individuals, free, untrammeled. They made a battle of being independent. They charged head on into life. True, times were changing. There was a lot of talk about the sexes being equal, about women's rights and that sort of thing. But to Sybil being right wasn't the main thing, but getting along with people was. You could, she reflected, be right and keep it quiet. A woman's job was to manage, and keep things easy.

Julie, she thought ruefully, was stupid. After seventeen years of living with Alden, why didn't she know how curious he was? Why didn't she tuck that fatal letter under the mattress? Also she knew how jealous he was, so why hadn't she been tactful about Mike? At first she had flaunted him in her father's face. Julie would have to learn to get along with Mike one day if they got married.

Alden was stupid too. If he let this affair alone, it might wear away. Putting Julie on the defensive would help Mike more than anything. It made him a cause. Julie was a torchbearer for everything from a stray kitten to a friend flunking out of college.

She sat so still, the rabbit hopped back, flipping an ear to the wind. She could see him lipping the clover. She went on with her thinking, wishing the rabbit could talk with her. She wished she knew exactly what was between Julie and Mike, for one thing. She had to keep guessing, like a game of charades. She might be able to help Julie, but now Julie was a stranger. All she knew of her child was that she hated squash, adored chicken, would not wear mittens, thought math hideous and her clothes too childish for words.

Was this the end of being a mother? You bore your child in agony, walked the floor a thousand nights with a croupy baby, went through all the ailments from whooping cough to bilious attacks. You survived the first day of school, the first party, the first dates. You survived mysterious fevers. And by the time you were through with shaking down the thermometer, you faced Michael. For him, no thermometer was at hand.

Leaves stirred as the wind rose. She knew she must go in, for Alden and Julie must be in the last stages of battle, no doubt crying by now. Also, she thought dryly, she had fifty cakes still to decorate. The practical aspects of life had to be dealt with. She must get to the hospital to see poor Ella, for one thing. If Ella could never walk again, Dr. Jim must have help in the office. Who was available? Suddenly she thought that Miss Nelson had nowhere to turn when she was retired —could she do small jobs, answer the phone, and sleep in one of the back bedrooms? Then when Jim went out in the night, Ella would not be alone. It would provide a small living for poor Miss Nelson too.

It was worth thinking about, if Ella was willing to try it. She'd talk to Jim. Also she must get a boy to take off the storm windows for him, get the screens on. Mike would do it. She should look at poor Ella's garden too, and pick the peas, do the weeding. And when he brought Ella home she must have the icebox full of food ready to warm up. He'd have to get a country girl to cook, for a while anyway.

She took a last look at the tranquil night sky, and went slowly to the house. It looked pretty, she thought, with the ivy covering the stucco and lights shining out. It looked like a happy house, not like a battlefield. She would rather stay outside and look than go in. She braced herself, opened the screen door, and stepped into the kitchen. They were in the study, which was a good sign. A shift in the battleground always was hopeful. She peeked in and saw Julie sitting on her father's lap, and both of them were mopping their eyes.

Had Julie given up? Somehow she doubted it, but she must at least have temporized, dodged the issue someway. Perhaps she was growing up after all. She went to the kitchen and grated bitter chocolate, melted it, heated the milk. Her cakes would have to wait. When the chocolate was done, she spooned whipped cream in the cups. Then she called them, and they came in, sheepish. Julie's eyes were swollen, Alden's nose beet-red. But they drank their hot chocolate with the usual gusto. She asked no questions. Alden would give his version of the battle later, and Julie's she would have to guess.

Now they argued peaceably about whether there were people on the moon. Julie felt there might be, Alden said it was impossible.

Then Alden began to talk about the camping trip. "I'm getting new mosquito netting for the tent fly," he said, "and I'll

114

cut new tent pegs. The canteen cap is rusted, I'll try to get another."

He looked so eager, Sybil felt a pang. "A fine idea," she agreed.

Julie stared at her empty cup, farther away than the uninhabited moon, Sybil thought.

"Well, better get to bed." Alden pushed his chair back. "Got to get an early start tomorrow."

As they got in bed he said, "I straightened Julie out."

"Did you?" Sybil smoothed her pillow.

"Won't have any more trouble in that quarter," he told her.

15.

The church bells rang sweetly that Sunday before Commencement. Cars chugged down the street and puffed to a stop. Some families still walked, believing it a sin to drive a pleasure vehicle on the Lord's Day. Alden reasoned that it was lawful to drive to church, but not to take a ride in the afternoon. Church was God's business and wasn't pleasure.

Men, women and children moved slowly up the steps to the open doors of the Methodist church, talking softly as they approached the church of God. The men were already sweating in their Sunday suits and stiff shirts. Alden kept a handkerchief tucked around his collar until the last minute. The women, held up by stiff corsets, walked stiffly, their flowered hats pretty, their skirts sweeping gracefully. Julie walked behind her parents, partly because she had difficulty walking in her new high-heeled patent leather slippers. They made the backs of her legs ache. She wore her green print and a white straw hat with daisies around the brim. She was hot, and longed to pull off her white gloves.

Sybil had a way of looking cool. She wore a cinnamon-brown dress and a brown straw with narrow brim. Her needle-point bag was darker brown. Her face, shadowed by the hat, looked pale and pensive. Alden puffed ahead of her, sweating and muttering. The truth was church bored him. He hated sitting still, and he didn't like being part of an audience. He preferred to do the talking. In church, the best he could do was raise his clear tenor and drown out everyone else. But today, on the whole, he was less peppery than usual, for he had settled Julie, once and for all.

Moreover, a new idea had come while he was shaving that morning. As he dabbed at the cuts which he always gave himself, it occurred to him that he could keep Julie away from not only Michael, but all boys. He could send her East to a women's college, where she would be safe from distractions and give her mind to her studies. When she graduated, she could come back to Westerly for her Ph.D. and then join the faculty. Of course the idea of parting with Julie gave him such a turn that he sliced his chin badly, but as he applied the court plaster, he felt that maybe desperate measures were required. That letter had shaken him badly.

As they filed into their pew he stole a glance at his daughter. She was looking off into space, dreamy-eyed, and he had an impulse to shout, "Look at *me*."

While Mark Allingham battled the ancient organ, the congregation dipped heads in prayer. Alden shut his eyes but would not bend his head. He met God face to face. There were times, indeed, when he tried to dictate to God. Now he wished Mark would get over that mumbling music. Finally Reverend Mallory stood up in the pulpit. He was too young, Alden felt, to shepherd a flock, and besides he was too handsome. He looked like a boy with that shock of sandy hair and rosy face.

The First Methodist church needed a solemn, elderly preacher who would concentrate more on hell and less on God's love. As the sermon began, Alden peeked at his watch. Two hours would end the service and he could go home for a good chicken dinner with giblet gravy and whipped potatoes and new peas and salad and Lady Baltimore cake; a nice plain meal, he thought, but he was hungry already.

"Praise God from whom all blessings flow—praise him all creatures here below"—he let his voice out on that, ignoring Sybil's warning pinch.

Sybil was resigned to the sermon, for it had to have the Commencement theme. Even Reverend Mallory had to conform and preach on go forth into all the world and show thy light. She kept attentive eyes on him, but let her mind drift. She was glad to sit down, even in the uncomfortable pew. Since it was so hot, one of the stained-glass windows was half open, and the air came in on a feather of breeze. The church smelled of toilet water, plush, and perspiration. She uncapped her silver bottle of smelling salts and breathed the sharp scent gratefully. The word of God seemed far-off. She wished she were outside, away in the bright spring, alone, walking in a meadow, picking violets. She was tired of listing her blessings, and tired of praying for forgiveness of her sins. (Those dreadful moments when she wished she had never laid eyes on Alden Prescott were truly sinful. And it was sinful to have those moments of wishing to give Julie a spanking as if she were six.)

"God make his face to shine upon you and give you peace."

God seldom got around to making his face shine on her and give her peace, she thought rebelliously. The benediction over, she followed Alden and Julie down the aisle. The Reverend Mallory had whipped out to stand with outstretched hands greeting his parishioners. Sybil put out her hand and his big paw engulfed it.

He looked down at her, his eyes smiling. When she tried

to comment on the service, he laughed. "Sermons come and go," he said, "but it is a good thing to look at God now and then no matter what the words be."

At the bottom of the steps, Alden was wrapping his handkerchief around his collar again. "Confounded heat," he grumbled. "Why can't they let some air in that mausoleum?"

Mark was on the sidewalk, music under his arm. Miss Nelson flapped her hands at him, talking nervously. Sybil waited until she tripped away before asking Mark to come to dinner. Alden would not put up with Miss Nelson. They piled into the car, and Sybil tied a scarf over her hat and put on her goggles. Julie took her hat off and let the dusty air blow on her hair. They braced themselves as the car shuddered and leaped away. Alden had quite a reputation as the most daring driver in Winnebago. When they reached the house he hauled on the brake, throwing them against the dashboard and the back seat.

The house seemed cool, for Sybil had drawn the shades early in the morning, and the dim light made it even cooler. Alden took off his tie, loosened his collar and sank down in his favorite easy chair. Mark sat on the rosewood sofa. Julie and Sybil went to put dinner on.

"Sermon too long," said Alden. "I could have said it in half the time."

Mark grinned. He was fond of Alden, as so many were. He admired his courage, his daring, his brilliance, and possibly even more, the fact that Alden was so utterly masculine. But as he looked around the charming room with perceptive eyes, he thought it reflected Sybil, not Alden. Possibly Alden did not care to impress himself on anything mundane. Or was the quiet Sybil really the strong one? He admired the carpet, with its faded pink roses, the pale curtains falling softly, the rosewood furniture upholstered in lilac and ivory. There was no paper fan in the fireplace, only a few branches of fresh pine.

There were no heavy oils on the walls, just a single water color, a bouquet of pinks over the mantel. The lamp shades were neither fringed nor beaded. Sybil had made them of plain ivory silk. The piano top was bare, uncluttered with photographs, urns, Persian silk scarfs. A milk glass vase filled with white lilacs gave fragrance to the room.

Listening absently to Alden's dissertation on the state of Westerly, he thought suddenly that in some way Sybil reminded him of his mother, during his early years. He ventured to say this, later, and Sybil said thank you, without enthusiasm.

She was tired of being everybody's mother. And Mark's mother, she recalled, died at the age of seventy-nine chasing a stranger from the house with a butcher knife. Then she thought she was being silly, for obviously Mark had forgotten the bad years. To a child the mother was initial security, warmth. Her own mother, long since dead of lung fever, appeared in her dreams now and then, young and beautiful in lilac silk, her dark hair rolled elegantly in a pompadour, her eyes gay.

This remained, not the memory of her mother wasted and with blood-red cheeks.

So she said gently, "Thank you, Mark, thank you very much."

While Julie and Sybil washed the dishes the men went to the parlor and Alden delivered a lecture on politics. By the time the dishes were done, Sybil opened the curtains, for it was cooler. Mark suggested Julie might sing, and sat down at the piano to accompany her. She sang *"Du, Du Liegst Mir Im Herzen,"* and although her German was only passable, her voice had a wistful sweetness. Then Alden decided to sing too. He began with "The Harp That Once Through Tara's Halls," followed with "Come Where My Love Lies Dreaming." Then Mark played a movement of Beethoven's Fifth, the music swelling into splendor as his long fingers compelled it. But as he played, he was considering the rumor he heard at church that the Director of the Tri-State Music Conference might come to Commencement to look over what talent there was at Westerly. If so, after he heard the program there wouldn't be a chance that Mark would get even a minor offer for next summer. And he couldn't do a thing about it, not without Marjorie.

Sybil loved the Beethoven, it lifted her out of herself. She could not carry a tune but she had a passion for music. And Mark played beautifully, although he had a troubled expression. When he finished playing he stood up and said quickly, "I must be going along. It's been a real pleasure." Sybil's eyes made him uncomfortable. He felt she saw him too clearly. "So nice," he commented, "a bit of family life ameliorates a bachelor's life, you know." It sounded silly, and he blushed.

"Yes, I know," Sybil said.

What did she know, this disturbing woman? He gathered his music.

"Glad to have you any time." Alden put the piano top down. He was restless, having sat still so long. "And, Mark, could you persuade the Glee Club not to drag the Alma Mater so egregiously?"

"I can but try." Mark made his farewells and went out into the pale twilight. The wind was northeast now, and silky. There would be a break in the unseasonable heat. He was alone on the street, for most families were at supper. Even after the big Sunday dinner the men got hungry as usual. Women moved about slicing rosy ham and putting out bowls of potato salad, made the German way, spicy and glistening with oil. He walked slowly, as if he had no destination. But when he swung onto the campus the familiar buildings reassured him. He must not get vaporish before Commencement, Marjorie or no Marjorie. Possibly next year he might get a good voice again —who knew? And buoyed up by the beginning of a new dream, he went on briskly. It had done him good to be with Sybil, he realized. He wondered what she had ever married Alden for.

Later, Sybil set out cold chicken, stuffed eggs, salad and cake, made fresh coffee, dropping an eggshell in the pot. Julie and Alden helped themselves, for after all dinner was four hours ago. Sybil managed a wing and a bit of toast. Lately she was never hungry.

"You know," Alden said, "I think Mark bears down too heavily on the bass in the Beethoven."

"Why, I thought so too." Sybil looked at him with surprise. How comforting it was to agree with Alden!

"Everybody thinks he plays better than anybody," said Julie, not to go along with her father. "Papa, I have to go to the dorm to plan the Gamma tea with Marcy." Her eyes were innocent. "May I go now?"

"It's Sunday night." He was doubtful. But he had relaxed during the pleasant afternoon. "Don't be late."

"Marcy and Linda will walk me home," she promised.

She flew off, as if she had wings. Why didn't she stay at home more? Why didn't she play checkers with him, or ask him to help with her Latin translations? She was always off or shut in her room. He looked at Sybil, who was stacking the dishes. Well, Sybil was there, at any rate, and no matter what she did during the day, she always met him when he came home, with supper on time. She didn't desert him.

"I like that dress you have on," he said suddenly. "That kind of frill looks nice."

"Why, Alden." She looked pleased.

"Most women," he observed, taking a piece of cake, "have bony necks. I like soft necks."

"Why, Alden." She blushed.

"Can't you leave the dishes for Julie? She doesn't do much around the house any more."

"This is a busy time for them all," she commented. "Things pile up at the end."

"Time it was over," he grumbled as he went off to his study. She washed the dishes quickly and quietly, while the sound of his typewriter muffled the kitchen noises. She set the table for breakfast, made up the buttermilk pancakes and set them in the icebox to mellow. She would have liked an evening with her china-painting, but of course it was Sunday. Alden might work on his next day's lectures but nobody else was supposed to do anything. He did not even favor novel reading, for it was light amusement.

She went upstairs and poked around in the bedroom, laying out Alden's clean clothes and making up the laundry. Then she took her bath, creamed her face, brushed her hair a hundred strokes with the stiff-bristled brush. As she tied the silk net in place she looked at herself critically. She touched her throat, ran her fingers along the curve of her neck. Indeed it was true, her neck was not bony, it was really nice-looking. And there wasn't the slightest sign of a double chin, just a clean curve. Actually she had no lines to speak of in her face, except the crinkled ones from smiling. And the shadows of fatigue made her eyes darker. She never paid much attention to her looks except to keep well-groomed and neatly dressed. But it was nice to know she had a pretty neck.

She buttoned her nightgown and went to the window to look at the latticed moonlight outside. How lovely to be out in the night, just walking. But Alden would think she had lost her senses. He didn't take to prowling around at night.

Marriage was a strange journey, she thought, in which most women traveled alone. But some men did too. Dr. Jim and President Wallace, for instance. How would it be with Julie? She wouldn't be easy, ever.

Far off, a lonely freight blew for the crossing. It would be pleasant to get on a train and travel, or "go across the water" as they said. She had always longed to see Venice and float around in a gondola while the gondolier sang. Or to throw coins in the fountains of Rome. Or look at Buckingham Palace. But any travel she did would be to the desert or some mining camp or some arctic wilderness where Alden could study the path of the glaciers. Of this type she had already had enough. She would live out her life in this house, being sure the cakes were frosted for faculty teas and carpets aired and beaten in spring. She was still thinking of this when Alden bounced upstairs.

"Julie ought to be home," he grumbled, "—racketing around on Sunday."

"It's not late."

"I've got a hard day coming up, I need some rest," he said.

"I always wait up," Sybil said. "Don't fuss, Alden, this is just Commencement. Even the dormitory rules are eased."

He got undressed, thumped into bed and, as always, was instantly asleep. Sybil lay down, listening for Julie's step. Had Julie really gone to see Marcy? Better not to ask. When at last she heard the fifth tread creak on the stairs, she knew Julie was safe once more, and that should be enough.

Then, as she turned over in bed, she smiled suddenly and put her hand on Alden's shoulder. He thought her neck was pretty. Soft.

Smiling, she fell asleep.

16.

In the President's house Carol had packed the twins off to bed early because they got on her nerves whooping around. She had wanted to put them in a private school last winter, but

Dick had flatly refused to send them away. He said they were too young to leave home. Besides, the Winnebago public schools were excellent, and far more democratic.

This had been a dreadful day, right from the start. Like it or not, the President's wife was hostess at a tea for the class of '99. Dick had, in one of his rare stubborn streaks, insisted that they invite Mr. Finny for lunch (the chapel needed a new organ).

The gas stove sprung a leak around eleven. The repair men did not come until one. The salad plate, substituting for the steak, was a miserable failure as Mr. Finny did not eat salad.

Around two o'clock Minnie, the cook, gave notice simply because Carol was sharp with her about the size of the tea sandwiches. The tea was a catastrophe. The gas men were still clanking around in the cellar banging on pipes. Minnie had to go next door to boil water for the tea. In the confusion, no damp cloth had been laid over the sandwiches, so they were dry. The icing on the cupcakes was grainy.

And the class of '99 was a year older, a year duller. There were fifteen of them, fat, graying, badly dressed, and giggling over the same old reminiscences. As she looked at them Carol wanted to scream. Such a pang of frustration went through her that she sat down in a corner.

Dick was moving from one guest to another, easy, smiling, gracious. He belonged with these dreadful bores, she thought. He even liked them. But she would rather die than fit into such a group. The awful clothes, the flat Midwestern accent, the platitudes—it was just too much.

She knew very well how she herself looked—cool, elegant. Her figure was a major part of her existence, dieting her main preoccupation. She ate steak without butter on it, dry toast instead of the hot rolls Dick and the twins wolfed, lettuce with no dressing. Today she wore a plain cloud-gray dress and her grandmother's pearls. Her hair was drawn smoothly back (no frizzy marcel to ruin the silken look). Her stockings, sent from New York by her mother, were sheer, and the heels of her slippers were high. She was beautiful, and she knew it, but the effect was utterly wasted on this gathering.

Who was there to admire her? She was utterly miserable. Why had she married this tiresome man and got stuck in this wretched college in this dreadful town? As she thought of the years ahead with the same old grads returning for Commencement, the endless faculty concerts, the awful banquets, she felt sick.

Right now, if she were in New York, the matinee would be over, and she would come out laughing on the arm of—well— of a man who had money enough to take her to the Waldorf, order the right wine and entrée. Discuss the salad dressing with the deferential waiter.

Pêche flambée for dessert. Then a ride through Central Park in a carriage, with the lights of the great, mysterious city gay against the sky. The clop-clop of the horse's hoofs was louder, for a moment, than the voices around her.

She came from the dream because a plump matron wandered over and started a conversation. The weather. The changes on campus since the last reunion. What were they? Carol hadn't noticed any. And a wonderful new recipe the President would like. He looked thin.

Carol pulled herself together as the recipe was given.

"And first you separate the yolks from the whites and beat them well, and then gradually—"

Dick, passing by, gave her an imploring look. He wanted her to be charming to these people. She had an instant of feeling guilty, and this made her angry.

"I wouldn't cook if I had to starve," she said coldly. The woman backed away. Carol could not have cared less. But this reminded her of Minnie. Would she really leave? Cooks were hard to come by. Minnie was her fourth in two years, and the only one who could be called a cook. For most women in Winnebago did their own cooking, helped each other out for big parties. Occasionally the cleaning woman would come in to serve and wash dishes. But there was no servant class in town. And nobody who came to help would wear a uniform. The few wealthy millowners had to import their help from Chicago or Milwaukee.

Carol went to the dining room to check on the sandwiches and cakes, rapidly being depleted, poor as they were. Minnie, looking sullen, carried a tray of empty cups to the kitchen. She certainly looked angry, Carol thought, and if she left, the whole struggle would begin again.

Suddenly she thought, I am not going to keep on like this. Suppose she packed up and left? Went back to her mother and father. Didn't she have some right to happiness? Why not go home and begin to live again? The thought shook her, and she poured a fresh cup of tea and hurried back to a group, hiding her excitement.

Dick would have to resign, of course. The town would be crashing with scandal. He could go away and do something else. She would wangle the money from her father to send the twins to a private school. Maybe Dick was satisfied to pinch and scrape forever. She wasn't. He kept saying money wasn't everything, but as far as she was concerned, it was basic. She wanted Parma violets, dancing in a ballroom, not a gymnasium. Second-act curtains. She didn't worry about a man to replace Dick. She'd invested enough in her beauty to be sure of one.

Now she came out of her dream and back to the present in time to say coldly to the wife of the Bolt and Bearing Company president, "I cannot see why everyone makes such a fuss about Commencement. I find it a bore."

"I expect most of us like to return to our youth," said the

126

plump little woman, "and Commencement brings us back our youth momentarily. Or didn't you find it so?"

"I never had one," Carol answered, "as I left St. Agatha's in April. My parents took me to Paris."

"That must have been an interesting trip."

"I was bored," Carol said. "They dragged me around museums."

Finally the tea ended and the guests said what a pleasant afternoon, and they looked forward to seeing them again next year. Next year will be a different story, thought Carol, shaking hands mechanically.

Minnie had gone upstairs saying her feet hurt. A cold, indifferent supper was laid on the table. The twins were fretful, refused their milk, dropped silver on the floor. Dick was in one of his abstract moods and paid no attention.

So Carol had plenty of time for the plan mushrooming in her mind. She would leave secretly while Dick was tossing a spadeful of earth around the Class Day tree. Her trunks could be sent later, but she must take enough with her for a short time. The hatbox would hold her three favorite hats, the wide Gibson with violet ribbons, the pink feather toque, the black velvet with the bird of paradise wing. The big suitcase would accommodate dresses, one suit, blouses, and lingerie. The carryall she would fill with slippers, jewelry, gloves, toilet articles.

She would pack at night and lock everything in the upstairs hall closet, which had a key.

The main problem was getting away. She could not wire her mother, for there were no secrets in Winnebago's Western Union office. The telegraph operator was Miss Hansen, and telegrams were her own property. She read them, commented, passed the news around in a friendly manner.

"You have a telegram from that college in Ohio," she had told Dick over the phone. "They want you down there for a conference. You better turn them down. In my opinion they want you for their president. I wouldn't take it. Shall I read the message?"

And then there was the time she called Carol to say, sympathetically, "Your mother has the grippe so she couldn't get the nightgowns off to you. Shall I wire back not to bother?"

No, she dared not send a wire. What a maddening, silly obstacle.

Money was another problem. If she drew out the money in their mutual savings account, Ralph Knight would ask, "Planning a vacation trip after Commencement? Or will it be a new Oldsmobile this time? President Wallace was in yesterday and didn't say anything about it." Without cleaning out the savings she had just enough money for train fare, but no extras.

She pushed her coffee cup aside. She began to feel the trap closing in. If she went to the station to make reservations, the ticket agent would tell the next customer that she had tickets for New York right in the middle of Commencement. Kind of unexpected. Was her mother sick? Or some businessman on his way to Milwaukee for the day would comment to his wife when he got back, and it would be all over town.

The noise suddenly penetrated into her plans. "If you don't stop that racket," she said fiercely to the twins, "I shall not let you go to Class Day. Go upstairs and be quiet."

"Why do we always have to go upstairs?" asked young Dick angrily. "You never want us around, that's why."

"I don't feel good," young Carol said. "I don't want to go to that hot old upstairs. I want some nice chocolate ice cream."

Dick looked up from his untasted pie. "It's true, you know," he told her. "You are always sending them away."

"Why can't they behave?"

Dick sighed and left the table. He wouldn't go against her orders to the twins, for he believed they must respect her. But he would slip upstairs and play Rook with them, or read aloud.

Well let him. Her nerves were frayed as she darted from one impossible plan to another.

Could she, unobserved, take the streetcar to the next town, and the train from there? Could she risk a cab, loaded down with her luggage? And where could she scrape up more cash? Then she remembered the twins had been saving up for a pony (as if she would put up with a pony stamping around). Their horde was in a fishing-tackle box. And Minnie's wages for the month—in an envelope in her desk. There would probably be a few dollars in the church envelope. How large a check could she cash without drawing attention? Fifty? Possibly seventy-five? If she murmured something about Commencement gifts and entertaining, she might risk it without too much interest on Ralph's part.

She was sitting in the living room when Dick looked in. "I think the children are coming down with colds," he commented. "Might have Dr. Jim look in on them tomorrow. I gave them each an aspirin. I'm going back to the office to clear up a few odds and ends."

As soon as the front screen closed she flew upstairs. Like a ship being launched, she slid into the waters of change. She was on her way at last. She began to pack, swiftly and efficiently. When she finished, she carried the luggage to the closet and locked it in. It was heavy, but she must somehow carry it herself.

She couldn't do anything about the trunks, which were in the attic. Sybil would pack them, for although she would hate Carol for escaping, she would help Dick out. She was always helping someone.

Slipping silently into the twin's room, she found the tackle box and managed to open it without a click. They were breathing heavily, and every few minutes Carol made a choking sound. They had undoubtedly gone wading in the brook and were in for head colds.

She was weak with relief when she put all the money together. It was enough. She was ready. She bathed, creamed
her face carefully, patted ice water on to close the pores. Then
she took the bottle of brandy from the medicine chest and
poured a glassful. With all she had been through, she needed
it. She went through the usual search for a gray hair or a slight
wrinkle, and was satisfied that there were none.

She got into bed, lying flat, hands folded over her shallow
breasts. She believed this position kept her spine erect. She did
the breathing exercises which were so good for the bust. She
felt brave and strong about escaping from this place, but her
fear of growing older never left her. She would not grow old.
She would be as beautiful and as young always as she had been
before she met Dick. She had not changed. Her eyes often
ached, but she had never given in to that stupid doctor about
wearing glasses.

"Mother." Young Dick opened the door. "We don't feel so
good."

"It's not surprising with all you ate after the tea," she said.
"Go back to bed and get some sleep."

The clock struck eleven. It was odd that Dick had not come
in, but it didn't really matter. For it came to her that she could
ask the truck driver, who was to bring the newly upholstered
sofa tomorrow, to drop her luggage off at the junction "for a
friend." There she would pick it up and get on the train. How
easy things were when you were clever.

As she drifted off to sleep she dreamed of her childhood.
She walked along a silver beach with her mother and father.
The tide was coming in, and her father pulled her away from
it to keep her slipper dry. She stamped her foot and said the
tide should wait.

"Tides never wait," said her father.

The house was dark and silent. It was an old house, warm
and welcoming, but it had never welcomed Carol. For her,

doors slammed suddenly, windows dropped on her fingers, lights flickered. Keys refused to turn in locks. Porch steps gave way. Drains clogged.

The house was her enemy, and she had always sensed it. Long cherished, it resented this stranger. Now tonight it was still. The house breathed softly as Carol dreamed of her childhood.

Outside, the June bugs bumbled against the porch light and moths flickered in the fatal glow. The campus was dark, rocking at anchor in the night. Dick walked slowly, deep in his thoughts. He went over his problems. A sea of troubles. But they would be solved. Above them, and written between the lines, was the thought of Louise. She represented quietude, warmth, humor. As Carol represented selfishness, coldness, and no more humor than a grocery list. Perhaps the world was divided between the givers and the takers. Louise—and Carol.

17.

Saturday was hot and clear, and the Knight flat was stifling. Marjorie choked down two soda crackers for breakfast and promptly threw them up. She drank hot water with a teaspoonful of soda in it, and threw that up. Then she wiped her face with a damp washcloth and rested on the couch, battling the nausea. It wasn't much fun.

The bank being closed, Ralph had gone off to play tennis. He needed, he said, fresh air after being cooped up in a cage all week. He looked fresh and carefree as he dropped a good-by kiss on her damp forehead. Of course he could chase a ball around a hot court and come home hungry—while it was all she could do to stay on her feet long enough to do a minimum of housework and cook meals she could not eat.

Dr. Jim was encouraging. He told her she would soon feel fine. Babies were born by the million, he said, and morning sickness had yet to carry off a mother. But with her it wasn't just morning, but also noon, and night. In spite of the heavy swelling from the baby, she had lost seven pounds and her bones stood out. She looked like a witch, she thought, and her hair was awful, for it was always damp with sweat. She now wore shapeless housedresses and eased her swollen feet into a pair of old tennis shoes. It was a change, all right, from being trim and sparkling, and being admired everywhere she went.

In the early days, she had taken off Saturdays to play tennis too, her long legs flashing about the court, her serves fast. She had always been careful not to beat Ralph, but it was still fun. Afterward they always went to the drug store for double chocolate malteds, and she sang along with the records on the Victrola.

Now Ralph played with another bank clerk, and stopped at Joe's for hamburgers. She couldn't blame him for not wanting to hang around the hot flat. He was, she thought, a good husband, satisfied with his small job, pleased about her singing, not minding the inconvenient flat. He had no ear for music, but enjoyed the praise he got as the husband of a fine singer. He always enjoyed sitting in the auditorium when she sang, and receiving compliments afterward. He also enjoyed spending the money she made. He had been perfectly happy until this baby business began, his only ambition being to become a thirty-third degree Mason some day.

Now that Marjorie could not sing and no longer had energy to mother him, it was different. They both were changing under the impact of the baby. He was bored, irritable. She was despondent because she had failed Professor Allingham, who had meant more to her than anyone in her life. The fine-spun empathy between teacher and gifted pupil was a splendor, and now was over. When she thought about Professor Allingham the tears rolled down her drawn face. He had given her so much for so little in return, and guilt was heavy in her.

And the truth was, her marriage had been all right as long as she had the world of her music to lean on, but without it, Ralph was a bore. Suddenly she could not bear the flat another minute. She put on a clean dress, brushed her hair, and crept out. She walked aimlessly, lugging along the burden within her, but automatically turned toward campus. As she passed the Conservatory her glance winged up to Professor Allingham's studio. She could no longer race up the steps and run in, smiling and eager.

She lingered by the steps. Someone was practicing a Bach fugue. Someone else practiced an aria. A group in the front practice room harmonized the "Alma Mater."

> "Love the pathways to and from
> The classrooms and the halls,
> Ne'er shall we forget, though far we roam
> These hours within thy walls."

"Why, Marjorie, I haven't seen you in a long time!" Dean Richardson held out her hand. "What a nice surprise."

Marjorie smiled shyly. As a private person she was very timid, although as a singer she had the aplomb of a diplomat. "I've not been well." She reddened.

The Dean, with those gray eyes that never seemed to be noticing, but missed nothing, said cheerfully, "I was just on my way home to fix some iced tea. I would like some company, if you have time?"

Time—she had time. Tears pricked her eyelids, for she cried at everything these days. "Oh thank you," she murmured.

The Dean walked slowly so Marjorie could keep up. In her

SPRING HARVEST

living room, she put Marjorie in the wing chair which was by the window.

"I find tea a help on these hot days," she remarked, "and Commencement is always hot, isn't it?" She brought a tray with lemon and mint and set it on the tea table while the tea brewed.

"I won't be singing," Marjorie said.

"So Mark told me. But it is lovely about the baby!"

Marjorie burst into tears. The Dean reflected dryly that it would take an ocean to hold all the tears shed in this room. She pretended not to notice, and went about putting ice in the tall glasses. She felt a special sympathy for this girl. It was a bad time for her, and her husband was weak and dependent. Her career was in jeopardy: in fact it was doubtful whether she would ever sing much again.

"Try this." She handed Marjorie a frosty glass. Marjorie sipped and the tea was cold and comforting. And then, following the pattern of all the refugees in the Dean's room, she poured out her troubles. The Dean listened, not commenting. When Marjorie finished, the Dean spoke gently.

"We all have moments when we give in," she said thoughtfully, "and then we pick up and go on. It is always much harder for a woman to make a professional career than a man, because that is the way the world is set up. But I know you will find that having the baby balances all the sacrifice. You will see."

"Are you sure?"

"Yes, I'm sure. And I'm sure you will be a better singer, too. But even if you weren't, I wouldn't be sorry for you."

Marjorie thought about it as she went back across campus, a heavy figure in the midst of the slim golden girls. Dean Richardson seemed to think it was a fine thing for her to have the baby. The news had been such a blow to Professor Allingham that she had felt ashamed.

134

And after the first pride, Ralph had grown cross and bored. He didn't like the sketchy meals, the disordered flat and her eternal queasiness. Ralph didn't want the baby any more than Mark wanted her to have it. But Dean Richardson seemed to think a baby was something wonderful! The Dean wasn't sorry for her at all! Hope began to put out tentative leaves. Maybe she could yet finish her study and sing again—maybe—

She decided to go home by way of Main Street and get something special for Ralph's supper. She would do a Swiss steak, have asparagus, browned potatoes, lemon pie. And put on a fresh dress and set the table in the living room. After all, he hadn't had much of a time lately. There was a lot you could say about Ralph, she thought, as the butcher waited on her. He wasn't one to set the world on fire, but he didn't get drunk or run around with other women or gamble at the pool hall. He didn't even swear.

As she took out her quarter the butcher said, "I have some extra liver. I'm giving it away. They do say it is good for you."

"I like it," she said gratefully.

His kindness warmed her. She went home and cleaned up the flat. Even after the walking, she felt she wouldn't lie down to rest. She did some washing instead, and then fixed supper. She washed her hair while the steak simmered and brushed it until it was soft and satiny.

Ralph came in as she was making the salad. He sniffed. "What smells so good? I'm starved."

"Supper's ready. Wash up and we'll eat."

"I have my backhand in control," he said proudly as they sat down. "It's all in a twist of the wrist."

"That's good news."

"You all right?" He added butter to his potatoes.

"Yes. I went out this morning. I had iced tea with the Dean."

He stared. "Well, I never. With the Dean? How did that happen?"

135

"We just met. She asked me. She thinks it is wonderful about the baby!"

"She did?" Well, that was something. Thought it was wonderful, did she? He sat a bit straighter. Professor Allingham was fit to be tied, but he wasn't the whole world, by any means. Not half as important as Dean Richardson.

"I'm really going to work on my serve," he said, "and you know, when the time comes, I guess I can teach him a good game of tennis."

"Of course you can." This was the first time the baby had been mentioned as an entity. Marjorie was pleased. Not that Ralph would ever be good enough at anything to teach it.

She understood by this time that she had married him because he was helpless and needed her. She had known he didn't fit in with her career, but when he knelt and put his head in her lap and begged her to marry him, she could not help saying yes. She could encourage him, bring him out, polish his manners, choose his clothes. It hadn't worked out quite that way. True, he now wore plain dark suits like Professor Allingham, and conservative ties. A haircut like Mark's replaced the bush he favored. But the essential Ralph hadn't changed a bit. In the bank, other tellers moved up to front cages, Ralph stayed in the back one. He was honest, accurate, but slow and utterly without talent at charming the depositors. People lined up in front of the tellers easy with conversation, gay with women, quick and deft with the business.

As she thought of this, Marjorie felt the nausea begin again. It might have been the sight of the large spoonful of gravy Ralph added to his potatoes. She got up and stumbled to the bathroom. It was worse this time, the seasickness became a pain. Afterward she lay down on the couch and Ralph awkwardly mopped her face with a wet washcloth. He meant well, but he squeezed drops down her neck, slipped on the throw rug, broke the best ash tray. Suddenly she began to giggle, and

then to laugh, and then to choke. Ralph frantically slopped
the spirits of ammonia around, and finally, spent, she quieted
down. He looked so frightened, so helpless. Poor Ralph. She
put out her hand.

"I'm all right, honey," she said, "don't worry. Dr. Jim says
it is—natural."

"You look awful white." He mopped her face again. "I
thought this didn't go on all the time." He wrung out the
cloth. "You haven't caught anything?"

Yes, she had caught something, she had caught herself. But
she tried to smile. "Finish your pie," she said. "I'm fine. I'll
rest a bit."

She rested her head on the pine pillow, souvenir of their
honeymoon. I PINE FOR YOU, FOR YOU I BALSAM.

Ralph cleared the table, only dropping two saucers. "And do
you feel all right now?" he asked.

At that moment the doorbell rang. Then footsteps sounded
on the stairs. Marjorie knew them as well as her own. She
got up, straightened her dress, smoothed her hair. "Shut the
kitchen door," she directed Ralph. "Put away the towel." She
ran past him to open the door. Ralph stared openmouthed at
the change in her.

"I hope I am not intruding." Mark spoke in his precise way.

"Not at all. Certainly not," cried Marjorie. "Come in."

"I happened to be passing by"—he was hesitant—"and I
thought I might drop in, just to see how things are."

"We were just about to have coffee," she said gaily, "and
there is some of that lemon pie you like so much."

Ralph couldn't keep up with it. Ten minutes ago, she was
so ill and now she bustled around after coffee and pie. He
couldn't make head or tail of it.

Mark sat down. He thought Marjorie, with the flush in her
cheeks and the loose wings of hair, was more beautiful than
ever. In spite of himself, he gave Ralph a fierce look. What a

137

meaching little man to ruin Marjorie's life. But in spite of her figure, Marjorie had a dark radiance about her as she brought his coffee. He himself was miserable. He didn't consciously think that he was in love with her, and the truth was he did not love the woman, but the voice. But for him, loving the voice was as close to passion as he would ever get. Nevertheless Marjorie herself was an extension of the voice, so it was difficult to separate the two.

"I thought you might like to practice some this summer," he said diffidently. "I mean when you could—and it occurred to me that Miss Nelson might play for you. She could suit your convenience. Of course you've heard she is retiring."

"Miss Nelson play for me!" If he had suggested the devil she wouldn't have been more aghast.

"She does keep time," he reminded her gently, "and hits most of the notes part of the time. I don't mean she would coach you or that you would study with her. Not by any means. You wouldn't pay any attention to any suggestions she might make."

"No. I guess not."

"But it would keep you in practice. Then, too, it would make her feel—not entirely useless. It would be kind of you, Marjorie."

She looked sorrowfully at him. This was the summer she should go to Chicago and work ten hours a day at the Conservatory. So she would keep in practice with Miss Nelson.

"I'll be glad to—have her," she said. "You could choose what I should work on."

He nodded. It was a thread to tie her to singing. "Then I'll arrange with Miss Nelson," said Mark, who already had. "She'll get in touch with you. Now I'll run along."

"Did you good to have a caller," Ralph commented. "He really does take an interest."

Marjorie did not answer. Poor Ralph, there wasn't any use

trying to explain just how much of an interest Professor Allingham took, nor how much it meant to her. Ralph hadn't any idea, either, of what a gift she had. But somehow knowing how Mark felt no longer gave her such a heavy sense of guilt. Instead, she felt new courage. He believed in her. Therefore she would yet be a great singer, although how it could be managed she did not know.

Slowly, imperceptibly, she began building her dream.

18.

Julie sat on their special log by the edge of the river, and her eyes were swollen almost shut with weeping. Michael was going to State, and when he told her, the resulting storm was so catastrophic it made her battles with her father seem inconsequential. And when it ended, Mike flung away in a sullen rage.

That afternoon he took Marcy to Tree Day. This was the end of everything. Naturally nobody asked Julie, for she was Mike's steady. So she sat miserably on the damp log, without a tear left in her but with a sickness in her bones. She wished she were dead, and she wished Marcy were dead. Her best friend, going out with Mike! She wished Mike would break his collarbone and not be able to play football at all anywhere. That would fix him. They wouldn't want him at State then. Not that it mattered to her. Her neck was rigid and the pain sliced down to her shoulders. She probably would die.

Why did people keep saying it was so wonderful to be young? It was dreadful, nothing but suffering. Parents were enough trouble without trouble with the man you loved desperately, hopelessly. Now her father kept talking about the advantages of an eastern women's college and there was absolutely nothing left to live for. Well, Mike would have a fine time at State. All those rich Chicago girls would invite him to their big houses on the Lake Shore Drive. Their parents would welcome the big football star. In the end, Mike would marry one of them, a very rich one. He would spend his time cruising around on a white yacht—she could just see him sitting on deck sipping an iced drink or dancing in tropical moonlight. She found she could still sob, even without tears falling. It made her chest ache.

"I thought I'd find you here," said Mike, pushing the clover aside.

"Mike—"

"Speaking." He sat down and fished for his handkerchief.

"I didn't expect—" she hiccuped.

Mike held her hands. "Who else would it be?"

Now was the time to rise and flounce away, stiff with pride.

But all she could do was bury her face in his handkerchief. He lifted her face and kissed the tear streaks, in a way not in the books at all. "Let's have no more of this," he said.

"I—I gave you up."

"Sure you did. I gave you up too. I've spent some time giving you up like crazy. You're the silliest, most difficult, most unreasonable girl in all the world, and I'm nuts about you. Now I'm not going to give you up again. And I don't give a damn whether it's a square deal for you or not. I just don't care."

Julie came alive, feeling his arms tight around her.

"Made up my mind after Tree Day," he explained. "Marcy's a nice girl, and so pretty and all that, and no trouble at all. Her folks don't interfere either, they don't care who she picks. There is not one thing wrong with her, believe me. But she just isn't you."

He pushed her hair back and kissed her again. Her blotched

face didn't seem to bother him. "I don't go for substitutes," he commented.

"Me either," Julie whispered, clinging to him.

"So I walked around most of last night," he continued, "and figured things out. So this morning I wired the State guy it was no sale. It won't be easy, a hell of a pull, but I'm staying at Westerly. I'll be around, and your father can't help that, can he? I'll see you, one way or another."

Julie heard a new assurance in his voice. It almost frightened her, for it made him strange.

"Are you—really sure?"

"I hate cheating," he went on, in that decided voice, "more than anything. I've lived with a couple of first-class cheats most of my life. But I guess we'll have to cheat."

He drew away, broke a twig in his hands, tossed it. "We can't come out and face your father now. He'd get me shipped, on some pretext or other. So we'll just have to keep going the way we have. I've got some summer jobs in mind, and a room in the basement of Kennicott in return for odd jobs. I'm pulling out of my aunt's dump. Next fall I'll have to work every spare minute, and you'll have to take it, rough as it is. That's the way it has to be." He closed his hands on her shoulders. "But you've got to quit this fighting with me. It takes too much out of us. You got to grow up."

Julie looked up at him. His mouth was tight, his eyes tired. He looked older. And something in his voice woke a response in her she had never known before. She felt humble. She was not, she knew now, worth what he gave up for her, and would go on giving up. She was spoiled, selfish, childish, petty. She had never made things easy for him, she had taken everything and given almost nothing. But if she were not worthy of him, nobody else was either. And nobody, nobody, could love him as she did.

What could she say to him? Humility sat uneasily on her.

141

It would take a lifetime to show him how much she loved him. And so, as women have always done, she only spoke the beloved's name as if it were an incantation.

"Oh, Michael!"

It was enough. The lover heard the words and the meaning underneath.

A hunting hawk went over. A fisherman pulled upstream. The sun hung low, shadows lengthened. Time had no meaning, until the brassy sound of factory whistles announced the end of the day shift.

Julie jumped up. "Oh my goodness, Father will kill me if he gets home first. I had no idea—you just came a few minutes ago!"

He brushed the twigs from her skirt as she whacked a comb through her hair. Then they ran up the familiar path, reaching the upper road as the sun dipped behind the hills. They raced along. Passing Dr. Jim's house, they saw him coming out with his black bag, and they waved and ran on.

Poor kids, he thought, they are always on the run. I wish I could reason with Alden—how lovely that girl is, running like a Maenad. Alden doesn't know what a treasure he has.

Then he cranked the car and started for St. Mary's. He had worries enough of his own, the Lord knew. Would it work out to take Miss Nelson in the house? She was a nice mousy creature and would never make trouble. She could use the piano in the parlor and teach at odd hours. True, Ella had never been able to keep a cleaning woman, but Ella seemed changed since the accident. Expenses would be higher, but maybe a few patients would pay their long-standing bills when the crops came in. It was going to be a bumper year, they said. Miss Nelson could shop, answer the phone, Ella could plan and the oldest Novak girl could cook. (Maybe work off what they owed him?) Well, he could only try, and there was always Sybil to depend on.

After Julie flashed down Durkee, Mike went slowly in the opposite direction. He felt like a king. Even if he had a hundred dollars in his pocket he wouldn't feel any better. He whistled "Moonlight Bay," and kept time to the tune. Somehow he felt this wasn't like the other times when Julie had flared up; Julie seemed humble, not forgiving him but almost asking to be forgiven. In time, her father would get used to him. He would simply have to.

Julie reached home exhausted, and she hadn't even the energy to be afraid of her father. But he wasn't home. Commencement was wonderful that way. He was always getting held up.

"Papa's late," said Sybil. "Better wash up and we'll eat."

Julie put on a clean middy and dumped the wet one in her closet. She went downstairs, now ravenously hungry.

Sybil sliced the ham and served the scalloped potatoes (with onion and cheese the way Julie liked them).

"It's the last of the wild asparagus," Sybil said. She passed the creamy mustard sauce. Julie had that drowned, ecstatic look, so they had made up again. How she wished Julie would tell her about it. But she could only put the best slice of ham on her plate, crusty with brown sugar, spicy with clove. She could feed the body, she thought, if not the soul.

"I think Jim is bringing Ella home shortly," she said. "I must get in some groceries."

Julie came out of her dream. "Isn't she ever going to walk again, Mama?"

"I hardly think so. But one cannot be sure. One always hopes."

After supper Julie washed the dishes, humming. Sybil went in to finish the mending. I wish Alden would let her alone, she thought, taking delicate stitches in a ripped hem. Julie was not cut out to be an elderly spinster teaching at Westerly. Marry she would, no matter what Alden said. Her warmth and passion could never spend itself in Greek or Geology. If she didn't marry Mike, she would marry someone. She dropped the mending and looked out at the apricot sky. If only Alden weren't so childish, so temperamental, Julie's life would work out. His lack of understanding was dreadful, but then he didn't understand himself either.

At least the year was ending and summer would ease along. She had never felt so tired, but after the camping trip perhaps she could rest a bit. She would think of projects for Alden, grading the hillside, painting the house trim, repairing the cellar steps. He just couldn't endure idleness.

Julie came in, on her way upstairs. The pale light fell on her mother, and somehow Julie noticed how sad and tired she looked. It frightened her, as if the earth shifted under her feet.

"Mama, are you all right?" she asked.

Sybil smiled. "Just end-of-the-year," she told her.

Julie dropped down on the love seat. "Mama, I'm sorry I haven't helped out much lately. I'll do better."

For an instant, something trembled between them, a closeness, an identity. Almost Julie told her mother all about Mike, almost Sybil spoke from her inner being. But the shadow of Alden fell between them and Julie said quickly, "I'll get Papa's breakfast tomorrow, and you stay in bed until a decent hour."

Under the words Sybil read the meaning, like a palimpsest. Julie was saying, I must be careful, because of Papa.

"I'm going to bed early," Sybil told her. "I'll be up."

Upstairs, Julie took her bath, cleaned the tub carefully for once, hung the bath towel neatly. The look on her mother's face troubled her. Then she put on her muslin robe and sat down to work on the chapter letter from Gamma to the national magazine. As she wrote the new pledges' names down, she felt a pang about Liz Fowler. Her death was never spoken of. What was the meaning of it? Well, all of them, she reflected, had been affected. They were kinder, they were less selfish. They had realized a responsibility to other people which they hadn't felt before. For most of them the conception of death had made their own actions easy to criticize. They wouldn't, again, be so petty.

And so as another year draws to a close, she wrote, *Gamma looks forward to fall rushing and a year of striving to fulfill the ideals of Gamma.*

And she decided grimly, they'd be pretty careful about turning down some girl just because she wasn't a social smash! She folded the letter and put it in a long envelope, found a two-cent stamp. It was overdue, but most of them were. Hardly any chapter ever got their stuff in on time; the editor was used to it. The magazine was held up more times than not because of the chapter letters.

After she put the letter in her book bag, she sat at the window dreamily watching the progress of the moon. A few clouds feathered the sky. When she heard her father and mother come upstairs (you couldn't miss that fifth tread) she snapped off her light so they would think she had gone to bed. She didn't, now, want to kiss anybody good night. She had been careful not to wash Mike's kisses off.

Under the excitement, sobering thought came. She wasn't a child any more to be petted, put to bed. She was a woman in love. But she was fearful, under the glow of Mike's love-making. Since this afternoon, their affair was no longer a question of a steady beau for her, a football hero to date, the heady excitement of stolen kisses, murmured words. It wasn't the beating of her heart when she saw him, or the ache when they parted. Something more had come into it. It was now her job to be sensible, as well as loving. To share his burdens, since she was not a separate person, but a part of him. She must learn some practical skills from her mother who was so expert in all of them. Why hadn't she ever done this before? And above all, she must control her destructive temper. It wasn't fair to Mike. He'd been patient with her beyond all necessity; he too had spoiled her.

She knelt to say her prayers and as she prayed, she ended, "God please help me to be the right one for Michael."

Comforted, she got in bed. She longed for Mike, she wished he were beside her, his tousled head on the pillow where the teddy bear was. She suddenly tossed the teddy bear to the floor. He was only a toy and she was too old for toys.

But after a few moments she crept out of bed and put the teddy bear back on the pillow. After all, it wasn't his fault he was only a plush bear!

19.

On Minnie's day off, Carol was all ready to leave. She had successfully sneaked her bags down the back stairs and hidden them behind the trash bin. She had made a list, ordered meat and groceries delivered. Minnie would be back in time to cook dinner. She kept the twins in bed with their cold and gave them trays at noon. She herself had a glass of milk in the kitchen, which was a mess, but Minnie could clean up. Minnie hadn't been paid for a week, so she was sure to turn up.

She was breathless, and her left eyelid twitched as it always did when she was excited. She had put on her brown linen, which was inconspicuous, and planned to carry her light coat. And then, just as she felt triumphant, she remembered her mink coat. If she left it behind, Minnie might steal it. Servants always stole when they had a chance. Or when Dick shipped her trunks, he would forget to send it. Her father had given it to her, and he wouldn't be happy if she lost it.

As she weighed the problem the truckman came. He was

willing to take her luggage to the junction but he was in a hurry, and she saw him drive away with relief and resentment. She could have found a box, packed the mink. She put on her hat, took her purse, hesitated again. She had the coat remodeled only last season and the furrier said he had never seen such skins. She could not abandon it. She would have to carry it. Hot as it was, she could manage until she got on the train. And what a good impression it would make when she said, "I left everything, Daddy, but the coat you gave me."

She tiptoed upstairs, took the mink coat from the hall closet, and almost got to the stairs when the door of the twins' room opened.

"Mother, I think you better come see Dick. He doesn't feel good at all." Young Carol's eyes were frightened. Then she said, "Are you going to wear your fur coat now?"

"Never mind," Carol snapped. She went into the bedroom. Dick was tossing about, muttering. He seemed to be talking but the words didn't make sense.

"Get back in bed," Carol said to her daughter. "I'll call Dr. Jim. You need some pills for those colds."

Downstairs, she cranked away at the phone endlessly before she reached Dr. Jim. It gave her time to think. If she hadn't gone back for the coat, she would be away by now. But she had gone too far to turn back, no matter what.

"I'll be right over," said Dr. Jim wearily. He knew the twins must be really sick, for Carol was not one to call for minor complaints. She never noticed them, he thought grimly.

He was bone-tired after losing the appendix case which had been treated with drastic purgatives before he was called in. Fool people, he said. Probably the twins had caught the measles from that Jones boy. As he drove recklessly to the campus he reflected on how thoroughly he disliked Carol Wallace. She was a stone around Dick's neck, a vain, egotistical, shallow

147

woman with practically no good in her. Well, a man rushes ahead in youth and lives to pay the piper.

However, he put on a hearty manner as he walked in the Wallace mansion. (Draughty old dump, he thought.)

"They caught a bad cold," Carol explained nervously.

"No doubt. I'll have a look." His legs were tired as he climbed the stairs. I'm getting to be an old horse, he thought, mopping his face.

"I think if they had some pills—" Carol followed him into the bedroom.

He smelled the fever in the room. "Well I guess your school is out, so you aren't skipping," he said, dipping the thermometer in alcohol and sticking it under Dick's tongue.

After he took the temperatures he went to Dick and with a tenderness many people would not credit him with, lifted the sheet and looked at the rash on the thin body.

"I hear Chautauqua is having a magician this summer," he told him. "He makes things come out of hats." He tapped the chest. "Even saws people in two," he went on, "and then they walk right off the stage. What do you know about that?"

"I want—to see." Dick wheezed.

"Sure. Take your pills and you'll be in the front row." He fished around in his bag and counted out a handful of pellets. Carol seethed with impatience. He was so slow, she thought she would go mad. But he sat down and chatted until the twins began to doze. Then he stamped solidly downstairs.

"I want to talk to you," he said gruffly.

They sat in the parlor. "I think the twins have scarlatina," he told her. "Maybe you don't know what that is. It's kin to scarlet fever, not as common but, frankly, more serious. I'll know better tomorrow. The boy is very sick, the girl has a light case."

"But they can't be sick now!"

"I know, Commencement time. Could hardly be more difficult. I appreciate that. But you have to go along with nature, can't do otherwise."

"But what will happen?"

"I'll have to quarantine the house as soon as the diagnosis is definite. Mind you, it isn't definite so far. I am warning you the symptoms seem typical. Has your husband been with them today?"

"No," she said, "he went out early. He's hardly been home all week."

"Good." He nodded. "Now in view of the circumstances, I suggest you phone him and tell him not to come home today. Tell him to go to Kennicott and get the guest suite. I know it is empty. Pack his necessary clothes for Commencement and get them ready. I'll talk to the Dean and she can send a boy over to pick them up from the back porch." He sat frowning, considering the problems. "We don't want to start a panic this weekend," he said, "so I am not going to jump the gun. Any other time of year, I'd slap the sign on just in case. Now I want to be sure. So your husband better stay away until we know. I'll get a nurse for you, and be over early in the morning. Just keep them quiet."

After he went out Carol sat paralyzed. Was this the end of her careful planning, to have the trap close on her, just as she was almost free of it? It couldn't be, it was too horrible. She sat staring at the floor until the phone rang, and then she dragged herself to answer.

"I'll take care of everything," said Dean Richardson. "I have a boy on the way over now. He will go to the back door. Don't worry about President Wallace, I've set up the guest suite for him."

"Thank you," Carol managed.

"Don't forget the robe and hood," the Dean reminded her.

Carol crept upstairs and flung Dick's things into his Gladstone bag. At the moment she could not think, but she dragged out the robe and hood under the impact of the Dean's voice, and jammed them into a suitcase. The twins were asleep. She told herself they would be all right in the morning, this was a lot of nonsense. They had bad colds. She took the luggage down to the back porch, just as she had taken her own earlier. When the boy knocked, she pointed them out. He went off whistling.

Then she realized that Minnie had not come in to cook dinner. She went up to the third floor and opened the door to Minnie's room. Minnie had gone, bag and baggage, pay or no pay, that was evident. Only a few hairpins and a drift of powder were left behind to mark her passing. Carol sank down on the cot and began to laugh hysterically. Minnie, she thought, got away all right, and got away in time. Only she hadn't, and it was all because of the mink coat. She laughed and cried and gasped for breath. It was the first time she had indulged in hysterics with no audience. After a long time, she quieted and went to her room, undressed and got into the bed she never expected to lie in again. She must begin again. She was not yet defeated, only delayed. She would go as soon as the nurse came.

Miss Eldredge, the nurse, did not come until eight o'clock the next morning. She had waited for a replacement for her maternity case. Carol, looking haggard after a sleepless night, let her in. Miss Eldredge rustled in, carrying a small bag.

"Well, how are we this morning?" she asked brightly.

"The twins are asleep," Carol answered truthfully. "I'll show you to your room."

Miss Eldredge clumped up the stairs. She was a square firm woman with steely eyes and a wide mouth and gray hair pinned into a tight bun.

"You look peaked," she observed. "Worried no end, I daresay. No need. Dr. Jim is the best. Nice view you have here."

"Yes."

"Now don't worry about a thing." Miss Eldredge opened her

suitcase. "I get along fine with children, and I'm not too highty-tighty to cook if it's needed. Leave everything to me."

Indeed she would, thought Carol thankfully. She herself couldn't nurse sick children, or cook. "I'm glad you're here," she said.

"Dr. Jim picks me for the special cases," laughed Miss Eldredge. "I can see right off you're not a natural nurse."

Dr. Jim had made the arrangements as soon as he got home after seeing the twins. He hadn't liked the look of the twins. But there was nothing to do until morning, he had reasoned. He was starting to fry a couple of eggs when the phone rang. He cursed his weariness as he answered. But it wasn't a patient, it was Sybil.

"I'm about to dish up roast beef and Yorkshire pudding," she said. "Could you pop over for a plate?"

"Be there in four minutes," he said.

He washed up and ran out, whistling. Sybil was a hand stretched in the dark, he thought, but how did she always sense when it was dark? Now if he were married to such a woman —he checked the thought sharply. But the lighted, welcoming house and the sound of family voices made him beat one hand against the other.

Sybil looked like spring itself in a fresh green cotton. Alden looked rumpled, but amiable, for he was going to get his mastodon. Julie had color in her cheeks again. They were in fair shape, considering it was Commencement, he thought.

The roast beef was properly rare (why did Ella always overcook it?) and the Yorkshire pudding fork-tender, and crisp at the edges.

"Pretty good handout," he commented.

Over dessert Alden got to talking of prehistoric times, and made them as tangible as the plates on the table. Jim enjoyed it. The pterodactyls and mastodons didn't need his services, and besides Alden evoked the whole time, the great forests, the hanging vines, the slow march of glaciers, the rise of life from primeval seas. Never mind Alden's opinions and ideas about the time they were living in, he was on sound ground when he moved back a few ages. When he got Ella settled in, he'd take that trip to Fremont, and when Alden got back from his fool camping trip they could go off now and then on summer afternoons and dig up rocks or whatever Alden wished.

Mercifully, this dinner was not interrupted by phone calls, and he felt rested as he swung to the other end of town to check on the Schultz baby. The baby was better, the threat of pneumonia over. As he drove home he stopped to look at his town from the Cherry Street hill. How still the plumes of smoke from the mills were, as if they were painted on the sky. The dome of St. Joseph's Cathedral was a gold pearl in the moonlight. It was a good town, he thought, full of people who were good and who were bad but none all good or all bad. And all subject to pain, grief, death. They were his people, and he wished he had a son to take care of them when he himself had gone.

He wasn't getting any younger, he thought, as he put the car in Daisy's barn and went in the house. He turned on more lights than were necessary, for the house seemed as lifeless as if nobody lived there at all. Everything clean, Sybil had seen to that, but not a cushion out of place, not a piece of mending on the table. It was queer the difference it made just knowing Ella was in the house, shut away in her room, but there. Now he creaked up the stairs to the bedroom, easing his tired joints.

On his bureau was a scrap of paper. *I brought your laundry. Shirts in second drawer. Sybil.*

You couldn't beat that woman. How in hell had she remembered to tend to his laundry? And to bring it in and put it away. Well, he thought, dropping his shoes, Alden would never know how easy it would be to envy him. He drew the shades and got in bed. If there was trouble at the Wallaces' he'd call on Sybil. He must get to the Wallace twins early in the morning, and hope to God his diagnosis was wrong. Mrs. Wallace would be fit to be tied if she got quarantined. He hadn't had any bed of roses with Ella, but Carol Wallace could destroy a man.

But in the morning Mrs. Wallace was boarding the train at the junction, shaking with relief. She was out of the house before Jim was up. She knew better than to get caught by him. She justified her escape as reasonably as most people do when they break the rules. She had set out breakfast for Miss Eldredge and the twins, hung out a sign for fifty pounds of ice, checked on the supplies in the icebox. She also gathered the laundry, listed it, and put it in the bag by the back door. She even peeked in at the twins, who were sleeping heavily. Dr. Jim was an old fussbox.

There was no sense in her staying, for everything was taken care of. Between them, Dick and Miss Eldredge would dig up a cook, which would be easy now college was nearly over. One of the dormitory staff could take over.

As the train pulled out, Carol did not look back at Winnebago, hazy in the morning light. She did not see the green surf of leaves breaking against the sky, nor look for the farm wagons clopping in from the country. She sat rearranging the contents of her purse as the town she hated and the life she despised receded. As for Dick, she felt only resentment. Dick had ruined her life and she had done her duty long enough, stuck in this wretched place living this dull life.

Whatever guilt she might have felt was fleeting. She wasn't required to spend her life at faculty teas, suffering through amateur theatricals, entertaining stuffy grads. She didn't hook rugs, or burn wooden boxes with a stylus, or paint china, or make quilts. She hated football, and had spent some freezing afternoons at home-coming games when Dick insisted she must go. It bored her to watch boys slug one another.

She felt no responsibility for the twins. She hadn't wanted them, they wore her out, and they obviously only put up with her. It was Dick they loved. So she would give them to him. She was taking only her own belongings and surely she had a right to live her own kind of life now. She was still young enough and beautiful enough.

The train gathered speed and the town lay behind. Rolling farmlands spread their rich grass on either side and herds of Holsteins dotted them with black and white. Scenery didn't interest Carol, except on a stage. She took out her mirror and studied her face and saw it was unlined, smooth as marble, still flawless.

"Taking a trip?" asked the conductor.

Fortunately he was new on the run and did not recognize her. He only noticed what a well-set-up elegant woman it was who handed out her ticket in a gloved hand.

"Yes, a trip," Carol answered.

It was a trip indeed, she thought, a trip back to the life she never should have left, a trip leaving the frustrations of the past behind. She drew a long, triumphant breath as the train roared toward tomorrow.

Her only regret was that, in the end, she had left her mink coat.

20.

When Dick heard the news about the twins being sick, he wanted to drop everything and rush home. But the Dean persuaded him to be sensible, and before he knew it he was in the guest suite, unpacking his bags. He phoned the house and the nurse answered and said the twins were sleeping quietly. Should she call Mrs. Wallace?

"No, thank you, I'll call again in the morning."

For what could he say to her? Carol hated illness, couldn't bear confinement. She would blame him somehow. After Commencement he would go home and take care of everything, but now he had to think of his job. His heart was heavy as he shook out his robes. The twins were the most precious thing in life to him, and he was all they had of love and security. He should be with them, sitting up nights, reading aloud, fixing lemonade the way they liked it, making up stories. But Dr. Jim was right. You couldn't have a panic at Commencement. At the moment the President was not a father, not a person, but a symbol of Westerly. He hoped the twins would see it that way. They were very sensible, but when they didn't feel well they wanted their daddy.

It was too late to try to change Carol, persuade her to mother them a little. Too late to make an attempt at a halfway marriage, for Carol was a frigid and relentless woman with no warmth to appeal to. She never let him forget how she had suffered when the twins were born. Well, you couldn't go back. You could only go ahead, and even hampered with a wife like Carol, he had gone ahead. He was on the way up. Maybe Carol would be happier when he was called to a big university, but he doubted it. Happiness wasn't a place, it was within you.

He decided to eat in the dormitory, for he liked the sound of young voices, the laughter, and general confusion. "Bless this food to our use, and us to thy faithful service," he murmured. The round tables in the dining hall were already full when he came in. The chatter quieted a moment as he sat down opposite Dean Richardson, but not for long. Next to the Dean, the students loved the President. This was an unusual phenomenon; both positions were usually filled by hated figures. But Dick Wallace commanded respect without fear, and

managed to combine dignity of office with warmth and friend-
liness. It was, perhaps, his greatest gift.

Now he smiled at them, said grace, chatted with the student
waitresses, all of whom he knew by their first names. The plat-
ters of ham and potatoes went around, the milk was poured.
The food was like most dormitory food, nourishing but taste-
less. The ham was too dry, the potatoes were lumpy, and the
salad was a canned peach half with a dab of mayonnaise. Dessert was rice pudding.

As the conversation bubbled about him, Dick began planning
a new regime for the kitchens at Westerly. It would take some
doing to talk the hard-boiled trustees into anything as new-
fangled as a trained dietician. What was good enough for them
in their day was good enough for the students. Now take Miss
Ida, they always said, remember her fried chicken? But Miss
Ida was dead and during her regime it was fried chicken one
day and macaroni the next. As he sipped his milk he thought
four years of this kind of dinner was enough to discourage any
but the most hardy.

"We might have coffee in my rooms," said the Dean. She
gave the signal and the girls boiled out of the dining hall. Dick
stopped to thank the waitresses, clap the arm of the boy clearing the table. (We need more scholarships, he thought.)
Money, money, money. He'd get it, given time. The dining hall
was badly in need of repair, dark and dingy, and the kitchens
dreadful. He'd begin next fall, travel around to alumni groups,
give the witty charming speeches he was noted for, and get the
money.

In the Dean's room, he sat on the sofa as the knot of anxiety
loosened. He drew a long sighing breath. The Dean brewed the
coffee and watching her quick quiet movements rested him.

"I'm sorry about the twins," she said. "I could go over to
help if necessary."

"Miss Eldredge is Jim's best nurse," he told her. "We'll

know more tomorrow. It may be grippe. They have colds too often."

They talked then of the college, the curriculum, the students, as if the casual conversation were a protection against something. They discussed whether Mike would go to State on the athletic scholarship.

"I think not," she said. "Mike has integrity. He would, I believe, always need to respect himself. Which has nothing to do with Julie. I don't think he can be bought."

"He's a fine boy. What a fool Alden is."

"In the end Sybil's wisdom will win out, I expect."

He said good night and went back to the guest suite without their exchanging a single personal word. It was like a truce before a conflict.

The dormitory simmered with activity. Trunks were being hauled along the corridors and he stopped to lend a hand several times. Boxes were stacked near the stairs ready for the truckmen. More than half of the students would be off tomorrow, their destination summer. Of course, he reflected, they had all known for weeks the exact day and hour of their departure, but who ever packed until the last minute?

The noise went on most of the night, but he slept, being too tired to stay awake. He was up for breakfast in the half-empty dining hall. He skipped the gluey oatmeal, but had toast and coffee. It was too early to rouse Carol, so he went to his office and worked on the report for the Board meeting. Then he put in a call, and Miss Eldredge answered, cool and crisp. Mrs. Wallace wasn't in, she said, she must have stepped out for a breath of fresh air before Dr. Jim came. The twins were quite comfortable. Morning walks were not like Carol, but perhaps she was nervous about being quarantined and decided to get out when she could. He waited an hour and called again. The line was busy, so Carol must be ordering the groceries. He called in twenty minutes and got Miss Eldredge again. Mrs.

Wallace had not come back yet. The twins ate a good breakfast, the fever was down, he was not to worry. Dr. Jim phoned he had an emergency and would be delayed, but expected to get there in an hour or so.

It was maddening to be walled away from his house. Why didn't Carol get home and phone him? Had she gone shopping? Surely she would not stay away when the doctor was coming. All he could do was fume and swear and wait by the infernal phone. Meanwhile, he had a few calls to answer and this tied the phone up. The grounds man wanted to know should he begin cutting the lilac clusters off or wait until after Commencement?

The housemother at the men's dormitory asked whether the drapes in the reception room could come down now. Mark phoned to say he wanted an extra piano backstage for the program. Alden phoned he needed a crew to help clean up the museum at once.

Finally he was able to phone the house again. Miss Eldredge answered, and spoke at some length. She finished by telling him not to worry. Ten minutes later he burst into the Dean's living room without knocking.

"Carol's gone," he said.

She dropped her blue books, closed the door quickly.

"What do you mean?"

He sank on the sofa as if it might uphold him and might sink away. "She went out this morning and never came back," he said, his voice flat with shock. "She's gone."

"Oh no. She must have gone shopping."

"Miss Eldredge went to her room. Dr. Jim wanted to consult her. She thought maybe Carol had come in." His voice shook. "She has taken everything. Drawers empty. Bureau top bare. Nothing but a few winter clothes left in the closet."

The Dean sat down, turning pale.

158

"Minnie's gone too." His voice was a monotone. "Sinking ship, I guess."

The Dean went to the bathroom and brought back a glass of brandy. "Drink this and lean back," she said. She waited until he finished it. "Would she perhaps suddenly go to visit friends?"

"What friends does she have?" He let the bitterness out. "She's gone home, that's where she has gone." He moved his hands over his face and straightened up. "I must not bring my trouble on you."

"Trouble is for sharing," she answered. Her hands clenched, she wished Carol's neck were between her fingers. But she couldn't afford the luxury of rage.

"I'm trapped," he muttered, "trapped." His eyes were blank, his hands shaking.

She came to him and touched his hands, then rubbed the cold fingers. She refilled his glass, watching until he drank it. He must not faint, he must not! Her years of experience stood in good stead now, for in spite of the shock her mind kept working. The first and vital consideration was to keep this quiet, protect him, protect the college. This was a larger problem than any personal one. A scandal in the President's house now would be fatal. (I wouldn't send a child of mine to a place where such things go on. I've changed my mind about giving the money for the new playing field. I don't think Westerly exemplifies the best ideals of America. And so on, endlessly.)

"What shall I do?" he asked.

Her quick mind already was marshaling the defense. First, there was the nurse and Dr. Jim to deal with. They knew. Then Dick had to pull himself together, cover up.

"Well," she chose her words carefully, "I think we can manage." She stood as steady and calm as she had during hundreds of emergencies. "If—your wife went away, really away—only Miss Eldredge and Dr. Jim need know at present. Nobody else must know until after Commencement. First, I'm going to phone Miss Eldredge, then I'll see Dr. Jim. You stay right there until I get back. Don't move."

If someone came in and found him flat on the floor, it would be all over Westerly that he had a heart attack. "Don't budge," she ordered.

He didn't budge. For one thing, two tots of brandy made him lightheaded, for another he was numb with shock. When the Dean came back she spoke cheerfully. "The quarantine sign is already up. I've enlisted Miss Eldredge's help. She's going to locate Dr. Jim. I'll see him. Now nobody will know whether your wife is inside the house or out. This gives us a reprieve until Commencement is over."

"Why did she do this to me?" he cried.

"Never mind that. People do what they do."

"I never loved her," he said, "and she hates me. But the twins—leaving them sick—" He wept then, terrible tears. Finally he stopped and wiped his face and sat up. "I—apologize," he whispered.

She brought a cool washcloth and wiped his face again. "Pull yourself together," she said. "You've got a duty to perform. Concentrate on it." She kept her voice impersonal, cold. "You're the President of this college, and don't forget it!"

He looked better; at least he was listening to her words.

"Fortunately this is my year not to have to participate in Commencement," she told him, "so I shall go to your house and stay with the twins. Nobody has to know."

"But why should you do this? Why?"

Her sudden smile was like sun. "Because I love you," she said. She stood across the room. "Perhaps she will decide to come back, and then nobody will ever know she left. If she doesn't, we'll face it after Commencement. Meanwhile, I'll take care of everything but your own job. That's for you. Go back to your office and get to work. Be very busy."

He got up and walked to the door, turned and gave her a look so burning, so desolate, that her heart stopped beating. "Louise," he said, "I'll be all right. Just because of you."

After he had gone, she sank down, feeling weakness wash over her. Then she got up and packed a bag with essentials, went steadily down the hall and told Miss Denise, the French teacher, that she was going over to the Wallace house for a few days to help out with the twins, who had a bad case of grippe. So trying at Commencement. President Wallace would stay at Kennicott until after Commencement, germs were so catching and all. Miss Denise should take over, greet parents, say grace at meals. Miss Denise was a good choice, for she hadn't the sense God gave a goose. Not even the curiosity of a goose, thought the Dean, hurrying across campus. Moreover, she was flattered at taking Kennicott over.

The Dean walked around the back of the buildings, hoping not to be noticed. Being devious did not bother her at all, for she had been devious many times when it was for the good of Westerly or the students. A good many of them would never have graduated if she hadn't been. She knew very well she might lose her position if this came out, but she couldn't bother about that now. She only wanted to save Dick.

She went to the back door of the Wallace house and knocked. Miss Eldredge opened the door and started back, mouth open.

"I've come to help out," said the Dean briskly. "I hear Minnie has gone, and Mrs. Wallace is away."

"Skipped." Miss Eldredge nodded. "I figured so. Rats and ships, I always say."

"I'd like to talk to you about that. Could we have a cup of tea?" Discussions were always easier over tea or coffee.

"I've got the kettle on." Miss Eldredge gestured toward the stairs. "Take your pick of the three empty bedrooms. I'll tote your bag up later."

"I don't need to be waited on," said the Dean, carrying it herself, and seeing the flash of respect in the nurse's eyes.

Over tea and buttered toast, the two women smiled at each other. Miss Eldredge thought the Dean might have a high and mighty place at college, but she was easy as an old slipper, always ready to sit up with a sick student. "I'll keep my trap shut," she said, munching her toast. "If that worries you. I got enough to do without running around telling bad news. But I want to ask one question—why are you getting yourself stuck here in this mess? Why you?"

"The fewer who know about this, the better," said the Dean. "Things get around fast. I'm off duty this year for Commencement. I can cook, do housework, and am pretty good at laundry. Is there any food in the house?"

Miss Eldredge grinned. She wasn't born yesterday, she told herself, dipping toast in her tea because her false teeth just did not fit well.

"Some cold ham and a loaf of stale bread," she said. "Looks like Minnie and her had a run-in and Minnie didn't bother."

"I'll make a list." The Dean smiled. "We'll need some good soups and custards for the twins, and something to keep body and soul together for us. Now tell me how the twins are."

"They'll pull through," Miss Eldredge predicted. "They're the wiry type. Hard to kill. They're good, too, don't keep yelling for their mother. They just ask about their father. Boy's pretty sick, but holding his own I'd say."

The Dean went to the phone and persuaded the grocer to send out a special order, called Mr. Lutz and got him to stop by with an extra hundred-pound cake of ice, and finally, after considerable thought, called Sybil.

"I'll explain later," she said (not on a party line), "but could you manage to send over to the Wallaces' some of your wine jelly, beef broth, and a cooked chicken?"

"No trouble at all," said Sybil, asking no questions.

SPRING HARVEST

By nightfall the Dean and Miss Eldredge had the house in order, a laundry on the line and in. ("We won't bother ironing the sheets, they smell nice and sunny," said the Dean.) The twins were fed, sponged with alcohol, had their medicine and, drowsy with fever, slept again. Miss Eldredge and the Dean had an early supper in the kitchen, broiled chops and a salad. The Dean washed the dishes while Miss Eldredge sat with the twins.

Miss Eldredge had her own thoughts. So that's the way the wind blows, she reflected. When Dr. Jim came, she discreetly left him with the Dean but was not above listening to the conversation.

But you could have heard Dr. Jim all over the house as he barked, "You're a fool, Louise. But the kind of fool I like. I'll go along."

The Dean undressed in what she thought was the guest room. She folded her dress and petticoat, hung up her jacket, put on her sprigged nightgown. Miss Eldredge was bumping around the hall, and it was a reassuring sound.

As she sat at the dressing table, brushing her hair, she planned for tomorrow. The kitchen was filthy, she would clean it first. They needed more carbolic to soak the sheet pinned over the twins' door. If the laundry wouldn't collect from a quarantined house, she would need more naptha soap. She'd better write a note to Dick and get someone to deliver it. The phone was public property.

She got in bed, finding the pillows hard, the mattress uncomfortable. But she thought of Dick tossing on that dormitory bed. What was he thinking? Where would he go if he lost his position? If Carol came back, repentant, how could he live with her? If she didn't come back, what would happen to his career? Would the Board keep him on? Not likely, this was a conventional college, subsidized by the Methodist Church. Until death do us part meant exactly that. But if Carol did not want

163

a divorce, could they say she had gone to a spa for health reasons, and cover it up?

She got up and went downstairs where it was cooler. A breath of river air stirred the curtains in the parlor. She sat looking out, her heart darker than the night. How could she sleep when Dick was in such dire trouble? Now she would trade all of her scholarly success, her reputation, just to make his job secure. For loving him was like breathing.

Possibly because she had lived so many years without passion, her feeling for Dick was more devastating. Love in maturity, she thought, had a reality, an impact, that young love never had. Well, she was fortunate, for she could protect the man she loved in a crisis. She would have this to remember.

"Thought I heard someone," said Miss Eldredge, padding in. "Can't sleep, eh? Brought you a pill." Miss Eldredge was something to look at, with curlers springing wildly over her head, face glistening with vaseline, and wearing a purple muslin gown with crocheted pink lace.

"Take them myself when I get a dying patient." She held out a pink pill and a glass of water.

"Thank you," said the Dean.

Miss Eldredge sat down, crossing her knees. Her slippers swung in the air, displaying purple pompons on pea-green calico. "Seen most everything," she said, "but this beats all. Mother runs off with sick kids. You stick your head into trouble. Only one thing makes a woman do what you're doing."

"Well, you see, the college—"

"You're crazy about him," said Miss Eldredge flatly, "don't tell me different. I figure we're better off facing facts. Have you thought what's going to happen to you if this gets out?"

"I can't help it," said the Dean.

Miss Eldredge closed the windows, pulled down the shades. "No use running an ad you're here," she said. "You are an awful fool, pardon my language." She stood in the doorway, hands on hips. "And I surely do admire you for it," she said. "Good night."

21.

Dick Wallace could not sleep, no matter how much he argued with himself about his need for rest. He only grew wider awake, so he finally turned on the lamp and sat at the desk leaning his head on his hands. He had reached a point in his life when the pattern was so confused that there seemed no pattern to anything.

He had believed a man made his own circumstance. That a man set a course, pursued it with honesty and diligence and achieved, if not his goal, an approximation of it. Was there a flaw in him that had caused this tragedy? Was there a point at which he could have mastered events? Or was everything accidental and without meaning? Had he and Carol met as meteors might meet falling in space? Or was it his destiny to fail? He had done what he felt was his best, but he had made Westerly his wife, mistress, friend, and perhaps this was a sin. If so, Carol's true revenge would be separating him finally from Westerly.

If he could make some sense of what happened down the years, he might look forward, begin to build new defenses, but now he only faced the unbelievable present. His wife had run away, his children were ill, his position in jeopardy, and the woman he loved was risking her job for him. There wasn't much left by way of disaster. As he thought of Louise he groaned. How had he drawn her into this disastrous orbit? Was his need and loneliness a magnet? He had been so careful, so circumspect.

Actually, he wasn't aware himself of just when his feeling for her grew into love. By the time he realized it, it was as if he had loved her forever.

Of course he hadn't planned to let her know. There could be nothing between them except an occasional glass of sherry, or tea and biscuits, some conversation. Now and then a handclasp of greeting or farewell (how slim yet strong were her fingers).

But now she had spoken the words.

Love is a need not confined to the young, he thought, trying to analyze the mystery. In his matured mind and long-deprived body he felt passion no easier to check than a forest fire raging in a stand of dry pine. He was completely and terribly in love, and being separate from this woman was a death in life. His guilt was heavy, for he had brought trouble to her life, but his longing was greater. Young love, he thought, was nourished by hope and dreams. But what hope for him, what dreams?

He must stop thinking of her, and go back to his dilemma. Could he persuade Carol to come back, erect a shell again? What could he offer to her when she hated him and all he represented? He couldn't, from now on, offer her an open heart. Could they go on in any manner living a lie? If so, would the twins be better off? No, they would be better off if they never saw Carol again.

Where was a man's basic allegiance? To the service for mankind he was fitted for, to preserving the pretense of a marriage, or striving for personal fulfillment? He didn't know. One fact stood out in his mind, and that was the necessity for protecting Louise. She was innocent, and must not be sacrificed for him.

He got up and dressed and went out as if he could escape from himself. Walking to the bank of the river, he breathed deeply. The river, he thought, flowed on, changeless. Sometimes it carried extra silt from eroded banks, sometimes it bore logs for the pulp mill, proud murdered pines destined for crush-

SPRING HARVEST

ing. Often, in dry summers, it narrowed and the shale cracks opened above the water. In September line storms, the scant foothold of young thickets gave way and branches cascaded to the water. But the river itself moved on to the destiny of great waters.

It was indifferent to man's suffering, but it was life-giving also. The Indians had camped by it, caught the fish leaping in the riffles, drunk the sweet water, made pathways along the banks. Later on, trappers shot the rapids, their canoes lashed with pelts. And later still, it powered the mills and built Winnebago, and Westerly too. For Westerly was founded by a man who made a fortune running logs down the river, whole forests of them. Drought and erosion followed, wildlife diminished, but the gray stone buildings of Westerly rose above the river.

Dick sat down on a cedar bench known as the Spoonholder. A cool wind from the north dried the sweat on his forehead. There was a relationship between the river and his life, he felt the power of the current, the inevitable flow toward the sea, the direction. That was what he lacked, the direction. His life was full of backwaters, eddies, debris. The past and the future both clogged his spirit, but the river never flowed backward to the ferny springs whence it came, nor checked its course because of the sea ahead. A man's life should be like the river, he thought, flowing ahead but always in the present.

He was so still that Julie and Mike didn't see him as they came along the path.

"But, darling, nothing matters but us," said Julie.

"Well, there are some things except us—" Mike sounded doubtful. They went on, Julie's hands in his.

He sat motionless, for he was not of a mind to ask her why she wasn't at home or in the dormitory. Tonight he was a man, not a president, and his heart was moved by them. The practical male, he thought, deals with the world around him as Mike is trying to do. The female drives to the essential desire. Perhaps life must be a compromise between the direct savage feminine drive and the wary common sense of the male.

But if he could walk down that path with Louise, how much common sense would he have? Or would he take the night for their own? Sighing, he made his way back up to campus. He wished the young lovers well, although he felt the probability of their lives falling in a happy pattern was unlikely. Still there was a toughness in Julie as in her father and an underlying steadiness as in her mother. Who could tell?

The night watchman's lantern bobbled along the crosswalk. His steps were unsteady; he was another who should be retired. But a generation of students had been his friends, he was a tradition. The old grads brought him presents, kidded him about how they had sneaked in the dorms under his eyes. Well, thought Dick, I may be spared the ordeal of firing him at any rate. But Miss Nelson I can't duck.

Maybe he and Miss Nelson would go out together.

Too bad I didn't get that pension system in, not that I'd be eligible, but she would. He walked hastily up the stairs and to the suite. It was hard on the girls to have a man in the dorm, for they had to be fully dressed whenever they appeared in the halls. No swishing around in night robes was tolerated, even if the man happened to be eighty years old and a bishop.

He banged the door loudly to assure the girls he was out of the corridors and not likely to emerge again. He longed to phone the house, just to hear Louise's voice, but knew he must not. It was too late.

What he had to do, and had been putting off, was to wire Carol's parents. There wasn't any use now thinking she had gone to Milwaukee to shop and get away. She had no friends to visit anywhere this side of New York. He had to wire, phrasing the message carefully (thinking of the local operator). A long distance call was out of the question. All the operators would be interested and would pitch in to ask questions. The mechanics of living were difficult in a town like Winnebago, he thought, and, if he had known it, this was probably the one time he and Carol had shared a feeling.

Then he realized the Western Union would be closed down for the night, so he could put off wiring until tomorrow. It was like a stay of execution.

22.

Julie and Mike had walked past President Wallace and wandered to the river's edge. Mike spread out his sweater for her and she stretched out on it. Mike sat down close to her, looking down at her face.

"Let's run away. Get married," she said.

"We couldn't make a go of it," he said. "We got to be practical."

She waved the practical considerations away with one hand. Her instinct was to secure the man she loved. "Mike, let's."

"What would you do when your father turned you out?" His voice was troubled. "We couldn't stay at Westerly, married, you know that."

"We'd be together."

"Oh Julie." He bent to kiss her.

They might, in time, look back with wonder that it had been possible to build a world in a kiss, but now it was quite natural. Julie let her breath out in a long sigh as he crushed her to him. Before she closed her eyes, she thought the stars were whirling in the sky. Mike wasn't gentle this time. Her ribs felt caved in. Her mouth was bruised. As she gasped for air he bent her head back and his hands tore the collar of her blouse. She gave a cry, but whether of pain or joy she couldn't tell.

169

Then Mike pulled away, letting her fall back so hard her head smacked against the ground. He sat down, hands shaking, head turned away. The breath came laboring into her lungs again but before she could speak, he said harshly, "Julie, I've got to quit this. Right now. I can't get us in any more trouble than we're in right now. That's the size of it."

She sat up, pushing her hair back, wiping the sweat from her neck. What was the matter with him? A moment ago she dissolved in his arms and now he was hardly looking at her! It didn't make sense. An old tree root jabbed her back, and her blouse was ruined. She had a horrid fear that there were runs in her stockings and how could she explain that?

"I'll try to tell you," said Mike. Then he sighed and shrugged. "I wouldn't want you any different, you know that. But there are some things—I mean I've been around more than you—and well, it's hard to tell you how it is."

He mopped his face. God, how he loved her, and how difficult it was when she didn't know anything about—anything! Didn't she even know about the girls that got sent home sometimes? Did his darling think babies came over the rooftops with storks carrying them? But what could he say to her? "Look, Julie," he said, "I guess you have to trust me to know what's best for us from here on."

The spell was broken. Julie began to worry about getting back in the dorm safely, about her father, about her stockings. "I better start back," she said.

Without a word, he helped her to her feet. He knew she was both angry and confused; he too felt a dull anger, not at her but at the way life was. He felt it was all wrong, the world was punishing them for no fault of their own.

He was spent with the effort to dam up his emotions, and he knew he had come too near making their union a reality. He hardly knew what had saved him. Except he loved her more than anything. She was so little and soft as his hands went under her.

Silently they climbed the path and when Julie tripped on a stone, she righted herself. He followed her stiffly. As he reached the top of the path, she brushed the twigs from her skirt and said, "Good night."

She knew he stood there watching as she ran toward Kennicott and she almost turned back, but kept on. Tears rolled down her cheeks but she wasn't sure what she was crying about. At the foot of the fire escape she paused, for it was dizzying and she hated heights. But she bit her lips, and started up. It was terrifying to be in space, clinging to the thin iron railing, putting one foot above the other on the narrow treads. At the second story the fire escape went inside, and the door was propped open with a copy of Plato. Weak with relief, she slipped in. No monitor stood there, the corridor was empty, and she went on to Marcy's room. From the next room came the sound of sobbing so she knew Sandra had failed her make-up exam in History and would be handed a blank diploma at Commencement. But she was too worn out to worry about Sandra.

Marcy's room, as usual, was full. Marcy, in pigtails, sat on the window seat. The "sisters in fraternity" sat on the cots, the floor. Somebody passed Julie a toothbrush mug filled with pink cocoa. Somebody else passed a box of cookies. Julie sat down on the floor. Everyone was too busy talking to ask where she had been. Dances, dates and men occupied their attention. Especially men. Dottie, they said, was pinned but it wouldn't last, and Leslie was unpinned and that wouldn't last either. Peggy might be pinned before Commencement. Julie sat silent, drinking the lukewarm cocoa gratefully. Somehow she felt safe, back in the group she was used to, an ordered, understandable world. That other world with Mike was hazardous, troubling. Before she knew it she was giggling at Marcy's story of losing her underpants on the library steps, right in front of Dr. Peake.

"They just slid," said Marcy. "I thought I would *die*. Absolutely. He was looking right *at* me."

"Whatever did you do?"

"I simply scooped them up and ran like a whitehead."

They laughed uproariously. Of all men, Dr. Peake! Presumably Dr. Peake had seen underwear before during a long life, but honestly! Finally they trooped away, still giggling, and Marcy sank back on her cot, yawning. "Well, that's that. I'm not even going to brush my teeth. I'm dead. If it gets chilly in the night use my fur coat, I haven't got around to packing. Do that tomorrow."

They settled down, Marcy observing the mattresses must be stuffed with steel filings. They said their prayers. Then Marcy raised her head. "How was your date?"

"We just went down the path and right back," said Julie.

"Oh, that all?" Marcy thought it over.

The springs creaked as Marcy propped herself on an elbow. "You really are nuts about him, aren't you?"

"Oh, I don't know what to think." Julie sat up. "He kissed me and kissed me and then pushed me away—then we came back."

Marcy was considerably more sophisticated than most of the Westerly girls. Now she contemplated Julie thoughtfully. "Pushed you away, huh?" she asked, and turned on the light.

"And after all I went through getting away."

Marcy came to an abrupt decision. "Have you ever heard of sex?" she asked.

"Certainly," said Julie, "we've studied it in plants."

"Nuts," said Marcy. "Sex isn't just for plants. It's kind of general. I know it never happened to the older generation but in this day and age, sex is here to stay. I mean, you can get sort of carried away—and it turns out to be sex."

Julie was confused. What was Marcy getting at? What Marcy was getting at was that she knew the score having once been "carried away" herself. She did love Julie, and wanted to protect her and help her. But it was a problem, all right.

"What I mean," Marcy spoke slowly, "is if you are really nuts about a man and he is nuts about you, there's more to it than kissing."

Julie considered this. Was it possible the wild urge she felt to be part of Mike had a deeper meaning?

In her sheltered academic life, she knew people married and had babies in due course. In her childish dreams the rose-covered cottage loomed, and gay suppers, dancing, parties. Secretly you wished Mike's head on the next pillow to yours, instead of the teddy bear. But modesty made it impossible to dream further. The truth was Julie had not grown up to the knowledge in her heart, not yet.

"And if Mike loves you the way I think," said Marcy, "he's right to be careful."

"Oh," said Julie.

"Girls do get in trouble," Marcy went on. "Think it over."

Julie thought it over. Could it be that moment of dissolving into Mike—

"You're already in trouble with your father," Marcy pointed out. "I'd watch my step until he quiets down. Play it down."

"I wanted to run away and get married, but Mike wouldn't."

"He's got more sense than you have. Mike has to graduate. You don't want to marry a millworker and he's too good for that. You ought to help him along, not be a millstone."

"What shall I do?" cried Julie.

"Grow up," said Marcy shortly. "Manage your father until Mike gets established. And help Mike out. Don't give too much with the kissing."

"I love him."

"Then in the end you'll have to choose between your father

and Mike, but don't jump the gun. Lots of football games are won in the locker rooms, not on the field." She yawned and turned out the light.

"I," she spoke drowsily, "shall marry a rich man. I don't want to bother with cooking and housework. One man is a lot like another, as far as I am concerned. But you, if I may say so, are peculiar. I guess you have to have this one man. You haven't been pinned and unpinned every few weeks. And as for him, I wouldn't be caught dead going to anything with him again, not Tree Day or a rally. He just broods about you. Take my advice, and don't push him too far."

"I'll try." Julie pulled up the coat. "So you think he does love me?"

"If he didn't, you'd be in trouble tonight for sure," said Marcy. "Wake me up when the bell rings. I got to be on my way at nine."

"I'll be up." Julie flattened the pillow. "I'm having a marcel."

"This I should live to see." Marcy giggled.

They fell asleep, Marcy dreaming of mink and Julie of Mike. The moonlight walked across the floor, lighting Julie's face, shining on the gold of Marcy's hair. The practical worldly one slept without moving, the other sighed in her sleep. Next door, Sandra cried on all by herself and farther down the hall someone was still packing.

Westerly was no more than a few buildings bulking against the sky, a small college where the young were educated to go forth and minister to the world. The night watchman went into the basement of Science Hall and made cocoa on a hot plate, for there was nothing to worry about on his campus.

After Julie left him Mike went to town and stopped at the pool hall. His blood was restless and he felt keyed up. He wanted, now, a world of men and easy laughter, the haze of cheap cigarette smoke, the click of balls. He couldn't help being angry with Julie, just because she was what he wanted, innocent and pure. It was queer that having what you most wanted in a girl could also make you angry. As he went in he had no idea of doing anything but watch and go on home. But when one of the gang made a remark about Julie, he knocked him down. It felt wonderful to lash out and flatten someone.

"Hey, can't you take a little kidding?" asked Mac, who owned the joint. "Who's so high and mighty around here can't take a joke? Keep your shirt on, kid."

"Cheese, what's eatin' on him?" someone said.

"Just watch yourself," said Mike, folding his hands into fists. It felt good. A good punch—took the kinks out of him. He helped the guy up, grinned. "Try your wisecracks on someone else," he advised. He looked them over, the drifters, the punks, the gamblers, the uneasy married men sneaking out for fun, the few teen-agers who kept an eye on the back door in case the cops came. He didn't belong there any more. He didn't want them.

He went out, breathing easily. That was a good punch. Set him up. He'd had enough of Westerly, the people, the problems with Julie, the works. He just wanted out. He strode purposefully across town, reached the place where country began.

It was funny, the way it was town one minute, farmland the next. You couldn't put your foot on the dividing line. But outside town it was cooler, the meadows brimmed with moonlight. He took the side road to Schotta's farm. A brook wound through the farmland, and at one point there was a stand of hemlocks, probably saved from the plow to be a windbreak. An early cabin stood at the bend of the brook, a one-room log hut chinked with moss. Possibly it was the dwelling of the pioneer Schotta whose descendants now owned the great barns and silos and the comfortable farmhouse (less impressive than the farm buildings, for it was meant for humans, not stock).

175

Mike had fished the brook that summer he worked for the Schottas, and sometimes on stifling nights had crept away from his attic room to sleep in the hut by the brook.

Now he found the path easily. You could read a book by the moon, he thought. The cabin door swung loose on a broken hinge, but the pile of hay inside was still there, although moldy. A bat circled warily around the rafters and he swished it out. Then he tossed the hay out, broke a few branches of hemlock, took off his shirt and lay down on the sweet-smelling pile. Through the open door he could see the moon patterned with hemlock. The brook ran free, still fed by spring rains.

Mike didn't know why he had come here, it had been instinctive, a flight from the present, a return to a time when he had been free of his aunt and uncle and the pressures of his life. He only knew he felt better, off by himself in this secret place.

As the tightness ebbed from his muscles he felt tired, but it was a relief just to be tired. His mind stopped beating at his problems, and wandered. He wondered dreamily how many stars there were in the sky and whether it was true the moon pulled the tides. And what would the earth be like in a thousand years? How was it here before the settlers came? The site of the Indian massacre was now a cornfield and grew good crops. They still called the area Butte De Morts, but the Indians were long gone. Probably they didn't like being killed off any better than a white man would.

Before he met Julie, Mike was apt to think about a lot of things that needn't have concerned him. But of late his mind was bursting with immediate worries, or squirreling around on the wheel of Julie and her father. It was good to think about the Indians, he thought, pushing a branch aside. Good to be alone, himself. Maybe he'd like to go to the north woods and cut lumber for a year. Nothing to worry about but keeping the ax sharp and felling the tree in the right direction.

The mood didn't last long, for Julie came back into his mind. Next year would be tough, but when had he had it easy? He'd work like crazy, get by, fit her in somehow. Tonight he had felt such a need for her that he just missed getting them in a worse mess than ever. This was going to take all the control he had. You couldn't blame Julie. She didn't mean to lead him on, she was just innocent. And that was the way he wanted her to be, for he wanted to be the one to teach her the meaning of love. He didn't want a girl who knew her way around; enough of them did and they were not for him.

He didn't want to make her feel afraid, and he didn't want any behind-the-bush affair with her. He wanted to live with her, sleep every night with her, grow in understanding of her, build a marriage better than any he had observed. But he wanted "Until death do us part" said by the minister. He wanted this relationship with Julie sanctified by the church, and acceptable to society.

His love was the best of him, he knew that. It wasn't just the surge of physical passion, and it was nothing like the ordinary college romance. It was as if he had been born to love her.

He got up and went to the brook and cupped his hands and drank the minty water. When he lay down again, the moon had moved. The truth was, he thought honestly, he wanted to move into Julie's world, not drag her into the one he had grown up in. He wanted roots, an end to being an orphan from the Fifth Ward. He wanted a house, a family, a respectable standing in the community. And it could all happen, he thought miserably, if only Julie's father would give him a chance. Otherwise it would never work out. No matter how far away he and Julie went, her father would be in her mind. She might hate him, but she loved him. Mike accepted this and it was the final evidence of his maturity that he knew he had to live with it.

Well, nuts, he thought, I got to quit going over it all the time. I beat my brains out and just get tired. I got to go ahead, that's all.

He turned over. In a thousand years would there be anybody like Julie walking in the moonlight with another Mike? Or was this for once? He sure would like to know.

But it was now that they were living.

23.

It was after two in the morning when Mark heard the phone ring. He fumbled for the receiver on his desk. Nobody ever phoned anybody late at night in Winnebago, much less at dawn. He was furious, until he heard Ralph Knight's quavering voice.

"I hate to wake you up. This is Ralph. I don't know what to do."

"What is it?"

"Marjorie," said Ralph. "I can't get the ambulance, it's out. I can't start my car, battery run down. Dr. Jim is at the hospital already on an emergency—"

Mark exploded. "Well, why didn't you call me first? I'll be right over."

He was furious, letting rage blot out his terror. That Ralph. Just like him. But what was wrong? Marjorie had been fine when he dropped in. She couldn't be in trouble—he pulled his shirt on backwards, got the wrong leg in his trousers. For once in his immaculate life, he forgot his tie and ran out without even locking the door. When he got to the garage he remembered the keys were on the bureau. So he picked up a brick from a pile in the neighbor's yard and heaved it through the glass of the window. Being thin, he got inside without cutting himself, although he didn't know how. Once inside, he took the jack and brought it down against the garage door with all his strength. It gave way, and he rushed to crank the car. For once, the motor caught and he backed out in a hurry.

Within ten minutes he was driving down Main Street with Marjorie in the back seat, huddled in a quilt. Ralph tried to reason with her, and Mark could have killed him except he was too busy avoiding the ruts in the dirt road. He drove furiously when the road was smooth, abandoning his customary fifteen miles an hour. The car sounded as if it might fall apart. Ominous creakings and groanings came from the motor and steam rose from the radiator.

Why should a hospital be built halfway to nowhere? Why didn't Dr. Jim stay at home so he could be reached easily? What was the ambulance doing? The taxpayers' money went for it. And why was Marjorie in this condition anyway?

He drew up at St. Mary's with a jolting stop. He rushed up the steps, disregarding Ralph. A Sister appeared, calm and comfortable. He made an incoherent statement and immediately a stretcher materialized. Marjorie was lifted onto it, and rolled away.

"Now everything will be taken care of," said the Sister. "You may wait in the next room."

The two men sat down in squeaking wicker chairs. The waiting room was not encouraging, with the Crucified Christ on the wall and the smell of disinfectant heavy in the air. Ralph was crying and Mark turned his back. He was trying to remember what happened in miscarriages but his knowledge of biology was confined to the time he had dissected a frog and fainted. Its legs kept twitching.

Time went on. Neither of them knew how long. Mark knew the nurses changed, and new internes bounded in.

He lived through every hour he had spent with Marjorie.

That first day when she came timidly in and he was bored but said she could vocalize. His schedule was already full. Then the big golden notes swept out. His life was channeled from that moment.

At last a Sister came in and said Dr. Jim advised Mark to go home. He would bring Ralph as soon as he was through. They were not to worry, things were going well.

What did that mean? Mark drove home at a sensible fifteen miles an hour. Did it mean Marjorie was all right, or the baby, or both? He was beginning to have a strange feeling since the dreadful drive to the hospital. He did not want anything to happen to this baby. It was real now, a being. He had a vision of the christening, when he would stand by the parents of his godchild while Reverend Mallory dipped water from the font and said, "I christen thee Mark Allingham Knight."

The boy would, of course, be a tenor. And Mark would work with him as soon as he was old enough to carry a tune. His namesake would be famous, no doubt of it. Certainly this baby had to be born, alive, safe. Too much had been sacrificed for him already. He and Marjorie had given up more than anyone could guess.

At home, he made a cup of tea hoping to steady himself. His hands still trembled and there was a pain in his chest. Well, he thought, if anything went wrong, it was all the fault of that husband of hers, that good-for-nothing weakling. A man like that was a dissonance in life.

He ought to get a little sleep, but he was still awake when the rooster in Devine's yard began his abominable crowing. Finally he dozed sitting in the chair, a haggard rumpled man.

At dawn Dr. Jim shook Ralph awake. "You still around?" he said. "I'll take you home. Marjorie's all right and looks as if the baby would make it too. Come along."

Ralph blinked at the light as they went out. "Is—is—she really all right?"

"Yes, and no thanks to either of you, I may say." Dr. Jim bucketed down the road. "The next time she lugs a washing down those stairs of yours, I personally shall beat you up."

"Well, I have to have a clean shirt every day—"

"Wash and iron them yourself then. You aren't having this baby, remember. She is."

Now the fear was gone, Ralph began to feel aggrieved. After all, Marjorie had carried the washing out of her own accord. No use blaming him for everything. People were always putting him in the wrong. Look at Mark bawling him out because his car wouldn't start. It wasn't his fault the battery went dead right at this time. It just so happened he hadn't got around to having it checked lately, but it could happen to anyone.

The truth was that he was tired of this whole baby business. The first glow of having proved his manhood had long since faded. His routine was upset. Marjorie no longer waited on him. Half the time he had to wait on her. He also missed the attention he had had when Marjorie sang. "Well, well, Ralphie, you picked a winner. You sure did." Why did so many men call him Ralphie? Or, "Ralph, could you persuade your wife to sing a few numbers at the Elk's banquet? Like you both to be our guests."

It had added to his stature to be Marjorie's husband. But now his wife was just another woman going to have a baby, and hardly a day passed in Winnebago without a baby being born. It didn't set her apart, he thought resentfully, to be like everybody else. Furthermore, now that Marjorie and the baby were safe, he felt put upon. He'd been scared, had put in hours of sheer terror, with nobody paying any attention to him.

Dr. Jim pulled up at the corner. "Well, I'll give you a ring later in the day," he said. "You're a lucky man, I can tell you."

Lucky, thought Ralph bitterly, as he went into the disordered flat. Doctor's bills, hospital bills, nobody even around to clean up the mess, and God knew how long Marjorie would be away.

It was all unfair. He warmed up the coffee and gloomily ate a stale bun. Then he made the bed up with clean linen, put the laundry in a pillowcase, and went downstairs to consult the landlady as to how laundry got done when nobody was around to do it.

A new era was beginning for Ralph.

Miss Nelson knew she couldn't put it off any longer. The invitation to drop in at her convenience was a kind way of putting it, but President Wallace was a kind man indeed. He hadn't even said before Commencement, trusting she would know it must be before.

She tried for three days to go to his office, every day thinking of reasons she just could not make it until the next day. She had her music to sort, for one thing. And a few make-up lessons for another. She had to write to her sister, which always took a lot of time. *The lilacs bloomed early this year*, she wrote, *and the roses are coming out for Commencement. The campus lawn has been mowed a number of times. There is some talk of painting the trim on Main Hall this fall.*

She had learned, painfully, not to mention people. Poor Marylin was so notional. If Miss Nelson so much as mentioned passing the time of day with someone, the return letter was full of references to some people who have a gay social life. *And I would be careful not to speak to a man,* her sister wrote, *for one never knows.*

So Miss Nelson's laborious missives were chiefly about weather and what nature was up to on campus. It just could not be her fault that the lilacs bloomed early.

She spent part of one day going over her finances. No matter how she subtracted or added, it came out that she needed more money and even getting through the summer was a hazard with the extra bills for her sister.

She had nothing to sell, for her seed-pearl ring had gone to pay for extra nursing care when Marylin had grippe. She had nothing to borrow on, for even the most secure faculty member dared not borrow a penny against forthcoming salary. It was not considered moral at Westerly.

Finally she faced the dropping-in on the President. She wore her peony print. She had worn this at so many recitals that the back was definitely bowed out. Sitting on a piano bench and rocking about while playing accompaniments did wear a dress in the wrong place. The peonies had faded from being exposed to too many garden parties in full sun. They were no longer red, but a pale bluish-pink. The white background was on the beige side now. But she pinned in her Irish lace collar (lace did not wear out). She planned to carry her gloves with the worn thumbs turned in. Oh dear, she thought, there are so many things to think of!

She wasn't able to fortify herself with a cup of tea, for her stomach seemed to have a cement block in it. Well, she would drop around and perhaps President Wallace would simply want to discuss the giving of extra credits for Voice. Or they might wish to repaint her studio (it was ten years since it had been done). Possibly she should decide on a color, something fresh and new—pale green. Or would blue be better? No, the north exposure wasn't right for blue.

She walked slowly to the campus. For some reason, her knees were shaking and her mouth was so dry she stopped to sip at the drinking fountain, although this was difficult. She always spilled the water. But her tongue took up so much room in her mouth, she had to try the fountain.

She walked around the Administration Building twice, admonishing herself to be steady. Steady does it, she kept saying to herself. But her knees betrayed her. Once inside the building, she sat down on the bench under the bulletin board. "Tempest in a teapot," she muttered.

Perfectly reasonable for President Wallace to want a conference with her. Quite in order. She held an imaginary conversation with him, nodding her head. He appreciated her years of service and her fine musicianship—Westerly was hoping to raise the salaries—

Then her natural courage asserted itself. "Just remember you are a lady," she said aloud, and got up and went down the corridor. The secretary was too polite. The President would see her in a few moments, if she wouldn't mind waiting. Miss Nelson sat and stared blankly at a calendar. They had forgotten to tear off April but April was gone forever. Just leaving the sheet on didn't make it April.

Why couldn't it still be April?

She felt quite ill and bent over to secretly sniff her smelling salts. The sharp quickening smell made her eyes water and she wiped them hastily. She was not crying at all.

"Go right in," said the secretary warmly.

Her eyes were blurred so she could not see President Wallace distinctly. The smelling salts were a mistake, she thought.

"Do come in and sit down," he said, rising to shake her hand. How warm his hand felt to her cold paw!

She sat on the edge of the chair, opening and shutting her purse and trying not to.

She coughed delicately. "Lovely weather," she ventured.

"Lovely," he agreed. Then he sat down behind his desk and laid his hands flat on it. "I've been wanting a little talk with you," he said gently, "for some time."

He looked dreadfully pale and she felt pale, as if all the blood had pumped down to her feet. The room had a greenish light, as if they were under water.

He fidgeted with papers on the desk, took up his pen, laid it down, and smiled painfully.

"Miss Nelson," he said, "I—we all feel your contribution to Westerly has been of immeasurable value in the past years. Your faithfulness, devotion to duty, interest in the students—"

He paused. He cleared his throat, looked out of the window, looked down at the littered desk. Then gave her another wretched smile. "I personally appreciate your service to Westerly," he said.

"Well, I—" She snapped her purse again.

"Of course we all realize that, we realize that—"

Miss Nelson suddenly felt sorry for him. "Of course we do," she said bravely.

"There does come a time when, a time when we—" He was quite lost.

"You mean a time when we must retire," she said.

"Yes," he said. He added fiercely, "I have, as you know, battled for a pension system. It must come. But for now, I haven't been able to get it through."

"But—but what's to become of us?" cried Miss Nelson suddenly. "What's to become of us?" Then she bent her head. The involuntary cry shamed her. It was like the sharp sound made by a small animal as the trap jaws snap down. "I beg your pardon," she said.

President Wallace was scribbling on a pad, not writing anything. When he looked up his eyes were compassionate.

"I wish I knew the answer," he said. "I wish I knew."

Miss Nelson tried to smile but her lips were stiff. The room was out of focus, the President's figure blurred.

"In view of your long years of dedicated service," he said heavily, "it is with reluctance I have to tell you the Board will make no exceptions as to retirement, for the Board feels that —that Westerly should be—"

"I understand perfectly," she said.

"But in appreciation of your devoted work for Westerly, a small token of our gratefulness—" He pushed an envelope toward her. "And of course we shall continue to look on you as a member of the Westerly family."

"Thank you," she said.

The Board had not given a token of any kind. If they began giving away money to everyone who left Westerly, where would the budget be? The customary watch was given to the heads of departments and this wasn't too expensive as one member could get watches wholesale. But Miss Nelson was only, after all, an instructor, and in the Conservatory at that, not in the regular college.

After much thought, President Wallace had cashed his personal check for two hundred dollars, although he could ill afford it. It would see her through the summer, at any rate.

"Thank you," she murmured, "thank you very much." She put the envelope in her purse.

"And do let me know your plans," he said, "for the future. If there is anything we can do—"

"I haven't made up my mind." She was truthful about that.

It was over. She stumbled into the sunshine and sat down on the nearest bench. The sky was as clear as when she went in. The light was brilliant. Students drifted about campus, laughing, talking. The world had not changed a jot. She had lost her living, and still it was May. It wasn't fair! She herself must have looked the same, too, for several students waved at her, and Dr. Peake stopped to comment on the beautiful day. The panic in her breast was separate, special, belonging only to her.

Suddenly she couldn't bear it alone; somebody, somebody, must know. But she didn't want to go through Commencement with those sympathetic glances from her colleagues. Poor old thing, she's on the shelf. It was the most terrible part of the whole thing. She fumbled in her purse for a peppermint and there was none and this small loss brought the tears heavy in her eyes. She did feel the envelope and opened it and stared at the check.

The Board was generous, she felt. But how long could she

live on this? Oh, how long? She couldn't even go to a home, for then there would be nothing to send Marylin.

She walked aimlessly off campus, smiling mechanically when she passed Miss Finch. Ah, Miss Finch was young, she didn't know what lay ahead. The fear was simply dreadful, her whole body was a great lump of fear. Then she thought of Sybil who wasn't, after all, a faculty member, and who was known to be discreet, helpful, and gentle. In desperation she turned down Durkee and went to the Prescott house. If Professor Prescott were there—but he wouldn't be. He was at a meeting about fall schedules with other heads of departments.

Sybil was at home, alone.

"What a nice surprise!" she said. "Do come in." She knew too well that blank stricken look of people in dire trouble. Miss Nelson looked shrunken. "I need a cup of tea," she said. "Won't you have one with me?" Miss Nelson nodded and sat down in the living room.

Sybil wondered how many gallons of tea she had drunk just because someone needed tea. She brought a tray and gave Miss Nelson a cup. She didn't ask any questions. She never needed to.

Miss Nelson told her. And then she dabbed her eyes with her damp handkerchief. "I shouldn't bother you," she said miserably.

"Nonsense." Sybil kept her voice brisk. "Friends are for bothering, or they aren't much good, are they? Do you have anything saved?"

So Miss Nelson told the whole sorry story about the lovely man who just vanished and about her sister. It was such a relief to tell it. She felt weak but calm.

"Now then," said Sybil, "we'll just take a step at a time. Would you consider, just as a temporary measure, staying a while to help Dr. Jim out with poor Ella? It would be such a kindness on your part—"

"Oh dear me." Miss Nelson choked. "I shall have to move, shan't I? I hadn't thought—oh dear me."

Of course she would have to move. She didn't belong in the college any more. She was homeless. Someone else would be sitting at her piano in her studio and someone else living in her room. It made the world a terrifying void. She looked helplessly at Sybil.

"You don't have to decide anything today," Sybil told her. "You can think everything over and then if you'd like me to speak to Dr. Jim, I'll be glad to. But put it all out of your mind for a day or so. Change takes getting used to."

Miss Nelson nodded. "I must be going," she said faintly. "So much to do—busy time of year—sorry to take up your time—"

"Try not to worry," said Sybil.

Miss Nelson went back to the campus. She felt lightheaded. She sat down on the stone bench to catch her breath, and then a new fear came. Would everybody know? How could she get through Commencement if everyone knew? Could she hold her head up through the bitter hours? She must. She must go to the dining hall and wonder whether the students already had heard. She wanted to creep into a dark place and hide.

Then her pride came to help her. She clung to it, a spar to keep her from drowning in the sea of misery. Miss Nelson was timid, but she was no coward. She must put everything out of her mind except getting through Commencement.

Her natural common sense told her that President Wallace was a kind man and not likely to publish abroad the news that she had been dropped. Professor Allingham was probably already scouting for a new voice teacher, but he wouldn't tell the students either. The Dean undoubtedly knew, for her room would be assigned to the new tenant. And of course nothing had ever been a secret at Westerly. But for just a few more days, it might not leak out. All she prayed for was a few days.

I shall go down with all flags flying, said Miss Nelson to herself with great determination.

24.

It was a cool morning, with a light wind freshening. Sybil's roses were in blossom and the white pansies in the border of the garden opened surprised faces to the sun. Under the bridal wreath a robin hauled away at a worm, stretching it until it came in two and he fell back. Lutz's ice wagon came down the street, the hoofs of the horses clopping.

Alden, however, was not enjoying the day, for he was trying to jack up a corner of the house. He had noticed, when he went down cellar to assemble the camping equipment, that one of the main house sills was developing dry rot. He dug his jack-knife in to be sure, and the powdery stuff came out. Confound it, he thought, next thing the upstairs plaster will begin to crack, floors sag, windows warp. He was not in any mood to phone a contractor and have men swarming all over the place, costing money. They'd want to replace all the sills and they'd be around all summer. He'd have to give up the camping trip, for with strangers running in and out, things would get stolen.

He'd simply fix it himself, right now. He had some good timbers back of the garage which he had bought at the time he planned to build a boathouse for his rowboat. Alden was no procrastinator but the boathouse had never been built, for he had gone out on the river to fish the day before and had rowed too close to the dam. Fortunately the water was low that day, so he was not swept over, but the boat piled up against a log jam. He had to swim for his life, but he was a strong swimmer, and by angling his course finally came out on the bank. So far he had not saved up enough to replace the boat.

Now he went around the house and inspected the lumber. He chose a good, firm timber, and sawed off enough to replace the rotted part of the sill. The wood was chestnut and infernally hard, and he got hotter and hotter. He finally tied a handkerchief around his head to keep the sweat out of his eyes. Now, he thought, all I have to do is jack up the house, saw out the rotted piece, slide the new one in. His reasoning was crystal-clear. He was not going to raise the whole house, only one corner. Common sense had never been Alden's strongest point.

He had a crowbar which he used on field trips to pry out recalcitrant boulders, also a sledge hammer for breaking up rocks. He went back down cellar and lugged them up to the site of the operation, feeling peaceful now that he was in action. He was in a good mood anyway, for he had been able to pass all his favorite students and he had the camp gear pretty well in hand. So he was humming as he lifted the crowbar. It went in all right, but when he bent over and put his weight on it nothing happened. He tried again, putting all his strength into it. He puffed, and the tendons in his neck went rigid. A sharp pain sliced across his shoulders.

This was simply ridiculous. He bore down again and heaved at the crowbar, and it suddenly plunged under the timber. At the same time the handle jerked back and caught Alden in the chest. He staggered, gasped, and let go, falling back on the grass. When breath labored back into his lungs, he advanced again and attacked the proposition with the same fury with which his ancestors had attacked the British.

But the house did not budge. In fact, after twenty minutes more, he had to accept the fact that he could not jack up his own house. It was a bitter defeat. He dropped the confounded crowbar and managed to straighten up, although with great difficulty. Beaten, angry, he stumped to the house with pain still slicing into his back. He went to the kitchen, which smelled good. Something was in the oven. Sybil was upstairs, for he heard the pedal on the sewing machine. He moved over and flung open the oven door. If anything was cooking he wanted a sample.

What was in the oven were the meringues, forty of them, tiny fluffs, perfect until the cold air came in to flatten them.

"Alden, what are you doing?" Sybil asked breathlessly. She had heard the door slam but couldn't get downstairs fast enough. "My meringues. You've ruined them! Oh, how could you?" She looked so angry that he retreated.

"I just wanted to look." He spoke meekly.

"You've looked," she said fiercely, "and I hope you are satisfied now you've ruined all that work."

"But I never meant—" He was really at a loss.

"I wish sometime you'd learn to mind your own business," snapped Sybil, dramatically scraping the meringues into the garbage can. She turned to face him. "What in the world have you been up to, anyway?"

Alden sat down. On top of the house defeating him, here was Sybil attacking him. It was too much. He just was not used to this sort of thing.

"All right, what were you doing banging around?" She was adamant.

"I was merely trying to jack up the corner of the house, and then I came in and I was hungry," he said meekly. "So I thought I might get a slice of something to keep my strength up."

Sybil looked at this man whom she had married for better or worse (and so often it had been worse). She would have to do the meringues all over again, and she was so tired, and all those egg whites wasted, and eggs were expensive—twenty cents a dozen. But there he sat, looking sheepish. And he had offered what was, for him, a handsome apology.

She put the pans to soak, and went over and kissed his damp face. "Never mind, Alden. I'll make some more. It doesn't really matter."

He brightened at once. "I feel as if I might be getting lumbago. When do we eat?"

Lumbago! Trying to lift a house! Singlehanded. But there it was, this was Alden, the man she was married to. "I'll fix you a snack," she said, "and why don't you take a hot bath with Epsom salts in the water. That helps—lumbago."

"I guess I will," he agreed, standing up painfully.

"Take your bath first," she advised, "and then I'll have something ready. Get the water as hot as you can." She watched him go out of the kitchen bending over slightly, and she thought, At least he hasn't fallen off the roof the way he did when he decided to point the chimney to save money.

She got out the iron spider and heated it over a low flame, with sweet butter melting in it, while she beat the last of the eggs. (Julie would have to run uptown and get more for the next batch of meringues.) She didn't really see how she would have time to make a second batch of forty, tipping each one from a teaspoon, putting them in a cold oven, very slowly raising the temperature. But she would fit it in somehow. She always had.

When Alden came down, pink as a baby, she had his creamy scrambled eggs, hot buttered toast, and hot coffee ready. He eased himself into the chair. When he had finished, he said, "I think I need a little fresh air and exercise. I'll take a turn around the block and stop in to see if Dr. Peake has finished his memos."

He was stiff, all right. He went crabwise down the back steps. Sybil watched him through the glass pane in the back door. Well, she thought, there was no use trying to reason with him. She might as well try to anchor the wind. If he had strained a muscle or pulled a tendon, he would try to work it off with more exercise.

Alden limped along, confounding his lumbago at every step.

He was taking an unaccustomed route, and as he turned the corner of a high privet hedge he discovered Julie and Michael holding hands. Before he could take a step, Michael kissed the palm of Julie's hand and went away. Julie stood looking after him. Alden turned as fast as his aching muscles would allow and beat a retreat down the block. He needed time to think. The way this boy bent over her, and the way she looked at him —how many times had they stood there, saying good-by out of sight of the house? Unobserved. The fact that he walked with difficulty added nothing to his comfort. His lips pressed into a thin line as he thought of Julie defying him.

Alden was not perceptive, except with regard to himself, but the look on Julie's face made him realize that he must summon his resources. Sybil, he felt, would be no ally. She was soft as mush, and all she wanted was for Julie to have her own way. She never considered—as what woman did?—what the future would hold. She could not be persuaded that this running around with Michael might threaten Julie's career. But then, Sybil had not had a college education.

He must not mention this to her. He would handle it himself. Quietly, and with dignity. There was a scholarship available at Mt. Southampton, in Massachusetts, as he had found out. Julie was more than eligible, as an A plus student, and his daughter. Two of the admissions committee had been at Johns Hopkins with him. That would settle it. His anger at Julie made him want to punish himself by sending her away. At the same time he would punish *her*, and cure her of this foolish infatuation.

When he got back to the house Sybil was putting the new meringues in the oven, and he tiptoed past the kitchen door.

He went into the bathroom and took a pill or two out of every bottle in the medicine chest. If one didn't work, another would. Then he went to the bedroom, for he had an inspiration. He dug around in the bottom drawer and took out the locked steel box that held his precious and semiprecious stones. He paused to admire the amethysts, the pink pearl bought from a clammer for a dollar, the moonstones with fire in their hearts, the single ruby. Then he took out the bottom drawer, where he kept his Sigma Psi pin, his medallion from the French government (for special research on fossils), and the velvet box with his grandmother's diamond brooch. This was to be Julie's graduation present.

But now he took it out, held it to the light, wiped it with a clean handkerchief. Yes, it was good. The diamonds were well cut, and blue-white. The antique setting, heavy gold, set them off beautifully. He tested the safety clasp. He was not a man to dwell anywhere except in the now, but momentarily he saw himself a small boy again in tight velveteen pants, cambric blouse, and flowing tie. He sat in his grandmother's lap, which smelled of lavender and peppermint. He was again, after all this time, touching the brooch where it lay becalmed on the wide sea of her bosom.

The room was all garnet with velvet draperies, damask sofa, and the cover that fell to the floor around the table. The maid was bringing in the tea, with the crumpets he loved. He would have his own cup, with milk and sugar. His grandmother put her heavily ringed hand on his tawny hair and said, "So you like the sparkle?"

"It's blue," he said, "and moony, and icy." Gems were always to be like poetry to him, but he couldn't know it, or she. But she was pleased. "The brooch shall be yours someday," she said.

Now, as he held it to the light, he had a nostalgia for the days when he sat on her lap. This, indeed, was his only tangible heritage, for when his grandfather died of lung fever, it was discovered that he had invested all of the family stock in a gold mine from which no gold came. The house and furnishings sold, Grandmother lived by visiting relatives, "taking a short vacation trip" it was called. She became a withered old lady with a clouded memory. But the brooch she never sold or gave away, and when she died none of the relatives dared to disobey the faded note wrapped around the velvet box. The brooch went to Alden.

The box he put in his pocket now, and went downstairs feeling that all of his problems were solved. They were, for once, having supper at noon, so to speak, for tonight was step singing and they had to be early for that. Sybil carried in the platter of pork chops smothered in onions, and Julie followed with the whipped potatoes and green salad.

Since it was not Sunday, Alden omitted grace and began to serve. There was no conversation at the table. Sybil, hot and tired, was planning how to get a few dollars from Alden for the missionary fund. Julie was in the rose-covered cottage with Michael. Alden was going over in his mind the calm discussion he would have with Julie presently. He would be firm, controlled. He actually was making up a lecture, but this time on the advantages of an eastern women's college. He would, he decided, even sell his hoarded shares of Anaconda for this project.

He was so persuaded of his reasonableness that he asked Julie quite casually to come to the study while they discussed something. But she seemed to turn to stone. Her eyes, wide and fixed, had the same look of horror that they had had when she almost stepped on a copperhead on the last camping trip. She did not speak at all. He felt unaccountably frightened, and this made his temper rise.

His peroration died away as he began to describe the charms of a female institution. So he reached into his pocket and brought out the velvet box and said, with a final flourish, "And I have decided to give you your great-grandmother's diamond brooch to wear to concerts—and things."

He snapped open the lid, and the brooch seemed to give off light of its own. Yes, those were good, well-matched diamonds, and he must advise her to be very careful of them. But of course she must know how precious the brooch was, for he had let her wear it once for her sixteenth birthday party, pinned on the bosom of her rose satin dress. And Julie, he knew, had his own feeling for minerals and jewels, as well as for the fossils that spoke of lost ages. So, reassured, he held out the box and said, "Now you must be careful of it."

At last Julie spoke. "Did you think you could buy me?" she asked. Every word could have been carved from ice. She turned and left the study, and he heard her stumble on the bottom step as she started for her room. Then, as he sat silent, he heard her door bang.

Sybil heard it too, as she watched her meringues. Oh dear me, what is it now? she thought. She laid wax paper between the layers of edible cloud. Then she rinsed her hands, wiped them, and went to the study.

As she stood in the doorway she saw Alden slumped at his desk. She had never seen him like this, not in all the stormy years. On the desk she saw the velvet box, and the brooch, sparkling.

"Alden, what is it now? What have you done?"

He lifted his head and stared at her as though he had never seen her before. "What have I done?" he echoed. Then he roused himself to tell her what Julie had done.

"You really mean to carry through this crazy idea, and send her away from home?" Sybil's voice sounded queer.

"Yes"—his own voice sounded hoarse—"I won't have this going on. I know what's best for her."

Now Sybil looked at him in much the same way Julie had,

as if she had suddenly stepped on a snake. Her head was pounding, her hands shaking. But her eyes were steady. She did not speak again, but went out through the back door and sank down on the steps. How did Alden think he could arrange Julie's whole life without love? How long could he keep her a child, when she was already growing up?

But for Sybil the conflict was not a single one. Her whole self was torn in two. No matter how much her heart went out to Julie, sobbing in her room, she retained in her mind's eye the vision of Alden, bowed, crushed. Alden, defeated twice in the same day, by his house, and by his daughter. So after a time she went back in, and walked slowly to the study. She moved to the desk, and took Alden's head in her arms and held him warmly against her as if he were a baby, as indeed he so often was. He drew a long, sobbing breath, this unreasonable, difficult man.

"Alden, you should be proud of Julie." She spoke softly.

"Proud? Why?"

"Because she is so like you that she can't be bribed," Sybil said, and kissed him. If the kiss had more compassion than love, he did not know. My poor darling, she thought. She would tackle this eastern college plan another time. Meanwhile she comforted him.

"I shall make some nice, fresh coffee, and give you a meringue," she said. "I want your opinion of them."

25.

There had been a thunderstorm in the night. Black clouds scalloped the horizon at sunset and then boiled up in round formations. The valley brimmed with rain. Lightning struck the Obertauffer barn, and the glow of the flames could be seen on campus, although the farm was half a mile out. Thunder bowled along the river basin. Then the storm passed, the rain diminished to a trickle, a few drops. In the washed air the fading lilacs hung drenched. The bridal wreath shone like wet pearl as the sky brightened. Grass had grown magically in the night, and all over town men pushed lawn mowers. In the Fifth Ward, barefooted women picked the peas and bright strawberries. The asparagus, about to go by, revived enough to send out new shoots which were snatched for supper.

Washing hung on the line in every back yard. Housewives were catching up while the heat was broken. It was cool and fresh. Swollen feet fitted back into shoes. Women had energy to scrub the veranda steps. The campus, dressed with June breezes, looked beautiful. The homely buildings took on charm when every ivy leaf glistened. Roses bloomed. Boys and girls wandered along the damp paths hand in hand. Professors stopped to chat with colleagues, instead of hurrying past to get out of the heat. The college band practiced, but without much gusto, because every member wanted to get out and enjoy the day.

They gave up on "Pomp and Circumstance," which they were to play for the processional, and banged out the "Alma Mater" once more.

"To thee we'll e'er be true," wavered the trumpets.

Naturally, they didn't have much idea what it meant. "Never shall we fail thee," but the music sounded good. It would come to them in time that never failing Westerly meant kicking in money as long as they lived, and then, hopefully, leaving more money in their wills. "Alma Mater, Westerly," they played.

Julie and Marcy could hear it through Marcy's window. Julie was on the cot holding a wet washcloth over her reddened eyes. Marcy, though sympathetic, was hungry, and surreptitiously ate fudge.

"Why I think it is the most absolutely terrible thing I ever heard of," she said, fudge melting in her mouth. "Why you'd think this was the Middle Ages or something, sending you off to a convent like that. I never heard of such a thing."

"I won't go." Julie's voice was thick through the washcloth. "I'd rather die."

"Well, look at Lizbeth Fowler," said Marcy.

Julie took the washcloth off one eye and peered at Marcy. There was a moment of silence, rare for them. They both thought how Liz had gone, and did you really know what happened, when you disregarded the minister, and died a suicide? They thought of all Liz had missed, and would miss, just by not being there.

"Well, I don't know how you feel, but I'm too curious to want to die, no matter what happens. Take Liz. We'd have bid her next fall, sure as shooting. We needed her grades. Takes time for some things. Take you, you sit it out with your father, and it will work out."

Marcy couldn't help thinking that if Julie really did go East to school, Michael would be lonely and it would be her duty to comfort him, being Julie's best friend. I mean, she thought, a girl can't help thinking of these things. "Don't be silly," she said sharply, "you can't just pine away, no matter if you do go to Southampton. Have a piece of fudge. It's delicious."

Julie was torn between being a martyr and having a bite to eat. So she compromised on half a piece. She tried to eat it as though she were doing Marcy a favor.

"I know who blackballed Liz," said Marcy, licking her fingers. "Want to know?"

Julie peered at her. "Do you honestly know, for sure?"

"Hope to die if I don't. But it's a dead secret. I wouldn't tell a living soul but you."

Julie swallowed the last bite. What she wouldn't have given to know during her days of terror and guilt didn't bear thinking of. But now she wondered. If she knew, would she be able to go on in Gamma and act as though she didn't know? She had never been any good at concealing anything. Her face was open as a meadow. She was learning, indirectly, on account of her father, but she was still candid. She would, she knew, give it away by a look, a remark.

This would not do Lizbeth any good. Lizbeth must be working it out with God, one way or another. The prospect of death seemed less desirable suddenly. She had a vision of Lizbeth in the coffin, underground, when she might at this minute be getting her dress pressed for the Commencement processional.

"No," she said, "I'd rather not know. Then I won't act peculiar. Don't tell me."

Marcy nodded. "I know how you feel. That's why I didn't tell you the minute I found out. But it was the very last person you'd ever suspect. I'll tell you that much."

At once Julie began to wonder who *was* the least likely suspect. But she got up, determined not to ask another question, ever, about Liz.

"You look awful," Marcy remarked candidly. "Borrow my make-up. Use a lot. But I don't think he'll ever send you to that convent, if you are careful."

"It isn't exactly a convent—"

"Might as well be."

"What shall I do?"

"Just suffer silently all the way through the camping trip," advised Marcy shrewdly. "Play up that you can't stand being away from him, your father I mean. Not Westerly. Not your mother. Just him."

Marcy put the fudge away, and considered. "Just don't cross him all at once. But I would seem ailing. Don't eat much. Sneak off to eat when he is fishing or digging up rocks. Act delicate."

Julie looked at her doubtfully. She was always hungry, and

it was hard to look delicate. She was really blooming with health and energy, in spite of her troubles.

She went across the campus, thinking what she could say to Michael. They were going to meet at step singing, where they could slip away without being noticed. Here he had given up his scholarship at State for her, and now she would have to tell him her father might send her East. It was too much to bear. Could she put it off until they got back from this hideous camping trip? No. She simply had to tell him. She would work on her mother, wear her down. But could her mother manage her father? It had never, so far, come to a test. And if Mike gave up a good living and a State diploma to be with her, and then she was not there, how would it look to him? How could she conceivably let this happen?

She wandered around, trying to think. If she defied her father, and he turned her out, what would happen? She was so essentially dependent that the idea of asking for a job, even waiting tables, was unthinkable.

She turned into Demetrius' place, which was not a college hangout but a place where farmers dropped in after selling their produce. Traveling salesmen ate there, and workmen from the neighborhood. Julie slid onto a stool at the counter and ordered a hamburger and milk.

"And how's about a nize piece lemon pie?" asked Demetrius, grinning.

"No thank you," she said. She ate the hamburger and part of the stale roll and drank the milk, which was well diluted with water. She was learning a lot, for Michael often ate here, and now she knew what he was getting. Not much. It was cheap, greasy, and the counter was drifted with crumbs from the previous customers. As she paid the check she had a moment of indecision. Did one tip, or not? And if so, how much? This loomed momentarily, as large as any problem she had. Finally, she laid a nickel under the plate and fled. When she got home the house looked like a haven.

Her father was in his study, bent over the desk. She went by with her face turned away. For something in this battle was vital, and she sensed it. This was not like whether she could, or could not, go to a dance, have a new dress, invite Marcy to spend the night. She went upstairs and wrote Michael a long letter, which she tore up and flushed down the toilet.

This part of the battle was hers alone. Michael had made his decision; now it was up to her to stay where he was. Somehow she had to manage, but she would have a better chance when they were on the camping trip, and she must remember that.

When suppertime came, Julie set the table. Sybil was chopping parsley to sprinkle over the omelet. Alden had gone upstairs to change his shirt, and he was aware, as he climbed the stairs, that his back felt like a hot flatiron and the muscles in his legs tightened up every time he climbed a step. He suddenly felt that he didn't want to go out tonight. He wanted to stretch out on the sofa, and read the *Scientific Monthly*, and then go to bed. He was so full of aches that for once he didn't feel hungry. He was all in.

As far as Julie was concerned, he was sure he had made the right decision, but it worried him, and he did not like to be worried. Sybil would go along with anything he decided, for she was his wife, and in the end, especially after a good camping trip, she would come around. A change of scene would do them all good. Eating outdoors, driving to new places, sleeping in a tent under the stars—that was what they all needed.

Nevertheless, for once he was not quite sure of himself. Doubt bit into him. It wouldn't be much of a life with Julie gone. But if he kept her at home, could he really keep her from seeing this football player? Although he could forecast weather with his instruments could he forecast the future? Well, he could always decide to keep her at home at the last minute, if it seemed safe.

He decided to slip down cellar and look at the camping equipment before supper. When he saw it, stacked on the floor, he felt reassured. Sybil and Julie would be right with him. They would all be together.

26.

Step singing was perhaps the best part of Commencement. The first students who graduated from Westerly had gathered on the steps of Main Hall to sing hymns the night before Commencement. Gradually, as the years passed, such nonreligious songs as "Tenting on the Old Camp Ground" and "When You Were Sweet Sixteen" were added, and now almost any song was sung. Step singing was practically the only time that students and faculty gathered together as a unit. Tomorrow they would be separated by the dignity of the rostrum, by the class seating, and by parents. But now there was an air of informality and nostalgia as the students drifted across the campus in the dusk. The faculty assembled in a group. At this hour feuds were forgotten and everybody spoke to everybody. Music and Mathematics got together. Geology and Art stood side by side.

Mark Allingham stood at the top of the broad stone steps, with Miss Nelson behind him nervously fingering her mesh bag. The rest of the Conservatory members peered forth from the curtain of ivy. It was their function to keep everyone *on key*. President Wallace made himself conspicuous in front of a Doric column, smiling and chatting. He did a good job of it, too, visibly assuming his position as head of Westerly. As soon as the singing began, he planned to slip away and steal home to knock at the back door. But now he made small jokes, and waved the students closer as they moved dreamily to the steps.

They were all there, even Sandra, swollen-eyed but persuaded "she could make it up" and get a signature on her diploma by fall. Mark started the "Alma Mater." "Westerly, we love thee, to thee we'll e'er be true," they sang. The young voices rose clearly. The middle-aged voices skipped the high notes but came out with fervor on the low ones. The elderly voices hummed huskily, worn out by years of lecturing and answering questions.

It was an emotional hour for the seniors. For four years they had talked of graduating, being free, leading their own lives. But suddenly a good many of them were not quite sure they wanted to lead their own lives. It was, in fact, frightening to leave the accustomed routine, the pattern of college life. They were like sheep long fenced in, and bewildered because the fence was gone. "Never shall we fail thee," they sang, and the girls wiped their eyes while the boys looked morose.

Michael, standing beside Julie in the shadows, only longed to be up on the top steps with the seniors. Didn't they know how lucky they were? The time between him and the sheepskin seemed interminable. But Julie was crying away into her handkerchief. Sometimes he was hard put to it to understand her. Why should she cry because another class was graduating?

The moon rose, dipping the campus in silver. Moths flickered to the portico lamps, the inevitable June bugs blundered against the globes.

They sang "Moonlight Bay" and "Peg O' My Heart" and "Way Down Upon the Swanee River." They finished with "Auld Lang Syne." Should auld acquaintance be forgot—no, they would never forget. They would come back next year, and the year after, and they would gather for step singing, and it would be the same as it had always been. Now they began to look forward ("You can't stay in one mood forever," said Marcy), and to think of all the wonderful things ahead.

But Sybil, standing beside Alden, thought sadly, what would become of them all? How many would never achieve their dreams? This was the point of departure, but for what destination? She looked at the young faces illumined by the moon, and then she looked at the faculty, always left behind, and always a year older. President Wallace, she thought, looked half ill. She must ask him about the twins; but as she started across toward the pillar she noticed that he was no longer there. Miss Nelson stood where he had been, pulling a scarf around her neck. She thought Miss Nelson looked smaller somehow, diminished. Did one always lose stature as one grew old? Well, she thought, the mullein reefs her leaves as she grows old, making a small rosette close to the chilling earth. Possibly nature reefed people in the same way. I am too full of fancies, she told herself. But Miss Nelson still reminded her of the mullein.

She hoped Alden would not see Julie beside Michael in the fringe of the crowd. He was in a bad mood, for his back must ache terribly, even though he would not admit it. Someday he would break his neck doing something ridiculous.

There wasn't, she told herself, any use worrying about his notion of sending Julie East. The way to manage Alden depended so much on timing. She would work on it on the camping trip. If only Julie would keep quiet! Deep in her heart Sybil cherished Michael. He is a real person, she reflected—quiet, reserved, gentle. Although Julie is far too young, it seems as though their love is older than they are. They may grow up to it together.

Background may be a problem. But somewhere background has to begin. Possibly gentle stock needs reinforcement now and then. She herself used solid roots to graft fine roses on, and her grandfather had grafted buds on wild apple trees, and grown sweeter, sounder apples than any in the county. So Michael's stability might temper Julie's impetuous disposition. Sybil could only hope.

Step singing over, the students melted away. The faculty exchanged last words about the morrow, Alden arguing over some detail with the Marshal. Resisting the impulse to drag him off before he got into trouble, she started on toward home. Alden, she mused, attracts trouble like a magnet. But after all, things usually worked out, and everybody understood Alden and forgave him, no matter what he said or did.

She saw Julie and Michael slipping off behind Main Hall. Fortunately Alden would not expect Julie to come home early on this of all nights. She walked slowly, savoring the smell of night. The lights were on in the Wallace house, and that reminded her she must make custard and beef broth to take over. The news that Carol was away somewhere Sybil knew by now. It sifted inevitably from the trash collector to the iceman to the cleaning woman. But so far it was mostly suspicion. Sybil herself felt that Carol might have slipped away to Milwaukee to shop, being bored and restless. No doubt she thought the twins just had another spring cold. Sybil would never have left Julie with even a sniffle, but she knew Carol was not like her. Possibly Carol would be back tomorrow, before the rumor had grown to certainty.

She walked faster when she was off campus. After all, she might have time to get the custards in the oven while Alden was still expostulating. While she was in the kitchen she would make Ella some tarts. Poor Ella. Jim was bringing her home the day after Commencement, when the steel brace was fitted. She might in time, Jim said, be able to spend most of her time in a half-reclining wheel chair. Ella was perfectly content in the hospital, but it was time she came back home.

Why should it be, Sybil wondered, that when he has done so much for so many, this kind of marriage should be Jim's lot? He needed a strong, easy woman, a bevy of children. Instead, he had Ella and a wheel chair. You had to believe there was a purpose, but it was not easy to say "Thy will be done" when it seemed so unfair.

She turned the corner onto Durkee Street and saw the house, serene in the moonlight, the porch light on. The climbing rose was heavy with bloom. Sybil fished the key out from under the coconut-fiber mat and unlocked the door. The house contained her life, she thought. It was the first long-lasting home she had shared with Alden. Here she had really grown up and come to love this man for what he was, instead of what she had expected him to be. And this house was Julie's first real home.

A house, she felt, was like a person, filled with memories, with sorrow, and with joy. It held the secrets of the years. Someday, after she died, it might begin a new cycle with a new family, surely a more peaceful family. She went to the kitchen and tied her apron on, moving efficiently as always, getting eggs, milk, sugar, and bowl, beater, custard cups. She lit a match and turned the gas on, jumping back as there was the customary explosion. She really needed a new stove.

As she slid the custards into the oven, she was pleased that Alden had not come in yet.

When she turned the oven off, she cleaned up the kitchen and set the custards to cool and went out to sit on the back steps to cool off and wait for Alden. Her head was beginning to ache, a needle of pain stitching away behind her eyes. Bother, she thought, not now, not so soon. The headaches came more often lately. When she got back from the camping trip she must get a tonic from Jim. But now there was too much to do. Perhaps the headache came because the heat wave had been so tiring.

But I wish I didn't feel so frayed, she told herself. I feel like a well that has gone dry. A well fills up, but it has to be rested now and then. Suddenly tears began to sting her eyelids, and this frightened her, for she was not a crying woman. She cried silently, the tears falling between her fingers as she held her head in her hands. She could not say why she cried, for there seemed no reason. It was nothing, but it was everything. It was all she had missed and never would have. It was Julie and Michael and the sadness of poor Miss Nelson, and the wretched home life of Jim. It was for life itself, perhaps.

And it was because the night was so beautiful and so uncaring. The shadows of the maples, the spill of moonlight, the river air. The thunder of the dam became suddenly a reproach rather than a comfort.

Julie found her there. "What are you sitting out here for? The dew is falling."

Sybil wiped her eyes quickly. "It was such a nice night—" Then with a very human reaction, she was cross. Why couldn't she sit on her own back steps, dew or no dew?

When she went in, Julie faced her, flushed and with a dangerous look in her eyes. "Mother, I am not going to be sent away to that convent. I won't."

"I don't think it is exactly—"

"Convent," repeated Julie.

Suddenly Sybil was herself again, as if being needed armored her. "You leave your father to me," she said quietly.

"You always stand up for him. No matter how awful he is, you take his side."

"You know that is not true."

Julie flung out her hands. "Nobody can make me go to that convent. If he sends me, I'll run away. I'm going to marry Michael, and I don't care what anybody says, you, or father, or Michael."

Sybil said practically, "After all, Michael would have to agree, wouldn't he? For one thing, he'd have to stop his education, and it's meant a great deal to him so far, I think."

"Nobody thinks I'm any good," wailed Julie, "but I'll show them. I will."

"I doubt whether ruining Michael's chances would show that." Sybil spoke thoughtfully. "Love that is selfish is hardly love. It's not getting what you want but giving that matters."

"Oh Mama." Julie flung herself into her mother's arms and sobbed. Sybil cradled this unhappy child of hers, but kept a quick ear for the sound of Alden coming home.

Fortunately Julie was cried out sooner than usual. "Now"— Sybil looked firmly at her—"you leave it to me. If you can keep quiet and not stir your father up, I think it will work out. But every time you fly at him, you make it more impossible for him to give in. I don't see why you can't understand that. After all, he's your own father."

Julie gave a last gulp. Then she slipped across the room. Sybil heard Alden running up the steps and spoke quickly. "Go upstairs and wash up and fix your hair." Julie vanished.

"Well, I thought I'd never get home," said Alden, striding in. "You might have waited for me."

"I had some things to do before tomorrow," she said mildly, "and I thought I might as well leave you to your business, while I did mine."

"I got held up over all sorts of things," he admitted, "but everything is cleared up now the way I wanted it."

"We must call up in the morning and find out how the twins are."

"Somebody was saying something about Mrs. Wallace," he observed.

"People always talk."

Off on his own tangent, he said, "We don't want to get our start held up in the morning. I thought I'd load the car early, and we can slip away the minute Commencement is over. I'll slide out the side door of the chapel, and meet you and Julie at the car. If we don't get started, we'll never get anywhere tomorrow."

"I have tomorrow's lunch all ready. We'll have to eat, and we'll save time if we come home first. Mrs. Novak will clean up after we go. A good hot meal to start on will mean we can drive farther before we set up camp for the night."

She made him a sandwich and heated the coffee. As she sat opposite him, he looked up at her and put the sandwich down.

"My, you look pretty tonight," he commented. "Nobody at step singing could hold a candle to you. Nobody."

27.

Alden predicted a fair day for Commencement. He was an expert weatherman, with his barometer, rain gauge and charts. People phoned incessantly to ask what the day would be like. Actually there had never been a rainy Commencement except one. But everyone wanted to be sure. There had, in fact, been so many calls the past three days that Alden got tired of it and took the phone off the hook. "Can't be bothered," he muttered. This solved the problem, until the telephone truck drove up because reports came in that the Prescott line was out of order. After the men left, the phone began ringing again, but Alden had gone to the campus and Sybil took over.

All over town phones were busy. Friends called one another to discuss what they were wearing for Commencement, whether the relatives had come, and were they going to the college luncheon or having a picnic? The final comment was always a guarded query as to whether Mrs. Wallace was home. Rumor was growing. All along the line clicks could be heard when Carol's name was mentioned. Someone had it on positive authority that she was home and sick in bed. Someone else said she had gone to Milwaukee, and with the twins sick it was a *queer* time to go off. Someone said she was seen getting on the train at the junction.

"If you'd all hang up for five minutes," an exasperated voice broke into one such session. "I have to phone the egg woman. Will asked *fourteen* seniors for breakfast and I have only two dozen eggs. You know how they eat, like locusts."

For this emergency everybody hung up. Eggs were a crisis.

The night before Commencement, things quieted down. The die was cast, the deviled eggs in iceboxes, the fried chicken wrapped in waxed paper, potatoes cooked and cubed and cooling. The picnickers would be ready to drive to the lake after the services, with their assorted relatives. Those who decided to attend the buffet luncheon on campus had country ham and scalloped potatoes ready, along with cakes and pies, so that an early supper could be served.

All over town flowered frocks were pressed and hung in the closets, white gloves and beaded bags were laid out, white slippers cleaned. The men's suits were ready, and the stiffly starched shirts that would melt in a trice on the morrow.

Julie, however, had not yet decided on what to wear. She was going over her wardrobe, wondering what she would have for clothes in case she ran away. The prospect was discouraging. Her satin evening dress had lemonade spots on the front. Her best navy serge was split under the arms (a mistake to play tennis in it). Those Peter Thompsons were not suitable for eloping, they looked girlish. Last winter's coat was shabby. As for the footwear—the patent leather slippers were cracked and rubbing with vaseline did no good. The white satin ones were smudged. Her oxfords were all right, for she seldom wore them.

In short, everything was a mess. Normally, in the fall, her mother would outfit her afresh and Miss Powers would come for a few days to cut and pin and fit. The sewing machine would whir and new dresses be pressed as they were finished.

But if she left home, she wouldn't have a thing fit to wear. Would Mike still think her lovely in old middies or a spotted evening dress? A girl, she thought desolately, can't go far without clothes. She flung everything back in the closet except the white linen she would wear to Commencement. Then she sat down on the bed, and considered the prospects. If they got married, Mike must work, and she would have to "make ends meet" as they always said. Unless she went on to graduate, she couldn't even teach school to help out. And she couldn't cook, or sew. The only thing she was good at was loving.

And how would Mike feel, giving up his education? Wouldn't he, in the end, come to hate her?

She went to the bureau and looked at the snapshots of him which ringed the mirror. In the pictures, he was always smiling or laughing, and he looked carefree. Now he was sober and had a grave look. I have done this to him, she thought, and why, when I love him so, can't I manage things better for him? And why didn't I understand about Father? I walked right into it, she told herself bitterly. I bragged about Mike. And then I tried to argue. How dumb can I be?

Her mother knocked on the door and came in to say good night. "I'm going to stitch up the hem on my duster," she said, "but I'll close the sewing-room door so it won't be noisy. Your father is puttering around down cellar. I think he's loading the car. I left some sandwiches out for you."

"Thank you, Mama," said Julie.

Julie heard the buzz of the machine (I don't know how to run one, she thought). She went downstairs to the kitchen and took a pitcher of milk from the icebox. She thought drearily of tomorrow. She might not even be able to say good-by to Mike.

Suddenly a sharp explosion sounded in the cellar, as if the

house were being blown up. She dropped the pitcher and flew down the stairs, and fell back before the fumes filling the laundry. Then she rushed on to the main cellar.

"Papa!" she screamed.

The scene was appalling. Alden seemed enveloped in flames which he was beating with a broom.

"Shut the door!" He shouted at her. "Draught."

She flew back to slam the door and ran back toward him.

"Auto robe," he called, beating away like mad. Now she saw her father himself was not on fire, but the cement floor seemed to be blazing. She dragged the old auto robe from the shelf and Alden flung it on the fire. "Pail of sand in the fruit cellar," he panted.

Julie found the sand and ran back with it and Alden flung the sand on the edge of the flame. He was skipping around like a madman. Julie passed him the rug from the foot of the stairs and he alternated slapping the fire with it and pumping away with the fire extinguisher. Meanwhile, Julie brought two pails of water from the fruit cellar and flung them wildly, dousing her father as he came across the narrowing circle. Fumes and smoke still poured out but the fire itself languished and at last died out. Smoldering blanket, rug, and broom made a stench and sizzled as Julie flung more water on them. Then it was really over.

"Open the door," said Alden, "but not all at once. Easy."

She opened the door a crack and fresh air seeped in. Alden sank down on the charred workbench and wiped his eyes. He was black as a coal pit, and his eyelashes were partially singed off. His clothes were ruined and the cellar itself was a sorry sight. Even the cobwebs under the ceiling were black.

"Oh, Papa, what happened?" Julie sat beside him, shaking.

"Confounded stuff," he said. "I ought to sue them."

"Sue who?"

"Those gasoline people." He smeared his face with his handkerchief. "They make it too inflammable, no sense to it."

"But what happened, Papa?"

"I was simply cleaning the camp stove," he said with dignity. "That was all I was doing. So I merely poured a little gasoline over the rusted spots and that was all I did."

"But I still don't understand—"

He coughed. "Well, after that, I had to light a match to look under the bench for my rags."

"Oh, Papa, you never!" Julie was horrified. "You might have killed yourself!"

She stared at him, hunched there on the bench in his sooty clothes and with bits of charred wool in his hair, along with a few broomstraws. Sweat made a few clean streaks on his face, and his eyes looked queer with half-lashes.

"Do we have to tell your mother?" he asked anxiously.

Oh dear me, thought Julie, oh dear me. She looked at the devastation, and if it hadn't been awful, it would have been funny. Her father eyed her helplessly. She began to plan rapidly. Blanket and rug could be tossed in the old sea chest, broom stuck behind the garage until it could be disposed of. If they opened one window, the air would clear faster. But the floor—what could they do about that? As for her father—she couldn't hide him.

"Where's the camp stuff?" she demanded.

"I had it in the car and all tied on," he told her. "The stove was the last thing."

"You'll have to sneak out for a new stove somehow tomorrow," she decided. "Toss the old one in the back of the coalbin. Then you get upstairs quietly (mind that fifth tread) and get a hot bath and wash your hair too. Mama's in the sewing room with the door shut so as not to make any noise." She began to laugh, and clapped her hand over her mouth. She mustn't get hysterics.

"Throw your clothes downstairs and I'll tend to them," she told Alden. "I'll do the best I can with the floor and maybe we can keep Mama from coming down here before we go."

"My eyebrows—" he said.

"You'll have to kind of hold your hand up when Mama looks you over, as if you had a headache or something. And watch where you sit on the rostrum, sit behind somebody, not on the front row."

He got up obediently, almost too stiff to stand upright by this time. Then he looked at Julie with the appealing smile of a small boy who has made a mistake.

"That's a good girl," he said, and creaked up the stairs.

Julie flew about, possessed with energy. As she charged around stowing burned things out of sight, swishing down the cobwebs, filling a pail with hot suds to swab the floor, she did not stop to think she was protecting the man who had become her enemy. She was bent on saving her father from her mother's rare but dreadful anger.

For there was no doubt about what Mama would say if she found out he had poured gasoline around and struck a match. And trying to kill himself and burn the house down the night before Commencement, of all things! No, this was not the time to upset Mama. Julie climbed up and got the window open. This was the best she could do, she decided. Maybe when it dried, the floor wouldn't look so awful.

She found her father's clothes at the bottom of the front stairs and took them down and tossed them behind the furnace. Fortunately they were his old work clothes, although he might have had on his best ones. She went upstairs again and cleaned herself up. It was a near thing, for she heard the cover pulled down over the sewing machine as she ducked into her room. She got undressed hastily. Then she remembered she never had drunk her milk and she was terribly thirsty. Her

215

throat felt raw. She slipped back down to the kitchen and poured a glass of milk.

"Are you still up?" Sybil asked, coming in. "I thought I heard you going to bed."

"I just came down," said Julie brightly. "May I bring you a sandwich?"

"Just milk, please." Sybil gave her a suspicious look. Julie acted as if she were hiding something. What was it?

"Seems to me I smell gas." She inspected the stove. "It's stronger near the door."

"I don't smell a thing." Julie was truthful enough, for her nose was no longer any good.

"Why, it seems to be coming up from the cellar." Sybil kept on sniffing. She opened the door to the cellar and jumped.

"Julie, what was your father doing down cellar?"

"Oh, I don't know, packing the car, I guess." Julie was too casual. "I was down there a while. Everything's all right."

"It smells almost like gasoline," Sybil persisted. "Was your father doing anything with gasoline?"

"Oh just cleaning up a little," said Julie. "I guess he spilled a little and it kind of caught fire. It wasn't his fault."

Sybil decided to wait and get it out of Alden, who was never able to keep anything to himself very long.

"I hope God will protect us," she said, "for it's evident we need it."

28.

As Dick Wallace had slipped away from step singing, he kept in the shadows, hoping not to be seen. Of course there was no mistaking his tall figure and long gait, but most of the college was still at the singing. Possibly a few of the alumni who had already come might be roaming around, but more likely they would be in a saloon drinking beer. The family men, of course, were helping get the children settled with their mothers.

It was a pity, Dick mused, that the bulk of the graduates didn't seem to mature. They fancied themselves as gay blades. But after all what is maturity, how measure it? Possibly it is nothing more than the ability to keep the child within from crying out, wanting the impossible. I expect, he thought dryly, we always find ourselves fully mature but seldom find others so.

As he passed the stone bench, empty for once, he wondered how many vows had been spoken there down the years, and how many broken. What happened to the golden promises, and to the young who made them? He often skimmed the alumni files and from them gathered who had married, who had children, who had been promoted in their jobs, who had moved to California or Broken Bow, Idaho. Facts were there up to and including the black-bordered page inscribed TO LIVE IN THE HEARTS OF THOSE WE LOVE IS NOT TO DIE.

But the inner meaning of those lives was a mystery. Had the four years in the ivied halls equipped them in any way to meet the burdens of living? Would the memory of Shakespeare help ease heartaches? He had believed education made for a better life, and now his own years of study did not seem much of a prop. But if he stopped believing in it, he would be lost.

The Wallace house was lighted upstairs, dark downstairs. As he stepped lightly on the grass he could smell the roses, those he had put in so hopefully when they first moved to Westerly. The roses had flourished if nothing else had. He walked around to the side of the house and stood below the window of the Dean's bedroom. He had picked up a handful of gravel from the path, and he measured the distance. He had been once the basket shooter for the team, but that was a long time ago. He hoped his aim was accurate as he cupped the gravel in his palm; he didn't want to rouse Miss Eldredge. He tossed the pebbles and thought the sound against the glass was loud enough to bring the night watchman. It would be hard to explain why he was prowling around in the dark. But nothing stirred, so he tried again, giving more weight to the throw. This time, the shade was pulled up and he saw Louise's face silhouetted against the lamplight.

"Who's there?" Her voice was low. She looked out, pulling a robe around her shoulders.

"Come down," he said, relief surging through him.

The shade dropped, the light went out. He went quickly around to the back porch to wait. He was lucky, for she might have been with Miss Eldredge in the parlor. Probably she had been up the night before spelling the nurse and was now going to bed early. He hadn't long to wait before she slipped from the house, easing the door shut behind her.

"I had to see you." He spoke with urgency. "I had to."

"Are you all right?" she asked.

"Are you?" He stepped closer to the porch. He looked at her, his love, his darling, and was suddenly shy, for with her hair loose and the long robe whispering about her feet as she took a step, she seemed strange. But when she spoke, the familiar voice reassured him.

"The twins are much better," she said. "The fever has dropped and they are eating well, and feel more comfortable." She added practically, "You shouldn't be here. We're still in quarantine."

"I just don't care," he said recklessly. The porch and the steps were a barrier, and he moved again.

"Then you may as well sit down." There was a hint of amusement in her voice. "You may break the law comfortably."

He sat down on the bottom step and she came to the rail

so that only the dark fall of steps was between them. "You must be careful," she told him, "you simply must not catch anything."

"How about you? You're exposing yourself."

"I had it when I was a child. You only have it once, so Dr. Jim tells me."

But talking about the twins was not the reason he had come and they both knew it. Abruptly he leaned closer, so he heard the intake of her breath and caught the scent of lavender from her robe. He reached his hand toward her and spoke impetuously. "I can't remember when I first knew I loved you."

She made no silly protestations. "I think it has been longer than you might guess."

"It has been forever. And it is now."

"I know."

"I can't sleep," he said in despair. "I keep going over and over everything, and I come up against the same wall."

"I, too," she said.

"And when I think of the wasted years—"

"It's hard to judge whether years are wasted or not," she commented.

"It would need a whole lifetime to find my way in your heart." He moved to the next step. "And half is already gone." His hands closed on the hem of her robe. "I need you. For all the lost years and for the years left to me."

She bent down and took his hands. They sat quietly. He was, at this time, too absorbed in his need of her to consider her need. But she loved him for his selfishness, for above all she did not want compassion. It was strange, she thought, that for two who spent most of their lives using words as tools, words were so difficult to find now. Or was it that they needed none?

But there were a few questions to ask about the practical aspects of the situation.

"Have you heard from Carol?"

"No. Nothing at all. I wired her family and wrote a letter. The wire was a problem—you know the operators."

"Perhaps she might come back, and nobody need ever know. You could—could go on as before."

"How could I?" he groaned. "How do you think I could?"

"But she might"—she chose the words carefully—"she might feel she had been wrong, and want to come."

"She's never wrong." He moved up another step, so his eyes were nearly level with hers. "Whatever she's done, she won't back down. She'd be glad to have me lose my position, so it's unlikely she would feel an urge to save it. I'll be asked to go, Louise, and I'm not fitted for anything except teaching or being a college president. You know that."

"You—would have to go somewhere far away—"

"References," he said grimly, "are the backbone of the educational world. And nobody wants a man with even a hint of scandal in his life. I'll be ruined. Think of the Board meetings at which the Chairman rises to speak about setting an example to the young people—about the sanctity of family ties, etc., etc. You've got to remember the kind of society we live in. Maybe someday it will be different, not now."

"Even if you're right," she said, "you are strong enough to manage. I am sure of it."

"Would you take a chance on me?"

"I don't think you need to ask."

"With the twins too?"

"I've mothered a good many very young freshmen"—she was smiling—"and I have always wanted children of my own."

"Oh Louise." He came up the last step and his arms tightened around her. When he kissed her, the world was new again. There was momentarily warmth and security as well as passion.

The night watchman finally lumbered past but he did not see them. The moon dropped behind the chapel dome, and the

predawn wind rose. Finally, she drew away and whispered,
"You must go."

He pressed his face against her as if to shut out the necessity. Somehow she found strength to push him away. "Dearest,
you must."

He nodded. But still he did not move away, so she crossed
the porch and went inside the house, closing the door. Inside,
she leaned against it until she heard him start down the steps.
He just couldn't stay there any longer, it was madness. She
was spent, she was once more in anguish, but the singing was
in her, over and above everything.

She moved stealthily upstairs, trying not to rouse Miss
Eldredge. Once in her room, she crept to the window and
looked out. Dick was a long time coming around the corner
of the house, but at last she saw him. He looked tall against
the stars, she thought. She got in bed facing a sleepless night.
I am old enough to know better, she told herself. I should never
have said I loved him. I've only made things harder.

Whatever happened, she must go away. They couldn't now
meet daily, talk impersonally, maintain any kind of pretense.
Even if she could manage, Dick's eyes would betray him. After
all, being Dean at Westerly wasn't important, although it had
seemed so until she fell in love.

A woman can bear anything, she thought, if she is loved.
It would be like death to go away, never to see him again, but
neither time nor distance could diminish their love.

The situation was hopeless, whether Carol decided to come
back or whether she stayed away. And all they could do now
was wait. They had only one refuge, they loved each other.
Finally she slept.

Dick walked back to Kennicott slowly, his head bent.
He almost ran into the night watchman returning from his
rounds.

"Out pretty late, aren't you?" asked Tim, swinging his lantern.

"Just taking a turn around," said Dick.

Tim's face, in the smoky glow, looked sharp and watchful. But he sighed and set the lantern down on the grass.

"Damp tonight," he said, "makes my joints ache. And all the racketing around they do at Commencement. You'd think they had been penned up all year. You know what, Mr. Wallace? I get tired of that alma mater. I'm glad when they all clear out and I only got my regular work to do. Time for my coffee at midnight again and a good bun."

"Yes, I know how you must feel." Dick looked at him speculatively. "Been here a long time, haven't you?"

"Yup. I see them come and see them go," he agreed. "And I know things about every last one of them, they'd be surprised. Mostly, I mind my own business. The wild ones generally tame down, sometimes the tame ones perk up. It all comes out in the wash, I always say."

"Do you have a family?" Dick had never thought of this.

"Got three cats. A calico and a tabby and a roving tom. A man needs company, when he spends his life walking around at night with a lantrun."

"I expect it is lonely?"

"Well, it is and it ain't. My cats sit up for me, cats like the night anyway. We have a bologna or so when I get in, and then we call it a night, I always say. Not call it a day, as you might say." He took his pipe from his pocket and filled it with bad tobacco, tamped it with a dirty thumb.

"I've seen most of what goes on at night at Westerly," he observed, lighting a match. "They all think they fool me with their fire-escape pebbles and such. But I keep an eye."

"You have been very faithful."

"Used to have an idea I could do something really big"— Tim picked up his lantern—"but what's big? Who knows?

Westerly and me get along all right. Sometimes I keep a wild one out of trouble, talk, and watch. And they all know I'm around, in case they get scared. Never mind, old Tim's here, they say. Gives a man a good feeling. Figure it's a good thing to be president, but a good thing to be night watchman too."

He lifted his cap, gave Dick a shrewd glance. "Glad you could have a chance to see her," he said. "Didn't mean to bother you going by. Notice I kept the lantrun low?" He chuckled.

Dick held out his hand. "You're a good man," he said.

"Just figure to do my job and mind my business," said Tim, "same as you do. Good night, now. Maybe you ought to turn in, seeing as it's Commencement coming up."

Dick walked on slowly to Kennicott and sneaked up the front steps. Maybe, he thought, a young man wouldn't do as well as old Tim. Wisdom took a long time to acquire.

He didn't want to meet any starry-eyed seniors. He knocked the silver bowl from the hall table, and every step protested as he went up to his suite. But nobody appeared, and the halls were quiet. He undressed and sat on the bed, thinking about Louise. What had he done to her life and how should he plan? She asked for nothing, gave so much. But what had he given her except trouble? Surely his love was a burden. Why, when he loved her so, could he not protect her? He was old enough to know better, he told himself.

But this was no April love. He couldn't push it aside, forget it. Could he possibly make a home for Louise and the twins in some remote place? They couldn't live without money. He hadn't saved much, because Carol wasn't a saving woman. Aside from his insurance, there was a small savings account, a few shares of stock. Westerly owned the house. His salary had never been adequate.

There wasn't any use in trying to plan until he had some word from Carol. She might be punishing him by going off, in which case she might come back, ready to pick up where they left off. It was incredible to think he had lived with her so long and yet knew her so little that he could not guess what she might do.

She could at least have left a note or sent some word. This was a final cruelty, and anger was bitter in his mouth. He fought against it, for it would only confuse him. He must keep his head, get through Commencement. And wait to see what Carol was going to do. However tenuous the ties between them, surely she would answer his letter. Or surely her parents would answer his wire.

Both he and Louise were accustomed to meeting problems directly, as they had met various college crises. They were not, he thought, suited to indecision, temporizing. But this personal problem they had no way of solving. They were trapped.

He regretted his letter now it had been posted. Why expect Carol to worry about the children when she had abandoned them while they were ill? You couldn't build in a sense of responsibility in a woman—or in a man either. It was a thing never grafted on.

Then the memory of the night came back to him, his love, his darling warm in his arms. It was a mystery that made everything plain.

Because she loved him, he would fulfill his obligations with dignity. Because she loved him, he would not be defeated.

And finally he slept.

29.

Day dawned with a promise of heat, for the sky was a haze of pink. When Alden went outside around five-thirty, the grass was cool with dew but the air soft. He snaked around the yard potting squirrels, for he knew they would get in the attic while he was away and eat corners from his old *Geographics*. Confounded nuisances.

The sound of his gun woke everybody in the block, but they were used to it. It was just Professor Alden, and they all looked forward to a nice quiet vacation while he was away. He was not in top form this morning, for he wasted one shot. Jacking up the house and fighting the gasoline fire had certainly made his lumbago worse. However he shot several squirrels, went to check on the car, pump up the spare with the bicycle pump, tighten a few tie ropes.

He rolled the car out to the drive and routed Julie and Sybil up. It was already seven o'clock and no use lying around.

Sybil had the pancakes ready by the time Julie came down, looking martyred. "I don't see why we have to get up at the crack of dawn," Julie protested.

"Your father gets nervous on Commencement day." Sybil melted the butter. "He's anxious to get away. And he always hates to say good-by to his favorite seniors."

"I'm not hungry." Julie slapped the plates on the table.

"You'd better put some cold cloths on your eyes before we go," advised Sybil. "They look puffy."

Julie looked out the back door. "Mama!" she cried out. "We can't go to Commencement like that! It looks like a gypsy wagon!"

Sybil went over and looked out, and sighed. "It can't be helped," she said. "You know he won't unlash all those things now. He's all packed up to go."

"I'd rather be dead than go up to Commencement in that outfit," Julie cried. "I don't see why we have to put up with it!"

"If you want to influence your father about next year"—

Sybil was firm—"you'd better put up with almost anything. If you upset him, I won't be able to do a thing with him."

Julie ran upstairs to put cold cloths on her eyes, for she didn't want to look like a hag if she saw Mike. Afterward, she dabbed powder on her face and went despondently downstairs where Alden was already soaking his pancakes in butter and syrup. He stared at her as she sat down.

"What have you done to your face?" he asked sharply. "You look like an actress! Go wash yourself."

Outraged, Julie slammed the door.

"Alden, try not to badger her," Sybil said.

"What do you mean badger her? She comes in looking like a Halloween mask. She can't go to Commencement like that."

Sybil resisted an impulse to pour the jug of syrup down his neck. Why couldn't he, just once, be tactful?

"I don't think these pancakes are as light as usual." He added fuel to the fire.

"Go eat somewhere else," snapped Sybil. "I couldn't care less."

"What's the matter with you?" he asked. "I only said the—"

"Eat your breakfast," she said wearily, "and stop talking."

"Well"—he sounded hurt—"I work myself to skin and bones getting ready for a nice trip as soon as Commencement is over, and Julie comes down looking a sight and you bite my head off just because I remark that the pancakes—"

"If you don't hush, you'll be taking that wonderful camping trip alone."

"I plan a nice—"

"I know." She was already clearing the table. "I've heard it all. But you needn't think the trip is for me or Julie. You know I'd rather stay at home than go traipsing all over the country at thirty miles an hour and camping in nests of snakes."

"That was only one time." He spoke with dignity. "And they weren't rattlesnakes, just a few copperheads."

"Snakes," repeated Sybil, "snakes."

"Well, it wasn't my fault." He rose to the challenge. "If you hadn't insisted on seeing the view from Lover's Leap at sunset, I wouldn't have had to pitch camp in the dark. I told you at the time there are lover's leaps all over the state. I sometimes think," he added morosely, "that all the Indians did was leap in those early days."

He got up and glared at this impossible wife of his, mother of his impossible daughter.

"I," he announced, "shall go and get my robes on. I trust you and your daughter will see fit to accompany me." He strode out.

Well, we are certainly off to a good start, thought Sybil. A beautiful Commencement day. Then she felt laughter bubbling inside, for Alden did look funny when he stuck his chest out like a balloon. I ought to have more patience, she thought, and not fly at him like Julie. It's the heat and being so tired and nervous.

When she got upstairs, Alden stood by the mirror adjusting his robe. The mercury in his emotional thermometer had dropped to normal as he contemplated himself in the trappings of his office. He felt uplifted, important. But he looked no older than the seniors, thought Sybil, with his rosy cheeks, tumble of hair, bright eyes.

"I'll fry in this," he complained. "I'm not wearing anything underneath but my underwear."

"But suppose something happened and your robe blew up— or you fell down—how would you look, just in long underwear?"

"I won't fall down. I'll be cooler."

No, she could never understand him, she thought. At one minute his modesty was excessive, even to wearing shirts over his bathing suit. The next he was going to Commencement in his underwear.

227

"You aren't going to wear *those* shoes?" she asked.

"Certainly I am. They won't show at all and my feet will hurt if I stand around in this heat with my best ones on."

Sybil gave up. She should be thankful he hadn't decided on his bedroom slippers. Now he turned his back as she slipped into her pink dress and hooked it up. She put on her pearl earrings, remembering as always the day her mother pierced her ears and pulled the thread through.

Alden fussed with his hood as she tucked flyaway strands of hair under her net. She knew he wanted to be admired, so she moved over and folded the bands of the hood so as to show the rich colors.

"There, you look handsome," she said. "Remember to pull your robe down in front as you start the processional. It hikes up. Watch the tassel on your mortarboard too. You had it on the wrong side last year."

They went downstairs and Sybil pinned on her hat.

"Tell Julie to hurry up," Alden said.

"We have plenty of time. Why don't you go out and start the car?"

My goodness, this is going to be a hot one, she thought, for already perspiration trickled down her chemise. She called to Julie to come along. Why did she always keep them waiting? When Julie did appear, she looked sullen. As they went out to the car she could understand Julie's feeling about it. She did think he might have waited to lash the tent and the poles on the roof until after Commencement. The box of kindling on one runningboard didn't look well either, not to mention that coffin on the other.

The car was so jammed that Julie would have to leap over the front seat and perch on a pile of bedding in back. With an ounce more of luggage the car wouldn't run at all. Perhaps she could persuade Alden to park behind the gymnasium, and they could walk to the chapel from there.

228

"You go on," said Julie. "I'll walk. I simply cannot ride to Commencement in that—that junk pile."

"Let's not upset Papa any more," said Sybil. "Get in. I'll see to it we park out of sight."

"What were you doing?" Alden peered over the wheel. "Could have dressed five times by now."

Sybil braced herself as the car bounded away. One of her hatpins fell out, and she retrieved it and jabbed her head getting it back in place. It did seem to her that when she rode with other drivers, it was smoother. With Alden at the wheel it was more like horseback riding.

Already people gathered along the campus walk, the women shading their faces under the wide hats, the men already sweating in their best suits. The seniors milled about on the steps of Main Hall where the class marshal tried desperately to form them into a line for the procession to the chapel. He was having a rough time, for they kept breaking ranks, running back and forth, drifting away, wandering back. It was enough to drive a man mad. He kept waving his arms and pleading with them and blowing his whistle.

The faculty, assembled under the elm at the front of the chapel lawn, was no easier to regiment than the students. The faculty marshal rushed back and forth, gown flying, mortarboard slipping. With the faculty, the exact order of the procession was a matter of extreme importance. The members walked in pairs, preceded by the President. But this did not settle who walked with whom nor which department went first. The chart was in the marshal's hand, but it did him no good to refer to it.

When Alden puffed up (Sybil had won out on the parking) he discovered right away that he was lined up with the head of the Spanish Department. He had no idea of marching beside a nonbasic subject like Spanish, and said so. Meanwhile the Conservatory faculty was in a turmoil because they were directed to fall in behind the Art Department. That implied that

229

Art took precedence over Music which was ridiculous. (Somebody had to be last, thought the marshal wildly. They can't all be at the head of the line.) Arguing, appeasing, explaining, he went up and down.

Alden, however, simply got out of the group entirely and went to the marshal to deliver his ultimatum. The marshal gave in (and next year let somebody else take this impossible job). He mollified Alden with the head of the History Department as a companion. Alden felt the History Department was respectable, for the history of man was related to the history of the earth, though not as important.

This, however, aligned the Spanish professor with the head of the Greek Department, and made more trouble. There was a constant feud between these two. What Spanish literature could be mentioned in the same breath with Sophocles? asked the Greek professor. Aside from the highly overrated *Don Quixote*, what was worth studying? Nevertheless the marshal paired the two off, by conceding that Greek might be a step ahead. Dr. Alvarez fell in, not quite even with his colleague. He knew how peculiar Americans were, and all he really wanted was to get out of this unbearable sun and sit down. He was not in the mood to defend the splendor of Spain. He yearned to get this dull affair over for another year, and go home to the cold broiled chicken and bottle of wine his wife would have ready.

The fact was, he and the young French instructor took alternate trips to Milwaukee, boarding the train with empty suitcases and returning with heavy ones. By this means they kept themselves stocked with good wines, and did not endanger their jobs. So far, nobody had inquired why they went to Milwaukee so frequently. Their little dinners were a touch of civilization in this dull community.

When Mark scooted past, carrying his portfolio, the faculty straggled into a semblance of order. Mark had stopped to phone the hospital to check on Marjorie, so he was late. The boy who pumped the organ was late, also.

President Wallace stood waiting for the signal to march. How childish they all were, battling for precedence. What did it matter? He wondered idly whether Noah had an equal struggle getting the animals in the ark. It would be a relief to get inside and he wished that for once the faculty would behave.

At last the whistle blew, and Mark began the processional. The parents and townspeople were seated and as "Pomp and Circumstance" swept the chapel, President Wallace, tall and handsome though pale, walked with dignified steps down the aisle, followed by his faculty, more or less in step.

Then came the seniors, looking awed. It was an impressive sight. The faculty hoods shone with bands of gold, scarlet, green and deep blue. The robes enveloped them with dignity. The seniors, in the plain caps and gowns, looked suddenly too young, too vulnerable to leave the security of Westerly. A good many women cried in their handkerchiefs, and some of the men blew their noses as quietly as possible.

This was the hour, the end of the year, the culmination of four years for some of them. It tasted of victory also to the faculty, who had struggled day in and day out to provide a passable education for the graduates. Behind lay the endless conferences, the special help, the make-up exams, not to mention the private teaching of the gifted. Childish they might often be, and petty, but a singleness of purpose drove them on. They were called to teach, and for this calling they gave up much. Now, even to the casual visitor, they looked impressive.

Alden kept bumping into the man ahead of him, and muttered that they were going too slow. Why not step along and get there? he asked himself. Nonsense to creep down the long aisle like turtles. Finally they climbed the steps to the rostrum and pushed the chairs about, while the seniors filed into the first two rows in the nave. The boys held their heads up stiffly, and the girls were solemn. Even the rowdiest looked angelic.

Alden kept a sharp eye out as he chose his chair. There was invariably one chair that collapsed. They were folding chairs furnished by Marston's funeral home and had seen many years of service. This time it fell to poor Miss Nelson's lot to take the worst one, for her eyes were weak with crying. She teetered into the lap of Mr. Parker, who managed to right her before she went flat. Alden, for once, sat in the back row, hoping his singed eyebrows wouldn't be conspicuous. He also sat at the end nearest the steps so he could bolt the minute the benediction was over.

Despite all the airing and pressing of robes, a strong smell of moth balls rose. It set Miss Finch into a spasm of coughing so Dr. Peake, sitting next to her, had to slap her on the back. Finally a glass of water was passed along the row to her, along with some Smith Brothers cough drops.

When things quieted down, Reverend Mallory rose to begin the long prayer. Knowing what was expected of him, he stifled his impulse to give a brisk and brief one, and launched into the customary peroration. He asked God to bless these young people about to fare forth into the world seeking new and wider horizons. He blessed the parents whose sacrifice and vision made their education possible. He blessed the faculty (squirming uneasily behind him) who had steered another class safely toward a new shore, and he asked God to bless those still enjoying the benefits of the years in the shadow of the ivied halls. He asked God fervently to bless the good people of the town in whose midst Westerly dispensed moral, spiritual, and mental largesse to eager young people.

Then, with a barely perceptible sigh, he asked God to bless the land of liberty and all the people therein, especially the leaders of the country, granting them wisdom, strength in their difficult tasks, and inspired leadership.

Almost nobody listened. The seniors thought about them-

selves, astonished that they were really graduating. They left
God to Reverend Mallory. They were triumphant but fearful.
The parents and relatives were moist-eyed, alternately wiping
their eyes and pulling at their clothes, which were beginning to
stick to the newly varnished pews. Heat rose in a shimmering
wave, and many programs fanned. The faculty, reassured that
Reverend Mallory was keeping to tradition, creaked in the folding chairs. They went back to their own problems.

Alden was figuring how to get a new camp stove on the way
out of town so Sybil wouldn't notice it. He wasn't accustomed
to any kind of secret life, and it bothered him. And when she
cooked the first meal on it she was sure to notice it was new
and shiny. Mr. Parker was in a dilemma too. He had let the two
young teachers and the widow all assume he would escort them
to the luncheon. And he couldn't, at the moment, think of a
feasible excuse for skipping out. Miss Nelson was folding and
unfolding her handkerchief, thinking this was the last time she
would sit on the rostrum in her robes. She should be, and was,
grateful that she was to go to Dr. Jim's and help with his wife,
but this was the end of an era. Mark was surreptitiously pulling
out the stops for the anthem. Dr. Burghley, his head bent, was
going over the one page in his address he had been unable to
memorize. And President Wallace was agonizing over what to
say to the Board about Carol. Could he offer a vague statement
in case she did decide to come back? Or wasn't this ethical? It
would take, he knew, some time to find a new president. Why
hadn't he asked Louise? He must phone her as soon as Commencement was over, if he could sneak off to phone, and get
her advice without disclosing anything to the operator.

What with the luncheon, the alumni, the departing graduates and dozens of parents, he would be surrounded. He also
had to take care of Dr. Burghley.

Dr. Jim sat at the end of the front row where he could keep
an eye on the graduating class, for now and then a girl fainted,

233

and occasionally an emotional mother collapsed. He was also near the steps in case he was called out on an emergency. He was hoping he could get Ella home without its being too much of a strain for her. He hoped the Novak girl who was coming to cook would work out satisfactorily. He hoped Ella and Miss Nelson would get on. He had made it clear, he hoped, to Miss Nelson that it was an arrangement to try out. For himself, he felt Miss Nelson was an ideal solution. She was gentle, un-aggressive, and so eager. She could never make Ella jealous, and she would never be demanding. It would be pleasant to come home and find her fluttering about, friendly as a wren. Sometimes she could play for him if he had an hour or so at home. "Hearts and Flowers" and "Voices of Spring."

Hope-hope-hope, he reflected, was what men lived by. But everything possible had been done to realize this one. Sybil had the house shining, stocked with food, flowers everywhere. How had she found time to do so much? She had even sent Alden to fetch Miss Nelson's shabby luggage over. And the sun porch was finished and ready for Ella. Ella herself was in fine spirits, for although she hated to leave the hospital, she felt reassured that she wouldn't have any responsibility. Sybil was going to teach her china-painting and she planned a choco-late set with roses and forget-me-nots. And her interview with Miss Nelson had been most successful, for Miss Nelson had said how young and pretty she looked, almost a bride.

Sybil and Julie sat with the faculty wives and children just behind the seniors. Sybil wished Alden would stop fidgeting. Every time there was an instant of silence, you could hear his chair groan.

She wanted to think. She had to plan a campaign to keep Julie at home, and for this, Julie was a problem also. She must limit her dates with Mike, go out occasionally with other boys, stay home now and then. She would have to grow up enough to make sacrifices, that was what it boiled down to. A great deal depended on this camping trip. If Julie would try—make Alden feel secure—if she would.

Julie spent her time trying to see the back of Mike's head. By craning her neck she could see half of it, a curious green from the light through the stained glass window nearby. Even this was worth it. She was going to fly out the minute the benediction was over and meet him behind the laundry for a last few moments. Otherwise, she would die.

Mike couldn't turn around and look for her. But he knew she was looking at him. He was divided between absolute envy of the seniors who were getting that parchment, and anxiety about next year. Giving up the State offer had been a difficult decision, for Mike was practical. He was probably a fool to send that wire saying he wouldn't accept that gyp scholarship. But somehow, after he had made up his mind he ought to take it, he just couldn't. He didn't, after all, want a degree based on what his honesty knew was cheating, pure and simple. Even without Julie, he didn't think he would have gone to State, to be a chiseler. He had always stood on his own feet, and he guessed he always would. Favors he had never had. And he had a basic faith in himself which even Julie's father had not shaken. He would make out, and he would stay at Westerly and get an honest diploma. Like those piled on the desk up there, all tied with blue.

When Mark began the anthem everyone forgot their problems. The organ chose this time to give forth a series of screeching wails. (They needed a new organ.) Mark pulled and pushed stops and the sound only increased. Mark, sweating, worked away at it. Nothing helped. The chapel was inundated with raucous sound. Dr. Burghley lost his place in his papers. Alden jumped up and ran to the back where the boy was still pumping and hauled him off. The sound died away in a series of moans. The graduates began to snicker and giggle, with the relief of tension. Then Mark lifted his hand and started the anthem without the organ, and as the music rose, he skipped out behind, himself. The janitor was already working at the stuck valves and the boy was sniffling.

The anthem wavered away and by the time it ended, Mark had the organ supposedly fixed enough to finish the service. He slapped the boy into action to pump again and got back on the bench.

It wasn't a good beginning for Dr. Burghley, but he began his address bravely. For a controversial figure, he was terribly dull, just booming platitudes. It was unfortunate that the page was mislaid, and midway of saying, "and now as we look forward to a new day—" the new day was not there. He cleared his throat. "We look forward," he began again. "We look forward to—" Then he simply had to skip to the next page and ended, "and with God's help, we shall accomplish His will."

The violin solo was a welcome change and the organ responded. President Wallace spoke briefly, welcoming the seniors as new alumni. They would, of course, forget a great deal they had learned. (He waited for the laughter.) But some things they would remember. He hoped they would remember the friendships, the inspiration of their professors, and the excitement of learning. They would go on learning, for life itself was the great educator. And Westerly wished them Godspeed.

Then Mark pulled out every stop on the organ and boomed into the "Alma Mater." But at the beginning of the chorus the organ boy fell asleep and the vox humana faded away. Mark kept on hopefully pedaling but no sound came. This time one emotional graduate began to have hysterics and was hustled away. And Alden sped back and began to pump while whacking the boy with one foot. Not being a regulated pumper, he alternately pumped madly and stopped while whacking the boy, so the organ at one moment blasted everyone's eardrums and the next ebbed to a sigh.

The Valedictorian's speech suffered. He grew so pale that

Dr. Jim edged forward ready to catch him if he pitched to the floor. This had happened before. But the Valedictorian managed to steady himself by clutching the desk, only sending fifteen diplomas flying. Dr. Peake crawled up behind the desk and fished them up.

Then the graduating class filed up one by one to reach for the diplomas. President Wallace gave them out with a smile and a handclasp. Of course, as usual, nobody got his own diploma; they were all hopelessly scrambled. But they could sort them out afterward, so this wasn't a crisis.

Everyone stood up for the hymn.

"Fling out the banner, let it float, Skyward and seaward high and wide," they began rather fearfully, waiting for the organ to go off again. "The sun that lights its shining folds, The cross on which the Savior died."

Alden sang louder than anybody. It was about over. "Fling out the banner! Wide and high, Seaward and skyward, let it shine: Nor skill, nor might, nor merit ours, We conquer only in that sign."

Silly words, he thought, just mishmash. As if we didn't have skill and might and merit quite on our own. It's not all on God. During the final chorus, he saw a wasp circling around. Wasps had an affinity for the chapel, especially in the heat. Alden made a grab for it. He could always catch a fly with one swoop. But the wasp angled out of reach, settled on Dr. Burghley's bald head momentarily, then winged on to settle on Miss Nelson's hat. Alden crept back of the row, crouching. Once behind Miss Nelson, he brought his palm down with a lightning smash on her hat. Miss Nelson uttered a squeak as her hat fell over her face. Her chair tilted and Alden clutched at it. As the banner flung out the last time, so did Miss Nelson, pitching again into Mr. Parker's lap.

Mr. Parker was not prepared and narrowly missed going down the steps with Miss Nelson on top of him. Mark, sensing the commotion, peered around the console, and gave a tremendous all-out on the organ, and since he had been nursing it along, the effect was startling. A few timid souls said afterward they felt the building had exploded.

Mr. Parker and Miss Nelson were retrieved by willing hands, and Alden bumped back to his seat. He's gone mad, thought Sybil, creeping around and looming up and creeping back. But Alden was grinning. He'd fixed that wasp all right, dead as a doornail. Miss Nelson, shaking, got her hat back in place, although it was squashed.

Reverend Mallory rose to give the benediction. Nothing could shake his calm, for he was used to church. Small boys shot paper balls, babies squealed, and regularly old Mr. Bean had a fit in church. Also the recently bereaved usually cried it out during prayer. Well, he thought, God puts up with it, so I certainly can!

"Make his face to shine upon us," he murmured, raising his voice, "and give us peace."

Mark swung into the recessional, hoping for the best, and the now graduated class marched down the aisle clutching the diplomas and looking dazed. The faculty followed, moving faster than the music, anxious to get away. They all had appointments with summer.

The parents and guests gathered their gloves and programs and fished for missing bags and jammed the aisles on the heels of the faculty. A beautiful, memorable Commencement they all felt, never to be forgotten. The janitor, closing the windows, took a more rational view. "Same as always," he said. "They come and they go. Mite hotter than usual, though."

30.

At about the time Dr. Burghley began to speak, the telegraph boy wheeled past the chapel, whistling. "Get Out and Get Under," he whistled as he pedaled onto the campus. Nobody was around to observe him, but it wouldn't have mattered. Ordinarily a telegram was the talk of Winnebago; at Commencement they were common as grasshoppers. Congratulations came in by the dozen from relatives too far away to get to graduation; wires from previous graduates poured in. Parents wired about being met at the station.

But this particular telegram made the boy jumpy and he whistled to keep up his courage. He brought up at President Wallace's house and kicked the bike rest under and went up the front steps, the whistle drying up in his throat. He rang the bell.

Dean Richardson peered through the letter slot. "We are in quarantine," she explained. "Didn't you see the sign? Get back off the porch."

"I got a telegram," he said. "They tried to phone but couldn't get no answer."

"Any answer," she said mechanically.

"So when they couldn't get no answer, they sent me along with it. They said to see did you want to wire back or what."

"Leave it on the top step," she directed, "and go down to the walk and wait. You don't want to catch anything."

"No, ma'am, I don't." He dropped the message and scuttled out of reach of the germs.

The Dean stepped out and caught up the telegram. It was addressed to Dick, but she didn't care. It had to be from Carol, and she had to know what was in it immediately.

When she read it, the words jumped out at her, and she pitched forward. Miss Eldredge, bustling along to see who had rung the bell, grabbed at her and kept her head from hitting the floor.

"Stop that!" she shouted. "Stop it, I say."

The Dean swayed against her, Miss Eldredge's words slapping her out of the faint. Deftly Miss Eldredge hooked one foot around the nearest hall chair and pulled it forward enough to ease the Dean into it.

"Hold your head down," she commanded, "and sit there." Then she dashed off and was back at once with a glass of brandy. It was the last drop in the house, and she hoped she wouldn't have to try that cherry bounce as restorative.

"Swallow," she said, "and then put your head down again."

Some of the brandy spilled but some went down. She watched with a professional eye until the Dean drew a long breath.

"Now what's this about?" Without waiting for an answer, Miss Eldredge scooped up the telegram and read it. She made an odd clucking sound. "Well, don't it beat the Dutch!" she exclaimed.

The Dean began to shiver violently, and Miss Eldredge gave her the last swallow of brandy. "I'm—all right now," said the Dean.

"Just lean on me," said Miss Eldredge, and she half-carried the Dean to the sofa and covered her with a shawl. "Keep your feet up," she admonished. "I'll handle this."

Miss Eldredge herself was used to sudden death, shock, grief, in fact to everything life had in the books for human beings. But this, she admitted to herself, was a thing. This really was. The boy outside was getting restless and came up on the step and stamped his feet loudly. He didn't want to stand around all day.

"You hold your horses," called Miss Eldredge. "You get paid

by the hour." She took the pad from the telephone table. She wrote a sentence, crossed it off, broke the point of the pencil and picked up the lead. This wire had to be answered and fast.

"Now you take this down on your pad," she called, "and mind you copy it right. Same address as on the one you just brought. Ready? I shall come East immediately. Terrible shock. Richard." She waited a moment and said sharply, "Read it back to me."

"There isn't any last name," he protested.

"They'll know who he is," she said. "Get going."

She watched him wheel away and then went back to the Dean.

"I sent back a wire," she told her, "just to hold things off until the poor man gets through with Commencement. We could hardly drag him out of the middle of the speeches. I always say what you don't know won't hurt you."

"But I can't believe it's true." The Dean raised her head.

"Keep it down," said Miss Eldredge. "I'm going to fix you some broth in a minute and some toast. It's no time for you to give up."

"But I can't believe—"

"Nobody ever believes in death," Miss Eldredge commented, "no matter how it's wrapped up. But as for that woman, God rest her soul, I wouldn't go so far as to say she can't be spared better than some I could name. And as for accidents, believe me, I've seen enough to figure sometimes people make their own. I mean, recklessness and carelessness go all the way through."

"But there wasn't any reason."

"Reason enough, if you want to look at it. That one wouldn't stop to think about her children and husband, would she? She was just bent on where she was going. So she wouldn't be one to look around her when she crossed a street, would she? No, she'd expect to get to the far side. Now you lie back until I get a tray for you."

The Dean had no idea of disobeying. The idea that Carol had been killed crossing a street was incredible, her mind could not receive the fact. Carol was too young, too strong, and too beautiful, whatever else she was. Was her headlong flight destined to destroy her or was it unexplainable? If she had stayed home she would now be sitting in chapel, bored, hot, but alive. She would have gone to the luncheon, arrogant and withdrawn, pushing the chicken salad aside, nibbling a dry roll.

Now she was dead. And it was impossible to connect death with her beauty, with that flawless skin, disciplined figure, swift walk. Life had never nicked her loveliness, her youth was as if preserved in amber. The grave had no traffic with such a woman. And yet it had.

"I have faith," said the Dean, sitting up. "I believe in God Almighty Who made heaven and earth."

She did indeed have faith, and quite aside from her personal beliefs, she had studied enough philosophy, comparative religion and the history of Christianity to have a good deal more perspective than was in most sermons. So she wondered whether Carol had, in some strange way, finished what she was born for, or whether her own failure as a woman had doomed her.

"Now you drink your broth and eat the toast," said Miss Eldredge firmly. "You have to keep your strength up. It always makes sense to eat after a shock. Makes sense to eat after a funeral too. Kind of squares you away with living again."

The Dean sipped the broth. "You are a wise woman," she said.

"I'm going up now and give the twins their sponge bath," Miss Eldredge told her. "It's so hot today. Then I'll give them their trays. You stay put until I get through."

The broth was hot, the toast crisp. Miss Eldredge, thought

the Dean, must be lined with gold. A very present strength. She herself was all right now, ready to take up the burdens. She must protect Dick, she must attend to all the details— and there were so many. She had no business giving way. She got up and carried her tray to the kitchen.

Last night his love had swept the world away, and surely now she could justify his love, if love could ever be justified. She began to plan, and her years of planning stood in good stead.

She went to his study, which she had not entered before. It was filled with his presence. She sat at his desk and pulled a pad of paper toward her. First she must make a reservation for him on the late train. She must pack for him, hunting up fresh shirts, socks, underwear. Then there was the report for the newspaper.

She sat, tapping her pencil, thinking quite calmly. Once you decided to be devious, she thought, things occurred to you. For instance, Carol had been suddenly called home. (Don't elaborate on that. Methinks the lady doth protest too much was still true.) She hadn't been well, she did not wish to—no, never mind that. She was on her way to a business appointment, that was better. She had evidently not noticed the policeman's signal at a crossing and had been run down.

It was amazing how it fitted together. She could almost believe it herself. There would, inevitably, be curious phone calls, some gossip. But nobody would know the truth, that Carol had deserted her children and her husband.

She finished the news release and decided to send it early in the morning. By then the campus would be given over to the reunions. The college students would be gone. By next fall, she thought dryly, they would hardly remember Mrs. Wallace, who had kept to herself so much. But as she looked at the report, she faced a new problem. Pinching her lips together, she wrote carefully, *Interment will be in the family burial plot in Bar Harbor.* It probably would be; if not, who would know?

There was one more thing to do. She took a sheet of the presidential stationery and wrote a statement for the *Alumni Bulletin. Carol Wallace, beloved wife of—* To live in the hearts of those we love is not to die, she thought.

Perhaps she was wrong, taking all the responsibility. But who had a better right to try to save Dick? Who indeed? She sealed the envelopes. Then she went down the hall to the twins, who were now well enough to be fretful.

"You oughta been in before," they said, in unison.

She sat down and made up guessing games for them, told them the story of the Ice Queen. She promised a surprise for tomorrow, kissed them warmly.

"It's nice with you here," said Carol. "I wish you'd stay."

"I don't want to get well if you go off," said Dick.

"Well, we're friends now, so we'll not be too far away."

"I like it with you right down the hall," persisted Carol. "You aren't ever too busy to come."

Miss Eldredge was cleaning up the kitchen. "Haven't done so much housework in years," she grumbled. "I got chops in. May as well eat early and get it over with."

"I'll fix the salad."

"You have a good hand with dressing," said Miss Eldredge. "Too bad you can't teach the dormitory cooks. Food is awful there."

"There isn't much money."

"Don't cost any more to cook something right than it does to cook it wrong," observed Miss Eldredge.

When they sat down, Miss Eldredge said, "I figured you wouldn't want to call him until he's through at college. Better let him finish what he's supposed to do."

"I thought I'd call in half an hour."

"Sensible," approved Miss Eldredge. "After all, what's happened is over. No use stirring people up. Far as I can see, he can keep on being president if this is kept quiet enough. You and me can manage it."

"I couldn't have managed without you." The Dean smiled.

"Likewise," said Miss Eldredge. "I'd as soon be quarantined with you any time. Feel free to call me. I enjoyed every minute, even you going out on the back porch half the night to meet somebody."

"Oh, dear—" The Dean blushed.

"What I say is more power to you." Miss Eldredge took a biscuit. "You know these are pretty good, considering we made them!"

"I want your recipe for smothering chicken," the Dean said.

"I'll write it down before I go."

Luncheon over, they washed the dishes together. And then the Dean went to the phone to locate Dick. If he couldn't make the night train, he would have to take the one tomorrow night. The best she could do was call around and leave messages for him to call his home.

31.

"I'll walk home," Julie had said to Sybil. "Have to see some people to say good-by—"

"Well, don't keep your father waiting too long," warned Sybil. "He won't like it."

Julie darted like a minnow through the stream of people. She made for the side door and ran into President Wallace, also hurrying out.

"Don't tell on me," he said, "I have things to do before the luncheon."

They both sped down the side street, missing the crowd in front of the chapel. Julie ran so fast her hair blew back in wings. Her dress was damp with perspiration and the skirt clung. The sound of the Commencement crowd died away as she crossed campus and it seemed suddenly very quiet.

But when she saw Mike standing there behind the laundry, the air was full of music. He caught her as she flung herself at him and for a few moments they just held each other, quite out of time.

"Oh, I'll simply die being away from you," Julie said at last.

"It won't be so long," he answered, and his voice was husky.

"It's like forever." She pressed against him.

"Well, it's all right," he said, "you're here now and you're real. That's the main thing. I had that dream again last night, a funny dream. I don't like it. I dream I'm in a battle and I hear the guns and it's dark and I'm scared. I keep calling to you. A silly dream."

"It's all that history you took," she said. "There's no sense dreaming about battles nowadays."

"No. We got our own and that's plenty." He kissed her. "You're a little thing. You take care of yourself while you're gone, hear?"

"I'll write every day," she promised, "but I'll have a hard time trying to mail anything. You write me every day and save the letters."

"I will. But you know I'm no good at words." He kissed her again. "I'm better at this."

"Oh, Mike, how can I go away?" she wailed.

"Just think of us. And you better go now. Let's be careful." She flung her arms around him. "Mike, this is for always."

"Always."

She pulled herself away and ran across the campus. It was almost deserted, for the luncheon was on and the picnickers off to the lake. A few stragglers from Kennicott lugged bags down the steps, and one or two day students carried overdue books to the library. When she turned into Durkee she saw the car was there, looking like a stuffed elephant. There was a finality about it. This was the end of the troubling year, the passionate spring. No matter what happened, there would be no year like this. She would go back to the worst days of it, just to have it again. There was something dreadful about the year being gone.

But as she hesitated on the porch, she took another step toward maturity. Next year she would have patience, make the best of things. Next year she would behave much better.

Alden was fuming. They couldn't leave right after lunch, he had to go back to college. Some of the Board members wanted to question him about his museum. As if he didn't know what was best for the college. And he wasn't being paid for staying on after Commencement either. It wasn't his fault they all lived in Chicago or Milwaukee and couldn't run up any time.

They had lunch and Sybil said it would give her time to do some odds and ends that needed doing. Alden ate his lunch and flew off in a terrible temper. He never liked his plans changed and this was too much, he felt. It gave Sybil time to pack the laundry, leave a note for the iceman, phone Mrs. Novak. It gave Julie time to write a long passionate letter to Mike and slip out to mail it.

Alden had a difficult time with the Board members. In fact, he almost lost his museum because some of them felt the top floor could be made into extra classrooms. He ran all the way home, for the day was practically ruined and they couldn't make many miles that night. Everything conspired against him. He hadn't even had a chance to get a new camp stove. They could breakfast over a campfire.

He dashed in, breathless. Sybil was at the phone and waved at him to be quiet. "Oh, I can't believe it," she said in a shocked voice. "Yes, I know. Yes, I understand. Yes, Miss Eldredge, you were right to call me. Yes, it has to be kept quiet." She listened briefly. "We'll take care of him. Don't worry. Yes, yes."

She hung up and walked over to Alden and spoke decisively. "Bring in the small suitcases, we are not going until tomorrow."

"But Sybil—"

"We have to put President Wallace on the midnight," she said, "and midnight is too late to start anywhere. We'll go tomorrow."

"But we could make a few miles—"

"Mrs. Wallace is dead," she told him. "An accident. You go and pick him up at Kennicott and stop by the house. The Dean has his suitcase on the back porch."

"Mrs. Wallace? What's she thinking of?" cried Alden. "She can't be dead! I saw her this week on campus and she looked fine."

"She was run over by a taxi."

"What was she doing? Where was she?"

"Nobody knows yet. There was a wire, that's all I know."

"Well—" Alden was stunned, and tried to gather himself together. "Why didn't she look where she was going?"

"Bring in the bags. You're to pick Dick up at Kennicott. Get his suitcase at the house."

Alden went out meekly and unloaded the small cases. Then he chugged away. Sybil turned to Julie. "You'll have to help me. I'm—so confused, I can't think."

With her mother needing her, Julie braced herself. "He'll need to eat something," she said importantly. "I'll bring up a jar of the chicken you canned last summer. Anybody can swallow some chicken soup. I'll run over to Brayton's and borrow some extra bread so Papa won't have to unpack that cof—that food box."

Sybil looked at her gratefully. "That will be just right. What would I do without you?"

248

Julie flew about. She put on an old cotton dress (no more spotting of her best clothes). She got the chicken, brought the bread, set a tray. She felt equal to anything. She brought aspirin for her mother, who sat by the window just staring out, not crying, not speaking.

"I'll have a cup of tea for you in a jiff," Julie said.

By the time Alden came back with President Wallace, Sybil had recovered from shock and was able to meet them at the door. It was a dreadful moment for them all. For once, Sybil lacked the right words and simply held out her hands. President Wallace seemed to cling to them. His face was ghastly, one would hardly recognize him. Julie took charge. "Leave the suitcase by the door, Papa," she ordered, "so we can pick it up in a hurry." She inspected President Wallace. Obviously he hadn't thought to change to a clean shirt. "I'll get out a clean shirt," she said. "You show President Wallace upstairs."

Dick followed Alden to the guest room and slumped down on the bed. Alden fussed around, opening the window, shutting it part way, opening it again.

Julie found the clean shirt on top of the suitcase, with a note pinned to it. She took them up and handed them to President Wallace. "Leave your other shirt," she said. "I'll tend to it."

He looked at her gratefully. "Thank you," he said huskily. "So thoughtful."

When Julie and Alden went downstairs, Sybil was stirring the soup. "Smells good," said Alden, for no emergency could lessen his interest in food.

"I'm saving some for you, "said Sybil. "Go and sit down."

They gave Dick an hour alone and then Julie carried up the tray and knocked at the door.

"Come in," he said in quite a normal voice.

He had the clean shirt on, and any traces of weeping were gone. Except for his deathly pallor he looked as if he might make it, thought Julie, setting the tray on the dressing table and pulling up a chair.

"Mama says she hopes you can eat a little of this," she explained. "Having missed supper and all. It's homemade."

"Why, thank you." He sounded humble. You would never guess he was the president of the college, an important man. He was just like anybody in awful trouble. It was Julie's first experience in the leveling power of tragedy, and it made her feel older.

"You come and sit down here," she said, and he went to the table obediently. He gave a despairing look at her.

"I know how it is," she said, "but Mama knows best. It'll go down easy, once you try."

He dipped the spoon in and began to eat. And it was true that the hot soup was good, the hot tea cleared his head. Julie waited until she saw him take a bit of toast and then she went out.

Time wore on. Finally, when it was time to leave for the train, President Wallace came down and asked to use the phone.

"I've forgotten my own number," he said apologetically, and Sybil told him what it was. The conversation was brief, but he had more color in his lips when he finished.

Number 99 was late coming from the junction. No reason it couldn't be on time, Alden fumed. The station platform was deserted as he took out Dick's suitcase and they walked to the end where the Pullman would be. Julie had stayed home, ostensibly because there wasn't room in the overloaded car, but really to try to phone Mike and have a last aimless conversation which said nothing and meant so much. She had to hear his voice again, and never mind his aunt and uncle. This was a special gift, an extra call, and being young, she never thought of it as a gift from a dead woman.

Alden stalked restlessly up and down the platform. "Poor

management all along the line," he grumbled. He just couldn't endure difficult situations except those he made himself. He wanted to get this over with, not hang around all night.

Dick stood quietly beside his suitcase, summoning what strength he had to face what lay ahead. The initial shock was over, and numbness gave way to grief and anxiety. His grief was a weight. Carol was too young to die. Had he really done his best in this wretched marriage? Or was he responsible in some way for what had happened? Must he bear a burden of guilt always? Reason asserted itself. He never had any choice as far as Carol was concerned.

And even now, in this dreadful hour, he was conscious that he must hold fast to the purpose of his life. Westerly had urgent need of him. This college, this town, were his destiny. He had made many mistakes, but none that could not be remedied as he increased in wisdom. He must not be defeated by Carol, not in death any more than in life.

Of Louise, his love, his darling, he could not think. But he could depend on her to save him. Nobody would ever know the truth, except Louise and Sybil.

The oncoming light of the train turned the rails to silver. 99 ate up the night and puffed to a stop, breathing smoke and flame from the stacks. Alden dashed about. "Better go farther down. No, better stay here. No, come back, they always stop so the Pullman is at the end, halfway back to the junction."

He ran back and forth with the suitcase.

Sybil put out her hand to President Wallace as the train stopped. "Dick," she said, using his first name easily, "don't worry. Westerly is safe. You will have some hard years of work ahead, but you will make it. God bless you."

As he took her hand he suddenly lifted it to his lips and kissed it. Then he ran after Alden. Sybil watched as the porter tossed the suitcase in and Dick swung up the steps. The wheels turned, the train gathered momentum, and 99 rolled down the track.

Sybil waved, and saw an answering wave from the murky window. Alden puffed back and urged her to come on, hurry up, no use standing around all night.

They drove back down Main Street, past the feed store with the white plaster horse in front, past the Sweet Shoppe and Joe's, the drygoods emporium, the hardware with the jar of nails in the window. Only the drug store was open, the druggist must be making up prescriptions. In the lighted window the glass jars filled with pink and purple water sent a cheerful glow in the dark street. Farther on they passed the campus, where only the light on the portico of Main Hall still burned. The streets were shadowy except for an occasional night light on a few porches.

There was a light on at the Wallace house, too. The Dean, thought Sybil, was up writing the correct notes to the right people, checking the news for release, notifying the Board. And probably sending a special to a New York hotel. No matter what happens to a man, she thought, women have work to do. And this was as it should be, for it was women's business to protect men.

"Well," said her own man, "I never thought this evening would end. I guess we did our duty. But it made me nervous."

They went in and found Julie still up, reading. "I wanted to be sure the train came in all right," she said. "You know, Mama, I can help out with the twins next year. I like kids."

"Humph," said Alden. He had to admit Julie was pretty handy in this emergency. She really took hold. He didn't mention the eastern college.

The Prescott family went to the kitchen for a snack. Even Sybil, with the day over and Dick on the train, felt like having a glass of milk. They sat around the kitchen table, each one, in his own way, being glad to be alive.

Then Julie, out of her new wisdom, got up and went over and hugged her father. "We can get an early start tomorrow, Papa," she said.

"Well," he said, hugging her back. "We've lost almost a day."

"It isn't losing time that matters," said Sybil, "it's what you do with the time you have."

"I'm tired." Alden finished his chicken sandwich. "This has been an awful hard day."

Julie stacked the dishes. "We'll have a lovely drive tomorrow," she said comfortingly. "We can start early and drive late. Make it up."

She went up to her room to write a final good-by to Mike which she might sneak to the postbox before they all got up.

All she wanted to say was that she loved him. It was about all there was to say.

Sybil and Alden went up the stairs together. Alden retired to the sun porch and got into his nightshirt. Sybil was too tired to brush her hair, she only got undressed as fast as possible.

When Alden flapped in, he came to put his arms around her, holding her with a kind of desperation. She felt warm, real, in his arms. She wouldn't go get herself run over. Much too sensible, he thought.

"What's that scent you have on?" he asked, sniffing. "Smells like spring."

"It's lilac." Sybil kissed him.

He checked his pistol, thumped his pillow, and slept.

Sybil pulled the sheet over him.

The day after Commencement, the sun shone on the deserted campus. The leaves of the lilacs drooped and the grass looked tarnished. The doors and windows in most of the buildings were open, however, for the cleaning staff was at work and the smell of ammonia and wax drifted out. Behind Kennicott

the housemen were beating carpets with wire beaters and the
sound was loud in the quiet air.

The Dean ventured out to the rose garden, for nobody was
around and the twins were playing Parcheesi. Miss Eldredge
was packing, getting ready to go on a pneumonia case. She
hated to go, she said frankly, for she had never had such a
fine time on any case as this present one. The Dean was sorry
too, for a strong bond had grown between them, a rare and
precious friendship between the hard-bitten veteran nurse and
the gentle scholar.

The Dean would stay on until President Wallace came
home. By then, she felt quite sure she could persuade Minnie
into coming back. The twins liked her and she was fond of
them. The twins were bouncy now and hungry. Broth and custards and wine jellies no longer satisfied them. They were also
noisy, enjoying the first freedom of their lives.

The Dean cut the dead blooms from the roses and decided
to water them if it did not rain by night. Dark blue-black
clouds were piling up beyond the river and there might be a
thunderstorm. She cut a few buds and took them in the house,
found a silver goblet for them.

The house already had a different air. It looked, somehow,
lived in. She had, in the last day or so, put away some of the
formal ornaments and her sewing basket was on the damask
sofa. She had been sewing buttons on the twins' blouses, and
darning the President's socks which were piled in the linen
closet.

She went back out to the porch and sat in the shade of the
trumpet vine. She thought about her love on his desperate
journey. But time, she thought, is a healing force. This year
is over, done with, ended. Summer will be for remembrance,
for regret. And then life will begin again as the students come
back to Westerly.

Nothing would ever be the same, and yet some things

could never change. And, with a little sigh, she went in to say good-by to Miss Eldredge.

Mike walked slowly across the empty campus. He was marking off the hours until Julie came back. Without her, the whole town was dreadful. He could watch endlessly for her flying figure and know it was not there. He could listen and not hear her voice. She would not run to meet him. But under the sharp sense of loss he felt in himself a new courage. He felt grown up. He believed he was strong enough to defeat Julie's father because in some way the decision not to take the easy way at State had given him a sense of controlling his life, and Julie's. He had faith in their future, which he never had experienced before. It was going to be pretty difficult for a while, but they were both armored with love.

Winnebago itself was quiet. The shops were deserted. A few salesmen ate at Joe's, an occasional farmer drove in with extra produce. The flow of malteds and banana splits diminished to a trickle. The drygoods emporium was empty. The young and eager no longer rushed in for a pair of silk stockings or new middy ties or petticoats. The few town students made hardly a ripple as they idled mournfully by the drug store.

Dust was beginning to settle on the white plaster horse in front of the feed store. The Elite advertised Warner Baxter for one night only. As Mike went past, he noticed that someone had punched a hole in the picture of Theda Bara right in the middle of her bosom.

Summer heat made the sidewalks so hot you could feel it through your shoes. Licorice whips melted in the candy store window. The butcher had drawn his window shades halfway down and moved all the meat to the icebox.

Mike stopped at the drug store for a glass of root beer.

"Kind of quieted down, eh?" asked the clerk. "Town's dead as a mackerel. You know folks fuss a lot about the college, and still and all, I guess the town needs Westerly much as Westerly needs the town."

"I guess," agreed Mike, fishing for a nickel.

"On the house," said the clerk. "First one in after Commencement. You going to be around?"

"I'll be around," said Mike, "working."

"Keeping in trim for next year's football games?"

"Sure."

"This was sure a good year."

"Yes," said Mike, "a year to remember."